NORTH KOREAN MEMOIRS

Mark D. Treston

iUniverse, Inc.
New York Lincoln Shanghai

North Korean Memoirs

Copyright © 2005 by Mark D. Treston

All rights reserved. No part of this book may be used or reproduced by any means, graphic, electronic, or mechanical, including photocopying, recording, taping or by any information storage retrieval system without the written permission of the publisher except in the case of brief quotations embodied in critical articles and reviews.

iUniverse books may be ordered through booksellers or by contacting:

iUniverse
2021 Pine Lake Road, Suite 100
Lincoln, NE 68512
www.iuniverse.com
1-800-Authors (1-800-288-4677)

ISBN: 0-595-34143-8

Printed in the United States of America

North Korean Memoirs

"The first step to knowledge is to know that we are ignorant."
—Lord David Cecil

"He was an anarchic figure in a world of his own order. He answered to no one and did as he wished, yet all had to follow his every command."

"God might be omnipotent, but the Kims rule North Korea"
—David's comments about Kim IL Sung and Kim Jong IL

Contents

Background to the Korean Peninsula ix
Introduction: Conversation with David xiii
Chapter 1: Growing up in Luxury 1
Chapter 2: Moving to South Korea 9
Chapter 3: The Plan 18
Chapter 4: Panmunjom 23
Chapter 5: Kim IL Sung University 31
Chapter 6: My First Class 41
Chapter 7: Sam, Matt, and Dr. Habibi 56
Chapter 8: How Does He Control all of Them? 60
Chapter 9: My Rise in the North Korean Regime 64
Chapter 10: Drunken Nights: Kim IL Sung's Birthday 68
Chapter 11: Profound Influences: Sam and Young Ae 72
Chapter 12: The Only Trip: Laos, Thailand, Japan 78
Chapter 13: Where is Sam? 104
Chapter 14: Kim Jong IL 108
Chapter 15: Rumors and Tours: Sam and Paekdu Mountain 122
Chapter 16: Kim Jong IL Studios: Hollywood and Socialism 132

Chapter 17: Dr. Han is Replaced/Struggle for Leadership 137
Chapter 18: Breaking the Myths: Real Tour of Pyongyang 142
Chapter 19: Disillusionment and the 1988 Youth Festival 147
Chapter 20: Eric Disappears 151
Chapter 21: Imprisonment 159
Chapter 22: Camp of No Return 172
Chapter 23: Escape 182
Chapter 24: Final Notes 196
Epilogue 199

BACKGROUND TO THE KOREAN PENINSULA

Following the breakup of the Soviet Bloc, and the end of the Cold War, the world headed towards a period of nationalism and ethnic identity as it did following World War Two. In the majority of these cases, nations were losing control over the nationals and ethnic groups within their borders. Nations such as the Soviet Union, Indonesia, Yugoslavia, and even Mexico, found themselves pressured by various religious and ethnic groups. The trend seemed to be toward dissection rather than unification. The ONE exception to this trend was the Korean Peninsula.

After fifty years the Korean conflict has yet to be resolved. A peace treaty between North and South Korea was never reached. The 38th parallel border between North and South Korea is the most heavily armed border in the world. Two million North and South Korean and 37,000 United States soldiers continue to wait on high alert on the infamous 38th parallel demilitarized zone (DMZ) between North and South Korea. Even a single shooting incident can spark another war. This time, both sides are armed with weapons of mass destruction.

The 1950–1953 Korean War claimed the lives of nearly 37,000 US soldiers and more than a million Korean lives (Exact estimates are hard to identify). Fifty years later, propaganda from both sides of the border is broadcast through loudspeakers, radio and television stations, and national news media. A few who have visited the reclusive North Korea have said they have seen dead North Koreans strewn on the sides of the road, supposedly from starvation.

One very sharp contrast between the two nations is the paths each has chosen. South Korea today is a vibrant economy with a democratic system of governance.

South Korea has climbed out of the ashes of Japanese colonialism and a bitter civil war to rank in the top fifteen developed nations in the world. These days South Koreans enjoy the simple freedoms such as traveling outside the country, voting for the representatives in government, even holding mass demonstrations against their own elected officials.

North Korea, on the other hand, continues to be ruled with an iron fist. Since the end of Japanese occupation, the Kim family has tormented the North Korean people by limiting even the most basic freedoms. Kim IL Sung and later his son Kim Jong IL have turned their warped sense of socialism into the first ever dynastic socialist dictatorship. Even Stalin and Mao Tse Tung never achieved such a long-term grip on their nations. Every aspect of North Korean life reinforces the ideology of the two Kims as Gods. Socialism is used simply as a guise for absolute control by the two Kims. After fifty years of such oppression, many North Koreans are oblivious to any other form of governance.

Reports coming back from North Korea are worrisome to say the least. Reports of Cannibalism, discontent, small rebellions, desertions, and mass starvation trickle out to the outside world. The government in North Korea is in disarray. Food rations are going directly to the ruling class while malnourished teenagers in the countryside have the physiques of children. Millions of North Koreans suffer from such curable diseases as tuberculosis and cholera. North Korea has resorted to illegal methods to infuse much needed cash. North Korea has been the mastermind behind counterfeit money for ages. Recent defectors and satellite images also point to the harvesting and exporting of drugs such as opium. North Korea is believed to be fifty years behind South Korea. North Korea lacks infrastructure, electricity, and phone lines. It will need to spend tens of billions of dollars to catch up with South Korean infrastructure alone.

The North Korean education system and overall knowledge of the world surrounding them is minimal (unless one considers *Juche* to be the only true system out there). Many North Koreans still believe most capitalist nations are on their last leg and in complete chaos. State run television in North Korea show a protest in South Korea from the 1970's and claim that it is another sign the "puppet regime" will not last long.

Nearly all North Koreans have never had the opportunity to travel outside their province, let alone the country. Most have never even tried the pleasures of life we take for granted in the West such as tropical fruit, using a cell phone, or driving a car. Access into North Korea is just as strict. The state propaganda media, a handful of defectors, and rumors are the only sources of information coming from North Korea.

North Korean attacks and subversive missions into the heart of South Korea and Japan have convinced South Korea, the United States, and Japan to distrust North Korea and suspect North Korea's true intentions. During one of my trips to Seoul, South Korea I remember seeing advertisements in the subways showing a black rat trying to get milk from a white mother cat and her white kittens. The ad was meant to warn South Koreans that anyone around them could be a North Korean spy. Most South Koreans today feel betrayed by the North Korean regime of holding empty promises for peace. Many believe it was just a ploy to get more aid from the outside world.

Only one regime in recent history-North Korea-matches the successful propaganda campaign conducted by Germany's Nazis during World War II. The survival tactics of North Korea despite the compounding odds have a lot to do with its propaganda campaign. The entire survival of the North Korean regime hangs on the intricate propaganda and security system that has exists in North Korea since. The purges of hundreds of thousands of North Koreans, the elevation of the North Korean leader to a god-like figure, and the constant spying of half of its population explain why a nation of hungry and abused people do not react negatively against their own government. It also explains why North Korea is known as the "Hermit Kingdom."

Recently, the focus has shifted back to the "Hermit Kingdom" with American President George W. Bush's comment about North Korea as one of the "Axis of Evil" nations. A wave of tit for tats between the United States and North Korea followed, leading to the coldest relations between the two nations in twenty years. North Korea has since kicked out nuclear inspectors and resumed their nuclear program. These actions, coupled with North Korea's admission of kidnapping Japanese nationals for decades have left North Korea more isolated and desperate than ever. For these reasons I believe the following story is crucial in order to understand the geo-political situation in Northeast Asia.

INTRODUCTION
CONVERSATION WITH DAVID

"They are watching me."

November 16, 1996

I never thought my life would amount to much. I always felt as if I had sold myself short. Of course, this was just my own interpretation of how my life was going. I decided to go to a local college in Pennsylvania instead of American University in Washington D.C. because I wanted to save money. After college, I took a job with the Foreign Service instead of pursuing a business career. There I was, in a remote post far away from home, filing library cards and making sure the magazine stands were in order. After completing my training in the Foreign Service training program, I was assigned as information officer to the United States Consulate library in the coastal city of Dalian in China.

Dalian was everything I hoped China wouldn't be. It was a polluted port city with very little cultural significance. The city rapidly industrialized in the late 1980s to serve as a source of cheap labor for Japanese and Korean firms. It was an ideal city for business with Korea and Japan because it was on a main shipping route to the two nations. I managed to make the best of my situation by using my generous vacations and weekends to travel around China and East Asia. I continued my Chinese studies as well as studying Korean and Japanese. I found some Korean and Japanese businessmen who were interested in language exchange programs. I would usually meet them in the cafes in the only real "cosmopolitan" area of the city, down by the passenger port terminals.

The Chinese were busy trying to make the whole country seem "modern" by building monstrosities such as the financial district equipped with a shopping plaza right next to the port. The local Chinese figured that if they built tall buildings surrounded by shopping centers, tourists from Japan, Taiwan, and South Korea would want to take a ferry to their city and spend money. The plan was a miserable failure. Everyone knows the Japanese have high tastes and wouldn't be caught dead in such a gray and industrial city. Furthermore, tourists would not spend sixteen hours on a ferryboat just to come to a small and insignificant city, when they could hop on a plane and be in Hong Kong, Beijing, or Shanghai in less than three hours.

In my training in Washington D.C., all the diplomats-to-be were warned about our diplomatic mission. We were constantly reminded about the importance of maintaining the symbol of the United States through our actions and deeds abroad. The State Department taught us to be on our best behavior, showing the utmost courtesy to our guests. That, basically, eliminated my chances of living it up or doing the crazy things I was used to doing in the United States. It also meant that I could never say or do anything that might jeopardize how Chinese might view the United States. Deep down, I really wanted to find someone I could relate to about my experiences in China, someone I could talk to candidly.

My life seemed to have reached a low point. I felt that my great ambitions for my future were being wasted as a government librarian in the armpit of China. There were days where I just wanted to pack up and go. I wanted to travel to a distant land where I could explore and learn new things. My job was so mundane. The Chinese I met only wanted to learn English and were not very eager to talk about Chinese culture or history and, especially not about politics. The only fun I had was on weekends, when I would sling on a backpack and head out of the city. I usually didn't get too far because of the terrible traffic and hectic bus and train stations. It seemed as if I was just putting in my time in Dalian, waiting for my next assignment, hoping it would be more interesting next time around. Then David came into my life.

The first time I saw David was during my fourth month in the consulate library in Dalian. David looked like the many homeless people I was accustomed to seeing on the streets of New York or Philadelphia. His miserable appearance might have been normal for a Chinese, but he was a white guy, an American. He had long hair, a beard, and a tall, but slender figure. His clothes were shabby and old. They were the attire of neither a Chinese nor a Westerner. They were more a mixture of whatever was around.

His face resembled that of what I had always envisioned Robinson Crusoe would look like. His sunken cheeks and eyes did not fit the typical look of a foreigner on vacation. He had a bent back though he wasn't that old. His skin had a yellow tinge, as if he suffered from exposure from the sun and malnutrition. From the moment I saw him, I knew there was an interesting story though the magnitude of that story had yet to be revealed to me.

I was cataloging the old magazines when I saw him out of the corner of my eye. At first, he looked around hesitantly, as if he did not trust what he saw. My Chinese coworker, Vivian, asked him if she could help with anything. He seemed to avoid her and continued to glance around the library with suspicious eyes. Then he quickly walked into the other room and disappeared out of my site. I could tell that his looks also surprised my Chinese counterpart. Vivian looked back at me with a puzzled look; as if I was suppose to know everything about every Westerner.

David began to come every day, around the same time. He would usually go directly to the classic books section or the newspaper and magazine room. He would normally only read the New York Times or magazines that were related to science, history, or the National Geographic. I myself read the National Geographic religiously, so I thought this might be a chance for me to strike up a conversation. Like clockwork, David strolled in that day at three in the afternoon. It was as if he was following a rigid and busy schedule. Yet, he appeared to look like someone who was obviously unemployed.

I approached David and asked him if he needed any help. He just kept his head down and shook his head. I noticed he had the most recent copy of the "History Journal" on the table and I asked him if he had read the article in there about the new findings on Francisco Pizzarro. Not a word! David did not even look up. I went on to explain that the article reveals that Pizarro was even more ruthless than once thought. Following Pizarro's death, his family continued to bicker over the looted treasures from the Inca.

"Pizarro knew how to conquer a civilization."

David interrupted me.

"I respect him for that. It seems as if people are bound by traditions and superstitions, therefore easy to manipulate."

"Much like the Chinese today?" I asked.

"These days the Chinese suffer from a much stronger vice: Greed!" David retorted.

"One interesting exception is the Japanese. They seemed to harness their traditions and culture and created a modern society from it." I responded.

"Yes, the Japanese are unique in that manner. However, even they suffer from not being able to break from the norm and individually think for themselves." David answered.

We continued to talk for about an hour before I realized that my Chinese counterpart was patiently waiting for me. Vivian was like that. She would not interrupt what I was doing, but would simply wait until we established eye contact. She wanted my help with an order form. I left David for just a few minutes. When I walked back to chat some more with David, he was already gone. He came back the following day, though. We continued to chat about history, philosophy, and travel. Every time I would ask him a personal question, he would get quiet, and act as though he wanted to leave immediately. As I said, I'd noticed he was extremely thin and bore scars on his face and hands (Which was all I could see of his body). He was also missing some teeth, his yellow skin looked dark and leathery and his hair was thin and long.

David came by a couple of other times. Each time I hadn't even noticed his entrance until I made my rounds. I always found him in the back, with the chair pushed so that our view of him was obstructed. Vivian glanced suspiciously at his direction. She commented a couple of times about the foul odor and appearance of our new patron. I really didn't care, David was interesting and I was dying to talk to someone about something. Of course, as we became more familiar with each other, David and I also openly disagreed about some topics. I sensed that he was extremely pessimistic about the future prospects of humankind in general. I sensed that he never was a very optimistic fellow.

However, on this particular day, David was not as talkative. He seemed to have something on his mind. While I was telling him about my travels in Eastern Europe, he suddenly pulled out a pile of papers. I recognized the papers because David was helping himself to our copier paper for the last two weeks. Vivian tried to stop him from taking the paper, but I intervened and let him take the paper.

David handed me the pile of paper, which by now, was full of scribbles everywhere.

"Read this!" David said.

"You must let people know what it's like in there."

"Where is there?" I asked.

"You have to make these papers public." David interrupted.

"Even if only a few people know. It will mean a lot. Innocent people are dying."

I was taken aback by his request. Where is there? What is there to know? Was he talking about China? Maybe he was an activist for Tibet. But Tibet was way across on the other side of China.

"Just promise me that you will let people know about this horrible place, promise me!"

David was pleading. It was the first time I saw him show any emotion. His eyes softened and exposed the innocent fear of child.

"Okay! I promise." I responded.

Suddenly, David turned his attention towards the front desk where Vivian was sitting. He looked at Vivian for a split second, turned back to me and pulled me towards him. Although he was extremely skinny, I could feel his hand crushing my arm as he whispered in my ear.

"They are watching me. They follow me everywhere. I have to go."

Without an explanation or even a goodbye, David left. That was the last I ever saw or heard from him.

That night I read David's papers without a break until the early morning hours. I just couldn't put the papers down. I find it hard to believe that David made any of it up. The details, the vivid description, all are too difficult to invent. He knew too much about a nation that has been the most successful in keeping outsiders out and in the dark. Even today people can only guess what is really going on in the "Hermit Kingdom."

Over the last few years I have pondered whether or not I should publish David's diary. I have tried to put David's diary into somewhat of a chronological order. It seemed as if David simply jotted down his experiences as he remembered them. In some instances, there is a blank. Probably due to the torture or shock he had been through. I doubt that anyone could remember what happened following such excruciating pain. However, in no way did I stretch David's diary to fill in the blanks. As amazing as this story may sound, it is exactly as it happened in his diary.

Mark D. Treston

Chapter 1

▼

GROWING UP IN LUXURY

<u>Note to the reader:</u> Names (including my own name) and exact locations have been altered in order to protect those mentioned in the diary.

A famous Chinese philosopher once said: "A journey of a thousand kilometers starts with one step." That one step is what I have regretted to this day. I was raised not to look back and feel bad about mistakes I've made. Nevertheless, this mistake led me down a journey no person should ever have to travel. I don't want anyone who reads this diary to feel sorry for me. After all, I had betrayed my native country. All I ask is that people understand what it was like back then. The era and place in which I grew up taught me to be suspicious of my government. It advocated free speech and individualism. I was naïve, idealistic, and ignorant of my surroundings.

As I write these words, I constantly look over my shoulder for my many enemies. I am a wanted man. Wanted by all sides for my past doings. I am tired of running. Tired of keeping silent. My main concern now is the information that is within these pages. If this diary ever becomes public, I just hope that it will serve as a truthful account of what North Korea was and still is like. The only justice I could achieve in my life thus far would be that this diary helps expose the vicious and manipulative North Korean regime. The same regime I once admired.

Some people in America blame or credit their childhood for the paths they took in life. I only blame myself. My years of reflection in North Korea helped me realize that the only paradise that exists was my own childhood. I was born and raised in one of the most beautiful cities in the world, San Francisco. We lived in the exclusive Pacific Heights neighborhood overlooking the San Francisco Bay and Golden Gate Bridge.

My father was a very successful businessman. All he inherited from his father was a sizeable debt. My father came to the United States at an early age, worked hard at the docks of San Francisco, then saved enough to open his own trading company. His company mostly traded with the Pacific Basin nations. San Francisco was becoming an important business center, and my father knew how to capitalize on the growing needs of cheap Asian goods by American firms.

My mother came from a well-to-do family and taught English literature at a local university. My parents only had one child, me. In retrospect, I was a very spoiled child. My parents were very intelligent, but just didn't seem to know how to raise children. I was mostly raised by a black maid, Rose, and a black groundskeeper, Otis. They lived down the street from us in what was called the "Fillmore District." It was a predominately poor black neighborhood and was famous for Jazz and blues clubs. Rose sometimes took me there when she had errands to run.

The economic and cultural contrast shocked me, even at such an early age. This was the 1950's and there seemed to be an invisible barrier between the exclusive neighborhood on the hills where I lived, and the Fillmore District down in the gulch. It was as if we rich folk were looking down on the poor blacks, literally. I guess this was the beginning of my hatred towards my parents and society in general. I didn't like the way my parents treated Rose and Carl, and the way Rose and Carl were so submissive to my parents. Back then I blamed my parents for all the wrongs that were done to people because I felt guilty of our fortune (interestingly enough, many revolutionary leaders came from well to do families: Marx and Engel, Fidel Castro, Kim IL Sung, George Washington, etc.).

Another point of contention from an early age came from the Presidio Army base located just blocks from our house. Drunken soldiers would constantly walk by our house from the base with their foul mouth and prostitutes by their sides. I felt as if these men were animals, brought from the dregs of society and unleashed on the general population. As a lonely boy, my mind ran rampant with theories and conspiracies regarding everyone. The lack of real problems in my life materialized into my problems with society. I felt the government was corrupt and Americans ignorant of the many problems the world faced. I guess that was why I was so intrigued with the "Beatnik" and later the "hippie" generations. It was an alternative to the status quo I myself was part of.

I spent my high school days in the various alternative bookstores. The same places where Jack Kerouac himself frequented (I can't say I have ever seen him though). These places were hotbeds for alternative and leftist leaning people. I usually tried to pay attention to the various groups meeting there, but I always seemed to drift away (I just couldn't focus on the arguments the Anarchists had regarding who should chair the discussions) and find myself alone in the travel or history sections of the bookstores or libraries, reading endlessly. I would usually lose track of time and get home late. My parents were fairly liberal and let me do as I pleased. My friends were always shocked at that.

I always had a knack for languages. From an early age, my parents taught me Spanish and French and were shocked at my early progress. I also learned Latin and German in school. But my interests were in far off and exotic places. Being that I lived in San Francisco, I took advantage of the fact that I could learn both Mandarin and Cantonese Chinese. All I had to do was take a bus or simply walk over Russian Hill and I would be in an entirely different world. A world where open markets and bartering was the norm. A world where people ate turtles, snakes, and crickets, and played Mah-Jong in the back alleys across from the Buddhist Temples. This was the world that interested me the most. The world of the unknown, where I would have to learn everything from scratch.

That was exactly what I did. I hung out in the alleys and street corners, the bakeries and cafes. I picked up the language remarkably easily. I was even able to read some Chinese characters at the age of 12. Being able to read some characters helped me put the puzzle together of what words meant. For example, I always saw the same character in front of the pharmacist stores, so obviously that character had something to do with apothecary (I also picked up some Japanese by reading the signs in the Japanese neighborhood by my house. It would later help me when I traveled to Japan). I made friends with some local Chinese kids and we helped each other with our language barriers. As I got older, I was asked by one elder to volunteer at the Chinese community center to teach English to immigrants and in exchange, they would teach me some Chinese. I jumped at the opportunity.

In the 1950's and 1960's many new Chinese immigrants were the result of the Nationalists losing Mainland China to the Communists. The immigrants who arrived were mostly from the losing camp. The Nationalist flags flew high on most buildings in Chinatown. During my English lessons, they would constantly remind me how terrible Communism was and how they were once rich. As a teenager in San Francisco, who spent too much time in leftist bookstores, I found it hard to believe that Communism could be that bad. I always thought that these

Chinese immigrants were bitter because they were forced from their vast lands and fortunes by the popular masses.

The 1960's in the Bay Area were full of new thoughts that questioned and contradicted what we were born to believe or taught in schools. I was swept up in this fervor and was convinced that a popular change was in the air. The newspapers and magazines constantly spoke of the "evils" of Communism and Socialism, yet all around the world revolutions were successfully overthrowing the unpopular, Western-backed regimes. Fidel in Cuba, the Red Army in Italy, the ANC in South Africa, and the new Socialist movements in third world countries inspired me. I felt as if the United States and Europe were purposefully trying to limit these movements simply to keep the status quo. I also used this belief against my parents as a tool to rebel against how they lived and how they wanted me to live.

The exception to the rule was the Bay Area. A rising affluence coupled with a rich history of openness to minorities provided an island of radical thought and action. I mean the hippie movement basically started a few blocks from where I lived: Haight Ashbury. The University of California, Berkeley was going through a major upheaval and seemed to have some sort of protest or demonstration every other day. This environment led me to believe, from an early age, that the bandwagon was anti-government, anti-institution, and anti-Western.

My family, on the other hand, was oblivious to this change. My father had my whole life planned out for me. I was to follow in his footsteps and continue his successful business. We argued about everything. I wanted to travel the world first and see all those places I had always read about in magazines such as National Geographic. I wanted to learn many languages and try to speak them in remote corners of the world. My father thought travel was a waste of money. He never traveled and he turned out fine. That was his reasoning.

We finally agreed that after I completed my Bachelors degree, I could go to Europe for a few weeks. I always tended to compromise with my father. My father was stubborn and I knew better than to try to get my way all of the time. I knew very well that I would take that opportunity and go to Eastern Europe or take a ferry to Africa from Italy or Spain. My father and I also compromised on where I would attend college. My father agreed to Berkeley because it was close to home and it had a good business school. I chose Berkeley because of its alternative education and its radical movements within the student and faculty body.

Berkeley just added more revolutionary wood to my proverbial fire. I was surrounded, both in classes and on campus, by radicals of every type. There were anarchists, atheists, Marxists, and those were the moderate groups. One thing they all agreed on was that the United States was responsible for everything that was wrong with the world. In retrospect, I believe one week in North Korea would have changed their minds immediately. Nevertheless, this was my lifestyle. I believed every conspiracy, and was convinced that the United States was purely evil. It's funny how people like me, who come from the highest echelons of American society, can be so critical of the establishment, which after all, made my family's life so affluent.

After I received my Bachelor's Degree, I was determined to travel around the world. I wanted to see, firsthand, the evils the United States has committed. My father wanted me to work right away. He tried to convince me to work part-time, and if I wanted to continue my studies, I could go to Golden Gate University at night. The University was right downtown so I could stay at home (which was what my father had wanted). The University was the first of its kind in California to offer evening courses for working professionals. My father wanted to surround me with the "real world" like he had when he was young. He made it through hard work and sweat and did not respect people who went to Ivy League schools but had no work experience. All I knew was that the University was surrounded with conservative business executives that wanted to enhance their own careers. That school was the opposite of Berkeley.

I knew that the only chance I had was to go to Graduate School, and then find a way to get away. I was a spoiled youth with my life handed to me on a silver platter. I just didn't want to work. I was a dreamer. I was accepted to the University of Southern California's (USC) East Asian program, which was famous for its Asian language programs. I convinced my father that if I learned more languages, I could be a better businessman and an asset to his business. My father agreed. One of his frustrations was not being able to understand his counterparts in Asia. He was also pleased that I showed interest in his business.

For me, it was an opportunity to go as far as I could from my parents without leaving California. Anywhere outside California was unacceptable. We Californians believed we were better than the rest of the country as far back as I can remember. I was, however, very disappointed with Southern California. It was a tradition for the Bay Area people to snub their noses at Southern California. I took this to a new extreme. I felt superior to my fellow students and new neighbors. In my opinion, Los Angeles was all about glitz and USC was all about connections.

During my first term I took several East Asian language classes until I found the language I wanted to concentrate on. The Korean language professor, Mr. Cho, was an excellent teacher. I also found the language intriguing. It was actually part of the Ural-Altaic languages, which included Turkish, Finnish, and Mongolian. Although it borrowed heavily from Chinese, it had its own unique alphabet. Mr. Cho was very cordial, and we would talk for hours about the situation on the Korean Peninsula. I told him that I thought that what the Americans did there was inhuman. They had divided the country and installed a puppet regime. Mr. Cho agreed that the South Korean government was not very democratic, but didn't think the North Korean one was any better.

I always believed that although Mr. Cho was a great professor, he was oblivious to the workers' struggle around the world. He was too cautious about the student movements in South Korea and Japan. He worried that the communist countries were using propaganda to entice students to cause upheavals in democratic countries. To me, a twenty something year old, North Korea was a workers paradise where the idea of wealth and money were replaced with equality and solidarity. It was the first time in history where the class system was eliminated. I was swept up in the Socialist and Communist cause. It was everything that America was not.

The graduate program lasted for two years. Towards the end of the program I was able to communicate proficiently in Korean. My knack for languages was paying off. I learned not only Korean, but also over seven thousand Chinese characters (Koreans, Chinese, and Japanese use these characters as well as their own unique characters). I had also taken a few courses in Spanish and Arabic. One day, Mr. Cho called me into his office. He told me how impressed he was with my achievements and asked me if I would like to use my language while traveling. He knew how much I wanted to travel. I agreed right away before even hearing what the job was. I just wanted a reason to travel. I knew my father would let me if I had a job lined up.

The job was with the United States Central Intelligence Agency, or CIA. I was taken aback. Me? Work for the CIA? It was the same organization that supports puppet regimes around the world? The covert organization that makes sure the workers and the poor are oppressed around the world? No way! I told Mr. Cho what I thought of his offer. I'd rather shovel shit for a living. Mr. Cho just calmly smiled and asked me how would I change the world unless I had an opportunity to change it from within. He also assured me that the job was clerical and would not involve any military or covert work. The CIA was then, and still is, the best source of information gathering. My job would be working for its publications department. I would be gathering information about the Korean Peninsula and putting it in the CIA's archives.

For one whole night, Mr. Cho and I engaged in a long conversation about whether it is better to try to make changes within the system or from the outside. We sat in one of the popular cafes in Santa Monica and defended our reasoning with quotes from various philosophers and ideologists. Mr. Cho argued well, insisting that being on the periphery in history had never achieved any meaningful changes. I countered that with the fact that being on the inside makes one biased, therefore, corrupted. Although I strongly disagreed with Mr. Cho, deep down I found it a fascinating idea to work for the CIA.

I definitely knew my father would welcome this opportunity for me. My father thought the United States was the best place in the world. It had given him a chance to rise from the bottom and escape the misery of his country of birth. Although my father was settled in the United States, he still possessed his Scottish pride. For him, it was important to see his son succeed so that the family name could continue with pride. I could see in his eyes how happy he was when I told him about the job at the CIA. My father was always worried about me. He realized my mother and he had spoiled their only child and that I didn't appreciate what I had. Most importantly, my father learned that no matter how much money he made, he could not control his own son's destiny. That irritated him and pleased me.

I was also excited about the prospects of going to live in East Asia. I had never been outside the United States, not even to Canada or Mexico. I decided to take the position, and then secretly work my way deeper into the CIA and make some big waves while I was there. I felt as if this was my crusade. I could make a difference in the world. On a side (yet very important) note, I was also assuring myself of evading conscription. I know this sounds crazy, but this was 1969. The Tet Offensive in Vietnam scared the hell out of Americans. Many of my friends were trying to run away to Canada or Mexico. Others even defected to Cuba.

These were trying times. Many Americans were watching the world change against their odds. With the exceptions of the stunning defeat of the Israelis over outnumbering Arab armies, the capitalist world looked bleak. Even within the United States, anger was growing among even the most traditionally patriotic crowds. This was a time of union strikes, the women's movement, rising black militant groups, the Hippie era. Just across the bay from us the Black Panthers were having shoot-outs with the Oakland police. Things looked apocalyptic. If I joined the CIA civilian division, I would be exempt and could travel the world (so I thought).

I don't remember much about my training. My mind is a blur about some sections of my life. My training in the CIA is one of them. I think that it was because of the severe pressure I was under. During my training, my expectations and perceptions of the CIA had changed little by little. It really wasn't the horrible place I envisioned. Even though American involvement in Vietnam was escalating, I couldn't find all the horrible things I wanted to find out about the CIA. It was just another place to work. I passed the background check of CIA employees and the physical. That was about all the cloak and dagger stuff that went on there. I was just another employee, working alongside some uneventful people. I was part of the CIA's Information gathering divisions. People just like me, ordinary citizens with exemplary bilingual skills, were asked to interpret documents, radio signals, and recordings all day long.

At first, I was given mostly South Korean documents and tapes. Nothing that was too secretive. I think the CIA wanted to find out how good I was and how truthful I was. After three months of this mundane work, the director of our department summoned me in for a talk. He knew that I really wanted to go to East Asia. He told me that there was an opening at the Eight Army Namsan Base in Seoul right away. At the time, not many trustworthy bilingual speakers in Korean and English existed. It was widely believed that there were hundreds of thousands of North Korean spies in South Korea during the 1960's. Not even South Korean government officials were trusted.

Chapter 2

MOVING TO SOUTH KOREA

August, 1972

I jumped at the opportunity. Within a week, I was on a plane to Seoul, South Korea. I was so happy to finally be on my way to the outside world. I thought that I was now on a mission to find the truth and tell the real story of the world's oppression by the well to do. Landing in Seoul was like landing in an alien world. Soldiers with machine guns and jeeps heavily guarded the airport. Driving in the US truck to the base in the center of Seoul I finally had a chance to see how the South Koreans lived.

Everywhere our truck tried to drive was blocked by something or other. Old women were squatting on the streets with their vegetables or fruit for sale. Men were pulling carts of stuff everywhere. Korean cars and taxis were constantly beeping at everyone and no one in an attempt to get to their destination a little faster. In the side streets, people relieved themselves in the gutters; there were no public toilets anywhere. There were definitely signs of heavy military and police presence. Once in a while, a nice sedan with a dignitary in the back seat passed by our truck. In the distance, I could see large apartments being built.

South Korea seemed very mountainous. Everywhere I looked sharp mountains jutted up above the small building in Seoul. On the way from the airport to the base, I also got a glimpse of the typical rice patties and terraces that I had envisioned. It was September and the leaves were turning yellow and orange. It was beautiful and spiritual. I was not accustomed to the four seasons. In San Francisco we only had two seasons: Wet and dry. I also noticed some traditional houses and temples. The houses had terraced style roofs with mud and hay in between the bricks or concrete. It reminded me of the Southwest's adobe style houses.

As we entered the center of the city, I began to see (what I believed at the time) the ills of capitalism. People seemed to be working very hard while a few were enjoying the fruits of their work. The side streets were littered with makeshift markets. Sometimes, one vendor only offered what seemed to me as tree leaves or bean sprouts. I also noticed how South Korean children would run after our truck asking for chocolate. That was Seoul in the early 1970's.

As we entered the Yangsan Army base, the disparities were obvious to me. The base had every type of luxury item Americans were used to at the time. Meanwhile, right outside the camp in Itaewon, young women were prostituting themselves to US GI's and older women prepared snacks for the drunken soldiers. The whole neighborhood, known as Itaewon, was a service area for the American Army. There were all the amenities of home, from bars to hamburger joints. South Koreans were not allowed to frequent these establishments due to the strict curfew imposed on them by then President Park Chung Hee.

General Park Chung Hee took over in a coup in the early sixties and had been ruling South Korea ever since. General Park was once a lackey for the Japanese during the Japanese occupation and was now once again in control. The South Koreans seemed to forgive all those who were involved in Japanese imperialism. I felt as if it were the opposite of North Korea. During my Korean studies, I learned that the North Korean leader, Kim IL Sung, was a former resistance fighter, as well as a cadre in the Korean Workers Party. To me, Kim IL Sung seemed like a hero compared to the South Korean leaders. He fought against the Japanese, while the others conspired with the Japanese empire. It was widely believed that Park Chung Hee had served as a military police officer for the Japanese during their occupation of Korea. Kim IL Sung was like the other leaders I looked up to at the time: Fidel Castro in Cuba, Allende in Chile, Ho Chi Min in Vietnam, etcetera.

I have to admit that I saw the world as black and white back then. Most of my leftist friends back home were the same. This naïve dichotomy carried over to my perception of the two Koreas. I immediately hated the American presence in South Korea. It seemed to me an obvious plot to maintain American domination over Northeast Asia. Don't forget, to the North were China and the Soviet Union, while Japan to the East was under increasing pressure from its growing Communist and Socialist movements. Socialism around the world seemed inevitable. To me, South Korea was another puppet regime, like that of South Vietnam, held up by the United States.

Meanwhile in South Korea, General Park was busy turning the country into another playground for Western imperialism. This was how I viewed the situation at the time. The smokestacks and factories that littered Seoul were evidence of how Park Chung Hee planned to develop his country: on the backs of the masses. I remember reading back in the San Francisco bookstore about the suffering of workers in Korean factories, especially textile businesses. Children, ages eight to thirteen worked eighteen-hour shifts at these textile plants. Sometimes the children were injected with stimulants to prevent them from falling asleep on the job.

At the time, South Korea was a far cry from what it looks like today. It resembled something out of a Charles Dickens book. People lived in horrid conditions and worked demanding and dangerous jobs. The Park regime pushed South Koreans to meet quotas in order to "develop" and become rich. It was the average citizen that suffered. Curfews were enforced, special brigades patrolled the streets looking for slackers, and North Korea was used as an excuse to limit free speech and democracy. This was the South Korea I despised. To me, it was just like another South Vietnam or a Franco's Spain.

It was 1972 when I arrived in South Korea. The North Koreans were now very bold in their guerilla attacks on South Korea. The North Koreans took their bravery from the repeated successes of the Viet Cong in South Vietnam and the general world feeling towards socialism and communism. Kim IL Sung, the leader of North Korea, was said to believe that South Koreans would soon rise up against the "puppet regime" in the South. This was my feeling as well. It was a dawn of a new decade. The 1970's looked as if the tide was going to turn against the United States and its allies. I truly thought so as well.

Only four years earlier, North Korean commandos stormed a theater in Seoul and attempted to assassinate General Park. Instead of killing him, they shot his wife. General Park was such a stoic man that the story goes that he continued to sit through the concert and forced everyone else to do so as well. Only after the concert was over, did he show any emotion. The same year, North Korea captured the USS Pueblo and held the American sailors prisoners for almost a year. As I arrived in South Korea, the attacks on South Korea were increasing. The North Korean commandos were highly motivated and seemed to put the living fear into the unprepared South Korean soldiers. It was obvious that without the US presence, North Korean troops could easily penetrate the South.

North Korea, emboldened by the successes of North Vietnam in South Vietnam, carried out hundreds of border skirmishes and penetrations during the late sixties. The United States Army was on high alert. One North Korean unit was even able to get to the Presidential Palace (known as "Chong Wa Dae," the "Blue House"). At the same time, Park Chung Hee used this as a reason to build up the South Korean army, with American and Japanese support. By the time I arrived, I felt something was going to erupt. Everyone on the base was tense, and the lines were divided regarding those who agreed and those who disagreed with American foreign policy. Even some soldiers (those who were young enough to experience the late sixties hippie movement) were questioning United States involvement in Asia.

The South Korean government did not seem to give any reason why South Koreans should resist such an invasion. To many South Koreans, their regime was not very sympathetic to them. That is why Kim IL Sung always believed that if it were not for the United States army presence, the North Korean army could defeat the South Korean army easily. Kim did not believe there was much support for Park and his regime. I don't know what the consequence would have been if the United States had not supported South Korea, but I can only speculate. At the time South Korea was not strong enough to resist an invasion from the North.

It's important to note that the North was historically always the industrial and productive section of the Korean peninsula. The South was agricultural and poor in nature. Pyongyang and Kaesong were once the industrial and cultural centers of Korea. Foreign influence first took roots in Pyongyang, giving it the largest Christian population in Korea. General Park was adamant about changing this stereotype. In the process, he was working South Koreans to death. Remember, he had children as young as thirteen working eighteen-hour workdays to make wigs and clothes for export to places such as Europe and the United States. He was more concerned about the South Korean image than he was about its citizens. Park had also signed a lucrative peace treaty with Japan without accepting any apology from Japan regarding World War II.

It was during my first year in South Korea that I grew increasingly disillusioned with my role there and with those around me. I made it my mission to learn as much as I could about what I believed to be the injustices committed by the Americans and the "Puppet South Korean" regime on the innocent Korean people. Most of my co-workers, on the other hand, indulged in the pleasures of being stationed in a poor undeveloped nation with people who "will do anything for US dollars." I think what disgusted me the most was how children could be bought to do whatever the hell you wanted. Some of the prostitutes were definitely younger than eighteen and already seemed to know the tricks of the trade. They matured faster than any woman I have ever met.

As I mentioned earlier, the famous foreign area, *Itaewon*, was right outside our base. During my first few weeks in South Korea I used to join my co-workers and hang out in *Itaewon* on a gaudy street strip with bars, brothels, and restaurants. I was really disgusted by what I saw. I considered it the most apparent mistreatment of humans. In the bars, drunken American soldiers would flash their dollars in front of the prostitutes and bar keepers to get them to do what they wanted. Most disgusting was the way money was being used to buy people. I watched the Korean girls flock to the soldiers who would wave their money up high.

When I first arrived, I also partook in some of the nightlife, but that quickly ended. One night, my colleagues and I took a couple of prostitutes with us to a sleazy "*Yogwon*" or motel. The room's walls were very thin and you could hear everything. As we were indulging in sex, I could hear the violence that was going on over in the next room. The men in the next room were apparently violently abusing the prostitute. I could hear her crying that it hurt her and that she didn't like it in her behind. They didn't seem to care and just told her to shut up. All I could think about was how I should go over there and rescue her. But I didn't. I was very idealistic. I believed that only Capitalism could be responsible for such evil. At the same time, I lacked the courage to do something about my feelings. I was raised as a spoiled brat and never learned about the values of life. I was a big talker, but did nothing.

I quickly grew unpopular at the intelligence center inside Yangsan Army Base. I felt as if I had to argue with everyone about our mission in South Korea, or the entire world, for that matter. Even my fellow leftists thought I was too extreme. I was reprimanded a couple of times by my superiors and was given special attention by the CIA's internal surveillance team. Still, my actions were only words so I didn't attract too much notice. This was the early seventies. Someone as critical of the government as me was considered the norm. So long as I did my job, I was considered harmless. No one took me too seriously. I'm sure if someone higher up in the CIA had voiced such remarks about the US, they would have been fired. Not I! I was simply a civilian translator at the bottom of the totem pole.

This made me angry. As an only child I was used to getting a lot of attention, whether good or bad. Sometimes I would think of ways to attract attention to myself by doing something radical. This was how it all started. I began to hear rumors from other GI's at the Itaewon bars about the unthinkable: American soldiers deserting to North Korea. This topic would always produce arguments among the soldiers. Some would wonder who in the hell would want to go live in North Korea. Others would say that those who defected were wanted by the police for a crime they had committed and that was the reason why they defected. Still others claimed that it was not possible because of the heavy security around the Demilitarized Zone (DMZ) on the 38th parallel dividing the North from the South.

One night my views on this topic almost put me in the hospital. I had joined a conversation between some Marines regarding the defectors. Most of them could not believe why anyone would want to go "be a commie." I commented that actually those at the economic bottom would benefit from such a system. As a matter of fact, I continued, most soldiers only joined the army because they were from the economic bottom of the United States and for them, a place like North Korea would seem like a paradise. It would be a place of equals where they would not have to fight the rich man's war.

"What do you know about the army? You're just a civilian?" One marine replied.

"Are you saying we are poor and don't know shit?" Said another marine.

"If you love it so much, why don't you move there?" Another soldier chimed in.

I could not have chosen a worse topic with United States Marines. I don't think the Marines liked any angle I put on the topic. The fact that a well spoken, educated, well to do person with no army experience was slandering the United States did not sit well with them. One of the drunk Marines began pushing me. The next thing I knew I was knocked on my head with some sharp object. I gathered myself and ran out of the bar. As I headed back to the barracks, I felt the warm blood gushing from my head. I kept away from the bar scene in Itaewon after that.

Those few times I did enjoy my stay in Korea were on the weekends and holidays. I usually packed a small bag and went on a trip to the countryside. The beautiful thing about Korea was that it was over seventy percent mountainous. Any mountain you climbed would culminate in a spectacular view and usually a Buddhist temple tucked away between them. The temples were always in tune with nature. Most temples followed three basic colors: Orange, forest green, and brown. The colors usually blended in well with the temples' surroundings.

The structures were built around the trees, cutting down as little as possible. The monks subsisted on what they grew and their surroundings. Of course, they were vegetarian and grew their vegetables and fruits. The monks were always very kind and would offer me some food and a place to stay. I was always very impressed by the patience and wisdom these hermetic monks possessed. I learned a lot about Buddhism and about the history of Korea from these monks.

I would also occasionally run into some "guests" at some of the temples I visited. Turns out that these "guests" were actually seeking asylum from the government. One man told me he was a student leader of one of the most radical student groups at Seoul National University, a prominent university in Korea. He told me about the connections he had made with North Korea and how he and his student body were planning joint demonstrations and even uprisings against the South Korean government. He claimed that he even had many blue-collar workers on his side. His group had even once planned to go to North Korea through China, and try to cross back through Panmunjom. However, they were denied permission to leave South Korea.

The man was very curious about labor and human rights in the United States. We sat up for hours in this mountain hideaway, discussing politics, philosophy, and other social issues. Between heated discussions, I would glance over the temple wall out into the distance. Korean mountains definitely have their charm. Their craggy ridges and deep valleys were always breathtaking. The maple trees in the autumn, and the cherry blossoms in the spring. The crisp air in the winters and the colorful flower dotted hillsides in the summers.

I maximized my weekends and holidays, traveling throughout Korea, from the Southwestern Island of Cheju to the alpine tops of Mt. Chirisan. I tasted the regional dishes, chatted with different Koreans, and visited the historic and cultural sites throughout the country, stayed in local inns, known as *Minbaks* and ate at local restaurants. I still cannot get over how diverse South Korea is. Although homogeneous, it varied in its architecture, food, history, and lifestyle from region to region.

I also took the time to learn the different dialects of South Korea. My knack for linguistics astonished the local Koreans when they heard a *"Waeguk"* (foreigner) speak their local tongue. This made me a lot of friends throughout Korea and really helped me better understand Korea and its people. Nevertheless, I also judged them. Although most South Koreans looked happy and content with life, I saw their plight as one of oppression. All those books by Karl Marx, Lenin, and Mao led me to believe that I was witnessing the natural process of a socialist revolution. As South Korea was industrializing, its people were working harder and harder under awful conditions. People were moving to the cities en masse, looking for any sort of employment. What they found was hard work and low pay.

Many South Koreans I talked with told me that I just didn't understand the situation. It was necessary, in their opinion, to industrialize quickly for the sake of the next generation. This was the Confucius ideology talking. Koreans closely follow Confucian thinking and believe that they must work and produce for the sake of the next generation. That was why they didn't mind working hard. They were only concerned about how their children would live. This unique trait coupled with the community psychology of Koreans, allowed General Park to push the entire nation towards industrialization. The Confucian notion of obeying the leader contributed to the fact that General Park went largely unquestioned or unopposed.

Most South Koreans did not care for my opinions on the evils of capitalism. One incident that still haunts me to this day happened when I was in a small village on the Island of Namhae on the southernmost tip of Korea. I became engulfed into a heated argument with a couple of fishermen at the local bar/restaurant/inn where I was staying. During my travels around South Korea, I wanted to find out what other people's opinions were regarding the Korean conflict. During one conversation, a quiet man in his fifties interrupted me. He had a huge scar starting at his left ear and circling around his chin. His eyes were worn out and his skin was dark and leathery. It was probably from spending years on a fishing boat.

He asked me if I had ever been to North Korea. My answer was of course "no."

"Then what," he continued, "do you know about socialism?"

"You don't have to live in a socialist country to know the benefits of the system." I retorted.

The man grinned, exposing his unkempt teeth. He poured another glass of *Soju* (Fiery Korean liquor) and took a shot, slamming the glass back on the table. He leaned over to me, placed his hand on my shoulder, and began to speak with a heavy Kyongsang regional accent.

"You learned nothing at your fancy school." The bar suddenly fell silent.

"Whenever a new system is introduced on an entire nation of people, no matter how good people believe it is, it is replacing something. That something, he continued, is what parents teach their children, and their children teach their own children. The reason they teach it is because they have experimented with it and it worked. All Kim IL Sung is doing is changing the traditions and installing his own insane system. As an experienced fisherman and farmer, I know that Kim IL Sung's system will fail. The difference between Park Chung Hee and Kim IL

Sung is that Park Chung Hee actually listens to those who count: Fishermen, Farmers, the 'real' working people."

The room remained silent while I took in this unexpected viewpoint. Another man poured us all another shot of *Soju* and we all downed it without saying a word.

At the time, I dismissed the man's comments, thinking that he was just an uneducated provincial who did not understand things that are worldly. I really believed that he was just uninformed and that he needed to listen to me, an educated man. As I write my diary now, I know that good advice sometimes comes from the strangest sources. That "country hick" was right on the mark. Too often intellectuals think they know what the rest of the world needs. Let's be honest, people like Karl Marx never even worked a day in their lives and did not suffer from poverty or mistreatment. Yet Marx preached about the plight of the oppressed as if he had experienced it himself. Those who complain the most are quite often from the well-to-do class themselves. They can enjoy the luxury of having time to complain.

Chapter 3

▼

THE PLAN

1973

I was still determined to do something radical. I still believed that I was a lackey of American capitalism. Every day that passed in South Korea, I felt more and more isolated from everyone around me. I even stopped writing my parents. At work, I was being watched more and more carefully by my superiors and even by my colleagues. A sense of curiosity was always strong in me, but now it was even worse. I was in search of something. One thing was clear, I just could not put my finger on what I was yearning for.

At work, I was growing increasingly interested in the "pariah" to the north: North Korea. Our job at the intelligence gathering office was to listen in to North Korean radio, both public and military, and translate what we heard. I grew increasingly transfixed with these broadcasts. Although I realized that they were coated with propaganda, I felt that it was probably for the same reasons we slanted our information. Since the end of the Korean War, we had been busy producing tons of propaganda to convince the North Koreans to drop their weapons and surrender. Another part of our job was to translate English propaganda into Korean. The propaganda was then aired in several different ways that were never revealed to us, but we figured it out. Since we interpreted North Korean propaganda, we just figured the United States used the same methods.

All of us used to laugh at the dogmatic propaganda we translated from the North, but secretly, I yearned to learn more about the socialist state. At that time I thought I was well aware of North Korea's advancements and pitfalls. I must admit now that I didn't have a clue. To the outside world in the early 1970's,

North Korea, and socialism in general, seemed to overtake the capitalist nations. A big reason for this was the control of the propaganda machines by socialist nations. I should have known better. I studied so much about the success the Nazis achieved using propaganda and blatant nationalism. I was just blind to the harsh realities. To me, these socialist systems provided an alternative to the existing systems in the United States and Europe.

My interest in the workings of North Korea, coupled with my disgust of our mission in South Korea, developed into a plot to visit North Korea. Of course at that time it was absolutely unheard of. No American was allowed to visit North Korea, let alone a government employee of the CIA. I knew that I would have to plan an escape, not a travel itinerary, if I wanted to see North Korea. Still, getting into North Korea would be an ultimate coup for me. In retrospect, I was delighted at the possibility of being the center of attention, regardless of its outcome. I began to think about possible escape routes and ways to cross into North Korea.

The border between North and South Korea was on the 38th parallel known as the Demilitarized Zone (DMZ). It was the most heavily armed border in the world. There were over two million North Korean, South Korean, and United Nations (mostly American) soldiers on its border. Between the two high barbed-wire fences was a slither of land known as "No-Mans Land." It was also saturated with land mines and checkpoints as far as twenty miles from the DMZ. I could count on my hand the number of successful escape attempts through the DMZ since its creation in the early 1950's. That was out of the question for me. I was not trained to conduct any stunts like that.

One story that resonated in the bar conversations concerning the two previous defectors was about Panmunjom. Panmunjom was known as the joint peace village where the truce between the North and South was signed following the Korean War in 1953. This was also the place where both sides could hold meetings without having to go through a third party. The area was referred to as the "Joint Security Area" because both sides patrolled it. Most interestingly, it was also open to give a select group of tourists a glimpse of the other side. Because of this, both sides had created their own version of a micro-utopia where each side could look jealously at the other side's "Paradise."

I knew this place well because my team and I translated a lot of the signs and messages erected on the North Korean side. We were even allowed access to the infamous room where a select group of tourists could glance firsthand at the mean-looking North Korean soldiers on the other side of the room. This room was known as the conference room. This was the heart of Panmunjom, a simple room with a large table in the center. A white line divided the room between North and South Korea. All one had to do was to cross the line to enter North Korea. This however was prevented because of the selection process and the physical barriers placed in the room: Mean-looking soldiers on both sides that stared down each other.

This room fascinated me even before I visited it. I saw a picture of it in a book I once read and could not get over the fact that this one room, this area of only a few cubic feet, was the epicenter of the Korean and Cold War conflict. When I first entered the room, I felt the tension in the air. Each side was very nervous and any wrong move could be seen as a threat. We were thoroughly briefed about the "room." The Marine sergeant warned us not to reach into our pockets or make any sudden moves while in the room. We were also asked in advance to dress conservatively. That was a South Korean concern because of the xenophobic notion Koreans had about Westerners. Many Koreans believed all Westerners were dirty and dressed "disrespectfully."

My only hope to escape to North Korea was through here. There was almost no information about the two other American Soldiers who escaped through Panmunjom. The only information was secondhand rumors. One elite Army ranger told me that his unit was told that the two who had escaped did it because they were wanted for criminal prosecution by the South Korea and US military police. He hinted to me that the crimes involved raping under-aged Korean girls. He told me that the military had nicknames for them, but never used their real names. When I tried to look up some information about the two, I came up empty.

Once voice of optimism for my escape plans came from an unexpected source. One of the Koreans I had befriended on the base was a former Korean special forces reconnaissance officer named John (as we knew him). John was more American than I was. He served alongside our troops for so long that he used profanities in every single sentence. John worked as the chief Korean security liaison on the base and around Itaewon. His job was to keep the peace among the American soldiers and the locals. John and I met at the Yongsan library because we shared the same interests in outdoor activities.

John sometimes accompanied me on my weekend hikes whenever his schedule permitted. After a few beers or shots of *Soju*, John's tongue would usually loosen and he would share his army stories with me. As a member of the elite reconnaissance team, John's missions would take him into the DMZ. Their outfit's motto was that for every one of their own killed they had to kill at least two enemy combatants. John had enough stories to keep a summer camp busy every night around the fire.

One day after a few drinks at a local mountain inn, or *Minbak*, John filled me in about the DMZ and North Korea.

"I'm telling you David, that is the only weak point."

So, if you wanted to attack the North, Panmunjom would be the spot? I asked John.

"No! Did you hear a word I said? I mean it is the only spot on the DMZ that is not heavily fortified because of its civilian access. But, If you were to send a column of tanks down that road, the North Koreans would be ready. Their troops are standing by just beyond their fake "peace village." No! The sea is still the best access. The Americans have the best navy in the world."

I poured John another shot of *Soju* as I thought about how to phrase my next question.

"If someone wanted to infiltrate North Korea as a spy, could it be done through Panmunjom?"

"What do mean? As a civilian?"

John had a confused look on his face.

"Yeah!" I responded.

"Sure! You could make it past the 'room' (the famous convention room where there armistice was signed), but the North Koreans would capture that person right away. They would not fall for anything. They would torture a confession out of you then use you for target practice."

"C'mon!" I interrupted. "Do you really expect me to believe they are that cruel?"

"Look, I have looked into the eyes of these soldiers, they are trained killers. They train on live targets. Their elite units even train on released political prisoners in the mountains."

John's eyes were lit and he stared right into mine with such conviction. I had no reason to doubt him, yet I thought he was simply trained to hate the North Koreans. I did not hear John's warning; I only heard the green light from a military expert regarding my plan.

I started to meticulously plan my escape. The whole time, up until the day I escaped, I saw the whole issue as a lighthearted expedition. I didn't really sit down and think what would happen to me once I succeeded in entering North Korea. The only thoughts I had regarding this was that I would be hailed a hero in the socialist world. I really believed that I would finally leave all the sorrows of the capitalist world and enter a kind of "Zen-like" world where I could help shape a new society. Since my high school days in San Francisco, I truly believed that there was a reason for my existence in this world. I believed that my purpose in life was to the rescue the wretched of the earth and develop a new society where money was not an issue and where there was only one class of people. A society where no one person ruled and no one relied on financial well being to survive.

Once I had begun to plan my escape route, I began to lighten up. Even my co-workers noticed the difference. They asked my why I wasn't complaining as much, why I was so happy recently. One of them came to the conclusion that I had found some whore that I fell in love with. I just kept quiet, happy that I was about to embark on the journey of my life. If only I knew what a journey that would turn out to be.

CHAPTER 4

PANMUNJOM

September 15, 1973

I arranged a tour to the region on the premise that I wanted to go and learn about some of the new signs that were posted on the North Korean side. Actually, because of my position, I didn't even need the excuse; I just wanted to cover all my bases. On September 15th, 1973, I boarded the shuttle bus from the Yongsan Base in Seoul to the border bases. We stopped briefly at the Uijoungbu base where I transferred to a smaller bus that was going with a group of tourists to Panmunjom. With me were a bunch of Australian tourists who I later found out were members of the Australian Embassy in Japan and a couple of their friends. Australians always seemed to me to be adventurous. They really helped me calm down with their friendly and cheerful discussions all the way up to Panmunjom. It took my mind off my growing worries.

As we drove into the compound, the danger of my plan suddenly dawned upon me. By now I was extremely nervous and sweaty. I also felt as if everyone was looking at me. The tough looking Marines and the formality of the place scared me. I felt that they knew everything; they were just waiting for the right moment to nab me. I didn't even feel as if I was walking. My feet felt like butter melting under my body. I stood in the back of the briefing room as the Marine gave the usual speech about what we were allowed and not allowed to do. It was the same speech I had heard before.

After the briefing we were escorted into the conference room. One of the soldiers recognized me from my previous visits and attempted to smile at me. I was so nervous that I just looked away. I thought that whatever I did would reveal my nervous behavior. I just kept clear from making any eye contact. As we stood in the conference room, I remained in the back of the group, inconspicuous. I remember the Australians taking the initiative and walking around the room, sitting in the conference chairs, and looking at the North Korean soldiers who stood just a few feet away.

All I remember next was spotting the white line dividing the room into North and South Korea and running towards it. My heart was pumping a mile a minute and my feet were moving on their own volition. As I was running, I yelled to the North Korean soldiers in Korean: "I am defecting, please don't shoot. I am defecting, please don't shoot." I also managed to yell out that I wanted to serve Kim IL Sung. Next thing I knew I was out the door of the conference room on the North Korean side in the open courtyard. All I heard was people yelling from every direction.

That moment is still very blurry to me. It all felt like a bad dream. I just kept yelling in Korean that I wanted to defect. I used every possible word in Korean I could think of to convince both sides I wanted to stay. I used all the propaganda I learned at my job. After a tense standoff between both sides, I was escorted away by the North Korean soldiers. I later learned that my defection almost led to bloodshed on both sides. The North Koreans told me that they were just inching for a reason to shoot some Americans and South Koreans for months. I almost gave them a reason. If it was a North Korean trying to defect, I'm sure the North Koreans would have opened fire. The South Koreans and Americans were taken by surprise that someone would want to escape to North Korea and I guess they just stood there, dumbfounded.

In what seemed as a split second, I was led into the North Korean compound that I had always seen from the South Korean side. This was my first glance at the reclusive North. The hallways were lined with the typical Soviet style paintings and sculptures of Kim IL Sung and the Socialist "struggle." As they led me through the building, I noticed all the military personnel were staring at me suspiciously and at the same time with amazement. People were coming out of their offices to look at what had made all the commotion outside that almost led to war. There I was, all on my lonesome, surrounded by military and government personnel. They began to debate what to do with me. I guess defections to the North were not included in their job description.

After an hour or so, one of the men barked out an order and I was escorted to a windowless room at the end of the hallway. They left me with three guards watching over me like hawks. I stood there silently, in a haze. I was still shaking and my heart was still beating fast. I myself could not believe what I have just done. It felt as if I was there for hours. I really don't remember how long it was. There were no clocks anywhere and I don't even think I was in any state to focus on such a small detail. Finally, a small man in a uniform with lots of medals on his chest entered the room. A taller, skinnier man followed him.

The short man began to talk in Korean to me, the taller man quickly translated. I responded in Korean that there was no need for translations. Both men were truly surprised. The short man gave a little smirk and asked me my name. I told him my name was David and that I wanted to defect to "The Democratic People's Republic of Korea." I knew better than to refer to North Korea as "North Korea." North Koreans hated that name. It insinuated that the North was a separate entity from the South. That was unacceptable to them. Kim IL Sung has always insisted on unification through any means necessary.

The men were not impressed. The short man asked why I wanted to defect. I told him that I was a sincere follower of socialism and the "*Juche*" ideology. For those of you who do not know about "*Juche*," it means "Self-Reliance" in Korean. This was a new twist on socialism created by Kim IL Sung to address Koreans in particular. It is a concoction of Marxism, Stalinism, and Maoism, but goes further in its zealous perception of Korea and the world. *Juche* encourages Koreans to be more self-sufficient and to rely less on the outside world. It is an extension of one man's xenophobia and paranoia into a political, social, and economic ideology.

Although I obviously did not believe in isolationism, I saw *Juche* as a last ditch resort by North Korea to break the shackles of their oppressors. The Korean peninsula had a long history of domination by the stronger nations that surrounded Korea. *Juche* was a reaction to the historical reliance of Korea on China, Japan, the United States, and the Soviet Union.

I also saw *Juche* as a method that other oppressed nations needed to pay attention to if they wanted to remain truly free. Although I was a socialist, I didn't like the idea that the entire world had to take sides. Both the United States and the Soviet Union were playing a game of chess with the smaller nations as their pawns. They were not really interested in the well being of those nations. North Korea realized this, and was not playing their game anymore. At least that was how I interpreted it.

I think my two interrogators were still in shock when I was explaining the reasons for my defection. First, they could not believe an American would want to defect to North Korea; second, they were in shock that I could speak Korean so well. To them, it was more likely that I was a spy. I was kept in the same room for hours. The two interrogators would ask me one or two questions, write down my response, and then leave the room. Each time they would disappear for almost thirty minutes before they came back with more questions. Truthfully, I was expecting a little warmer welcome than I was receiving. But then again, it was North Korea. Koreans in general always seemed a little suspicious of "outsiders."

As night was approaching, my interrogators returned for the umpteenth time. That whole time they kept me shackled to the pipe that ran through the room. This time they brought another man with them and some food. My first question was if I could use the restroom. They escorted me to the end of hall where a soldier was standing. The soldier saluted the two men then followed me into restroom. The guard watched me as I squatted in the small hole in the ground they called a toilet (it is very common to have a communal hole in the ground as a toilet. There is not much of a plumbing system because North Koreans use the feces as fertilizer. That is why North Koreans believe their vegetables and fruits are so delicious).

When I returned to the room, the third man who had joined us was smiling. He offered me a seat in front of a meal that had been prepared for me. He was very cordial and seemed to carry more weight than the other two (who still looked cold and mean to me). As I began to eat, the third man told me how brave I was and how I would be rewarded for my sincere desire to "break the shackles of oppression." He continued to assure me that in due time, I would find a welcoming committee for me in Pyongyang. There was just one little pit stop they would need to make along the way. He told me that because of the severity of the situation, I would need to lie low for a while in an undisclosed location in the countryside.

After my meal, the third man abruptly left and the other two signaled for me to follow them. They led me outside to a one-story compound that seemed to be where the soldiers slept. I was put in a room alone and heard the door locked behind me. The room had no windows and no bathroom. There was only a bed and a water basin (or piss pot, who knows!). There I was, my first night in North Korea, too excited to sleep, yet exhausted from the nerve racking experience I had just gone through.

The next morning, very early, the door opened and my two interrogators were standing at the entrance. Again, they just signaled me to follow them. They took me around the compound to a small depot where a big old truck was waiting. We climbed into the back and the soldier in the truck with us lowered the vinyl in the back so that I could not see anything. The truck then sped away (as fast as a North Korean truck could go).

All I could see was the road we were traveling on. There was a gap in the vinyl at the bottom and a small peephole where I could look through and see the roads we were traveling on. At first, the road we were on was paved, but after an hour, the road turned into gravel and dust. The three other people in the truck stayed quiet the whole trip. I tried to ask some questions, but I just got yes and no answer. My first impression of North Koreans fit the description of their propaganda: lifeless and stoic.

After three hours the truck finally came to a stop. I heard some noise outside and the soldier with us opened the vinyl. The sun blinded me for a second, and then I started to see that we were at some kind of army camp. I was led into a compound that was flanked by two beautiful pine trees. Inside, a short stocky man was waiting for me with two other men seated behind two tables. I was asked to sit down and the interrogations began.

They asked me every possible question: What is my mother's hometown? What is the most important place I have ever been to? Who is the governor of my state? What are the principles of socialism? The questions seemed to get more and more absurd by the minute. I was denied food and water the entire time. When I asked to use the restroom, the short man, kept saying "in a few minutes." When I was finally allowed to go to the restroom, the soldier interrupted me in the middle of urinating and shouted at me to finish up and come back immediately.

On the second day, I had a short respite from the questions when a camera crew entered the compound. They made me wear the new clothes. There was a pin of Kim IL Sung on the lapel. One of the crew put some make up on my face to make me look fresh. They then handed me a piece of paper and told me to repeat those words while they rolled the camera. The paper basically said that I escaped on my own free will and that I denounced all forms of capitalism, that I was happy to now be under the leadership of Kim IL Sung, and that I would do anything for the socialist cause. The paper also went on about how the American army was hindering Korean unification and causing so much pain to the Korean people.

The minimal psychological torture continued for two weeks. I was taunted by the short man, while the other two wrote down everything that was being said in the room. He demanded to know all about my duties at the Yongsan Base. When I told him the limited information I knew, he became enraged. He told me that I was holding out on him and that he would beat the truth out of me. I could tell that he was disappointed at the low level deserter that I was. I was certainly not the big fish he had hoped for. He became harsher and harsher with his abuse. He accused me of being weak and of deserting my country and my duties. He continued to say that I was not worthy enough to be a true socialist. Sometimes I got angry and yell back at him. "What the hell do you know? I was the one who risked my life to come over to North Korea."

After two weeks of degradation, lack of sleep and food, suddenly the short man's attitude changed. He began to speak softly and even smiled. Instead of insulting me, he was now offering his insights about the "glory of socialism and the dear leader Kim IL Sung." The short man (I never got his name) was now a messianic messenger for a Korean utopia. The entire day he talked about the great leaps forward that had been achieved by North Korea. Behind all these great achievement was Kim IL Sung. He concluded by saying that I was going to play an integral part in these amazing feats, as long as I was willing to sacrifice my time and passion to the cause. I assured him that I was ready to do whatever was needed. Now, this man, who two days ago was so vicious to me, beamed with happiness.

The next day I was again taken in a covered truck. This time there was only one guard in the back with me. I never saw those two goons or the short man again. This time, thirty minutes into the trip, the soldier lifted the vinyl in the front of the truck so that some light could come in. I could now see the driver and the front of the road. The soldier told me to put on a military hat and shirt. I did as he said. I asked him in Korean why I had to wear the hat and shirt. At first he just looked at me in shock. A few minutes later he explained that if a common North Korean person saw an American, they would most likely freak out or even attack us.

I now had a window into my future, literally. I watched as the truck made its way along the narrow road, up and down a series of mountains. On several occasions our truck was stopped at a roadblock. Each time, the man in the passenger seat got out and yelled at the soldiers manning the checkpoints. From his thick North Korean accent I could make out that he didn't have to show them the content of the truck. He demanded each time that they let the truck through immediately. As the truck barreled down one of the mountains, I noticed tall building on the horizon.

The high-rise buildings were getting closer and closer. During the ride, I struck up a conversation with the soldier and get some information out of him. He told me we were heading toward Pyongyang, the capital of North Korea. He told me that I was going to get a very warm welcome and that I should not worry anymore. He also told me a little about himself. This was only the third time that he was going to Pyongyang. He was from the city of Kaesong and was now serving in the elite armed forces of North Korea. He said it wasn't easy to get a pass to go to Pyongyang so he was happy he had this opportunity. He told me that after they dropped me off, he was going to buy some items that could not be purchased elsewhere in North Korea.

Pyongyang was the strangest city I had ever seen in my life. It made Seoul look normal. I remember reading the book "1984" by George Orwell and picturing in my mind what the city looked like that George Orwell had described. It was as if that vision had come to life. The highway leading into Pyongyang was almost ten lanes wide and brand new. The only problem was that there were almost no cars or any other type of vehicle on the road (except for the occasional military trucks that passed by). The whole scene was surreal. Before entering even the outskirts of the city, we were made to stop at a checkpoint and thoroughly searched.

The outskirts of the city were littered with closely built houses and buildings, most only had one story tall. The houses were all the same and reminded me of the tool shed in the back of our house in San Francisco. Those houses didn't seem to stand a chance if a nasty storm blew by. The weird thing about them was that I didn't see any people around them. I would later learn that North Koreans work so hard they were never home except to go to sleep.

One of the most bizarre scenes I had noticed was driving into Pyongyang. The workers on the sides of the highway reminded me of an ant colony. The workers were squatting and picking the weeds that were encroaching on the edges of the highway. Most of the weed pullers were women, while the men hacked away with plows at the longer weeds farther away from the highway. For what purpose I wondered. I would later find out that North Koreans broke their backs frequently for no good reason except to appease the "Great Leader."

I was very apprehensive at this point. Not only because of what I had done and what might happen to me, but because of my genuine interest in the unknown. I was not so naïve that I thought North Korea was a paradise, or that Kim IL Sung was a genius. You have to remember what kind of a person I was (and still am). I was a dreamer who spent most of his childhood reading and dreaming about far away places where only the truly inquisitive and a little crazy would ever want to go.

One of the most profound writers that really influenced me was Joseph Conrad. Conrad had a way of keeping his readers on the edge of their seats with suspense about the most eccentric people and places. He was a world traveler who wrote about conquering the unknown. His characters and places were always on the extreme edges of our "respectable societies." His books always seemed to follow themes of humans who had tried and failed to control other humans or nature. That aspect of his writing had attracted me. I had always respected human nature but not humans. I read some of his books, such as "Heart of Darkness" and "The Secret Agent" several times. It all depends how one interprets his books, but for me, they were a push in pursuit of the unknown.

What better pursuit could one wish for? I was one of the first Westerners to see firsthand the most reclusive and unknown nation in the world. By the 1970's, other Soviet block and communist nations were already open to hoards of curious Westerners and thrill seekers. Some Americans were even making their way to Cuba and China. I was a pioneer. No one dared go to North Korea. It wasn't just the Socialist rhetoric that interested me; it was also the unknown.

Well, there I was. Driving into the heart of the capital of North Korea, Pyongyang. Just before reaching the large (and only one that I could see) bridge crossing the Daedong River, the truck turned right. The truck was now heading directly north. Unbeknownst to me, we were heading towards my future home.

Chapter 5

KIM IL SUNG UNIVERSITY

1974

We reached a T-Crossing and turned off onto a paved road where we were stopped at a checkpoint for the umpteenth time. This time even the guards with me were searched. The road was lined with the most beautiful pine trees I had ever seen. Each branch on each tree seemed to have a different route it wanted to take. The imperfection of these trees was what made them so beautiful. Although, the government closely lined up the trees in rows, they obviously could not control the way the branches grew. I thought that was an interesting point, which later followed me throughout my life proved to be a valuable lesson.

We passed by a sign that read "Kim IL Sung University: The birthplace of Juche." Kim Il Sung University was the number one university in North Korea, thus very exclusive. Only the top cadres' children were allowed to enter despite the claim that it was "The People's university." Why was I being led here? Everything was a mystery.

The strangest thing was that I didn't see any students around the campus when we first drove in. Later I realized that everything and everyone was synchronized. All classes began and ended at the same time and no student had any reason to be wandering around during classes. When classes were let out, the campus immediately turned into an ant's nest. It probably looked just like an ants nest from a bird's eye view. The campus was my first look into North Korean life.

The school was not very beautiful compared to American universities and colleges. It was, however, surrounded by beautiful mountains and woods.

The truck stopped outside a small building, tucked away at the edge of the campus. I was led into this building and told to wait in the lobby. A smiling man dressed in a dark suit, and wearing glasses greeted me.

"Mr. Walker, welcome." he said in English. We have been expecting you."

He seemed very nice and I immediately felt at ease. Since I made my escape, my stomach was killing me. It was probably because of the stress and apprehension I was feeling up to this point. The friendly man introduced himself as "Dr. Han." He was the Dean of the Language program at Kim IL Sung University. His English was very good and it seemed to have a touch of a New York dialect. Go figure! A North Korean who speaks in English with a Brooklyn accent. He later told me that he had studied medicine at Cornell University Medical School in New York. Prior to that, he had lived with a friend's family in Queens and worked at a local grocery store they owned there.

Dr. Han showed me around the building. He gave me a tour of the small library, the classrooms, and the administrative offices. The building was known as the foreign studies building. This drab building was the gateway to the outside world for North Korea, but it didn't even look international at all. The staff was predominantly Koreans and the students were all Koreans. I was introduced to a Russian and two Chinese. The Russian, Victor, was the director of Russians studies. He seemed like a Russian academic type, with a Lenin-style goatee and a plaid jacket with elbow patches. The first Chinese man, Mr. Zhu, was a Chinese language professor, and the second man, Mr. Chang, was the director of the Chinese Studies program.

After this brief introduction, Dr. Han quickly led me away, asking whether I was hungry. Without even waiting for my response, he led me to his office where a meal was waiting for us in the corner. We removed our shoes at the entrance to his office and proceeded to sit with our feet folded. We sat on lavishly sewn pillows on the floor. A short-legged table between both of us was covered with all types of side dishes in the customary Korean fashion. Unlike in Japan, Koreans folded their feet in an "X" fashion. His "assistant," a pretty young woman, served us as we began to eat. I probably made a spectacle of myself because I wolfed down the food. I had not eaten a decent meal for a few weeks now.

In a typical Korean fashion, Dr. Han finished his food before me. Koreans are fast eaters. Mr. Han smoked a cigarette and pulled out two bottles of beer from his desk. He told me to try it. That was my first introduction to Korean beer. The beer label had a sickle and axe on it. Even the North Korean beer symbolized socialism. I can't believe I have forgotten the name, but I am almost sure it was "Rongyong Beer". I was surprised how good it actually was. Unlike almost everything else in North Korea, this beer was delicious. God only knows how they made it.

As I swilled down this surprisingly good beer and smoked North Korean cigarettes, Dr. Han filled me in on his entire life. It was customary for Koreans to talk about their family background because many could trace their family lineage for centuries. He told me how his family was able to escape to the United States during the Japanese occupation of the Korean Peninsula in 1910. They moved to California and opened a small shop in San Jose. They then asked their friend in New York to take of him while he studied at Cornell. His family decided to return to Pyongyang following the Japanese surrender in World War II. Of course, the Korean War then broke out. His uncle, a top commander in the North Korean army, died during that war. Dr. Han then enrolled in Kim IL Sung University and received his PhD in English.

Dr. Han didn't ask me too many questions. He just continued to talk about the University, North Korea, and his plans to expand the linguistics program. He seemed very impressed with me and I began to understand why this was my first introduction to North Korea. It seems that I was going to teach the North Korean elite all about the United States. I would later learn that the elite in North Korea knew a heck-of-a-lot more about the outside world than most North Koreans. It was my job to fill them in not just about English, but about the West. I mean, just from looking around at the top university in all of North Korea, it was clear that "We have been expecting you." they didn't have many individuals representing the Western World.

After Dr. Han monologue and the beer, he took me on a walk around the university. The university was totally lacking in charm and was nothing like the colleges I was accustomed to in the United States. I remember my childhood memories, playing hide and seek on the University of San Francisco's campus. It was only a few blocks from my house. The campus was well manicured and had classical European style buildings. Kim IL Sung University looked like factory buildings with lots of windows. The campus grounds were mostly concrete with small patches of plants and lots of statues and posters commemorating Kim IL Sung and socialism.

We had made a circle around the campus when Dr. Han stopped by a building that looked a little nicer than the others. It was ten stories high but looked new and well maintained. There were two guards posted at the entrance. Dr. Han showed his identification card and we proceeded into the building. It did not have an elevator so we took the stairs up five flights. Dr. Han led me to room 502. This room was going to be my home for a while. The room consisted of a small entrance area (where Koreans remove their shoes and place them in a cupboard), the main room, a small kitchen and a large bathroom. There were already a couple of suits and underwear in the closet. I was surprised to see that they had my size right. They had obviously prepared for my arrival. I finally started to feel welcomed.

Dr. Han followed me around in an approving manner as if to say: "Nice place, huh?" It was a pretty nice place for ordinary North Koreans. I even had a view of the North side of the campus all the way to a wooded area on the outskirts of the forest.

"Nice view, huh?" Dr. Han stood beside me with an approving face.

"Now make yourself at home and let me know if you need anything."

I was speechless. The entire week was still sinking in.

"Okay, I have to get going now. You should rest. You have a long day ahead of you tomorrow."

Dr. Han left and an empty silence filled the room. The only noise was the sounds of a band practicing far off on the campus grounds. I sat there in silence, feeling mentally and physically exhausted. For the past few weeks, I had been very disoriented with normal references of time, dates, and bodily functions. I guess those little things didn't seem important compared to what I had gotten myself into. I washed up, changed clothes, and fell right into a deep sleep that became very hard to wake from.

I began to dream, I remember, about my old high school friends. We were all playing in this big field that divided the Presidio from our neighborhood. Outlining the field, there was a thick forest with pine and eucalyptus trees fighting each other for better positioning. My curiosity got the best of me and I proceeded to walk into the dark forest at the end of the field. My friends warned me about going there. They were telling me that if I crossed into the forest, I would never be allowed to return. Then a bunch of Army soldiers from the camp came around the field and also began to yell at me to stay away from the forest. I panicked and ran right into the forest, ignoring my friends and the soldiers. Next thing I knew, I was in North Korea. In my dream, North Korea was just beyond the field in the dark forest that always gave me the creeps growing up.

Despite the torture I have undergone, I vividly remember this dream. Normally, I can't even remember a dream I had the night before. The pine and eucalyptus forest that always scared and calmed me down at the same conjured up the memories of my weekend walks with my father from our house to "Lands End" (literally the end of San Francisco that jutted out with sharp cliffs and incredible views of the ocean). My father knew so much about so many things. He used to point to that forest and tell me that even though it looked peaceful, it was a war zone. Even though the pine and eucalyptus trees seemed to be coexisting, they were on a lifetime struggle to survive. They were on a race to the sky. The trees that could shadow the other trees would eventually win.

For me, it was a sobering lesson that taught me that even beautiful things could be hostile. Like many fathers, my father was a wealth of information to me. I now understand how much I actually have learned from my father, a self-educated man who worked so hard to provide for us. I was saddened by what my father told me that day. To this day, I look at the simple forms of life with a different perspective. Even when I see some flowers encroached by weeds, I think about the slow death that is inevitable for all of life forms. I guess that's why I was always fixated with that dark corner of the forest.

In my dream I approached the North Korean soldiers in the dark forest. The soldiers seemed very wary of my advances, raised their machine guns, and pointed them right at me. For some reason, I wanted to turn around and run, but I just kept advancing towards them. The soldiers started to yell at me to stop, but I just would not listen.

Suddenly, I heard a voice call my name followed my some loud knocking. That was when I woke up and heard Dr. Han's voice outside my door. He wanted to know if I was doing all right and whether or not I wanted to have dinner with him. It was dark by now and I could see the guard-post lights through my window. He took me to the university's cafeteria where we were escorted to an area where we had more privacy. The cafeteria was full of people. While no one dared look at me, I could sense that everyone was very curious. I wondered if they knew about my situation.

The food served to us was *Kimchi* soup with several side dishes that included more *Kimchi* and vegetables. In both North and South Korea, the staple diet consists of rice and different kinds of *Kimchi*. *Kimchi* is made from pickled vegetables, in particular, cabbage. Koreans eat this for breakfast, lunch, and dinner. I liked *Kimchi* from day one, so I was very happy to eat it three times a day. I noticed, however, that the other people at the other tables were eating some kind of rice gruel with only two side dishes, but at the time I thought nothing of it. I was introduced to a couple of other professors, including an Australian named Eric. Eric towered over the rest of us. He must have been over six feet two and long arms. He had a resonating voice and not much table manners. Eric was already done with his soup and was on his third beer. Though he looked very anxious to talk to me, he kept his conversation to a minimum.

Following this hearty meal, Eric came up to me as I was getting up to leave.

"I hope you like *Kimchi*, because you will be seeing lots of it." He chuckled.

"Yeah!" I answered, not knowing what to say.

"You know, if you want, we can go get..."

"Excuse me, David!" Dr. Han interrupted us.

"We are late for the meeting." He continued.

Dr. Han grabbed my shoulder and led me away while he explained that I needed to be briefed about my work schedule. I already had the feeling Dr. Han did not want me to associate too much with the other foreigners, especially Eric. After Eric left, Dr. Han grabbed me by the shoulder and led me down the hallway. He had a habit of guiding people like this. We stopped abruptly in front of the boiler room. The noise coming from the boiler room echoed in the hallway, even shaking the ground underneath us. Dr. Han turned to me, leaned into me, and gave me a brief heart to heart talk.

"You must be aware this is not America. This is not even South Korea. You must be very careful what you say and to whom you say it. Nowhere is safe when it comes to discussions. Even if you don't mean anything in what you say, North Koreans might interpret it negatively. For example, if you and Eric joke around about something such as how the students walk in unison, others would read your joking as mockery. Mocking, in any way, the way of life here is punishable by imprisonment and our prisons have only one door: The entrance."

That said, Dr. Han grabbed me again and rushed me out of the building. I followed him across the quad and into another building in the center of the campus, where an old man and a middle-aged woman were waiting for us. Dr. Han introduced one man as Dr. Kim, the president of the university, and his assistant, Ms. Sohn. Dr. Han bowed deeply and shook Dr. Kim's hand. I followed in his footsteps. Dr. Kim looked at me suspiciously (which I learned is very normal among Koreans), and then asked me to sit down. Dr. Kim insisted on a translation even though Dr. Han assured him I understood Korean very well.

Dr. Kim began with a long speech about the background of Kim IL Sung University and its significance today. Kim IL Sung University was founded on October 1, 1946, as the first people's institution of higher education in Korea. It was located on the foothills of Mt. Ryongnam, just minutes away from the center of Pyongyang. The university had many faculties and departments of social and natural sciences, different scientific research institutions, and postgraduate and doctoral courses.

Kim IL Sung University was comprised of the main building, the No. 1 building, the No. 2 building and others simply known by a number. Some of the other numbered buildings included a science library with a stock of over two million books, reading rooms and study rooms, a natural museum, a publishing house, a printing shop, laboratories, and dormitories with sleeping accommodations for over 10,000 students. There was also a large hospital where the "best doctors in the world" studied.

Dr. Kim continued with the same bullshit I had already heard a few times since defecting to North Korea about the values of Juche and North Korean socialism and the pure genius of the great leader, Kim IL Sung. Dr. Kim then turned to the role I will be playing at the university. Most importantly, Dr. Kim babbled on about the important contribution I will play for North Korea as a whole. North Korea had just started to change its tactics when I defected. It realized that it couldn't survive on the support of its communist neighbors, China and the Soviet Union. The Soviet Union was already late on its payments and threatened to cut off aid to North Korea.

North Korea was now on a mission to win the hearts of what was called "the non-aligned nations" or those nations that did not fit into the Cold War chess game. This was always a tactic I admired about North Korea. By the early 1970's, North Korea was decreasing its military and terrorist attacks on the South and instead fighting the diplomatic battle. Kim IL Sung began a worldwide tour to gather support. How successful the mission was for that era is debatable. However, it did create some kind of alliance among third world nations for a while. Most importantly for North Korea, it spread the message of the unique North Korean socialism, which was now being called "Kimilsungism." A little conceited, wouldn't you say? No wonder! His son, Kim Jong IL coined the term.

That was where my role came in. I was to be a leading translator and editor of the Korean documents into English, as well as a lecturer at the university on all American affairs and the English language. I would be the dignitary foreign scholar at the most prestigious university in North Korea. Dr. Kim was extremely impressed with my academic background and with the fact that I could speak so many languages. The fact that I wasn't a top military or governmental figure didn't matter. They would make me look like a big shot. I would later learn that the North Korean regime built me up in the North Korean eyes and used me as a source for all sorts of propaganda. As if I agreed with the nonsense the North Korean mouthpiece broadcasts.

Dr. Kim continued to talk and talk, but I don't remember much. After the meeting, I was introduced to more of the university staff and led around like a dignitary. The first thing I noticed was that Dr. Kim and the top staff of the university all had Mercedes Benz limousines with their own chauffeurs parked right outside the building. This was the first of many disparities I noticed between the haves and have-nots of North Korea. Believe me, North Korea was far off from the "socialist paradise" it advertised itself to be.

After the tour, Dr. Han and I returned to his office. A couple of doors down from his office was to be my office. One worker was already preparing my nameplate on the door and two other men were carrying a bookshelf inside.

We sat in Dr. Hans' office all day and into the night talking about the curriculum he had in mind for me. He explained the different classes I would be teaching. My schedule looked full and it was all a bit overwhelming. But then again, defecting to North Korea in the first place was overwhelming. What did I expect? Didn't I want this? Isn't this exactly what I had planned? I told myself to shut up and take everything in stride. I was on a mission. I was here to make a difference. What I didn't realize was that it was already Friday. It was already eight in the evening and Dr. Han turned to me and asked if I wanted to come with him on a weekend trip. I jumped at the opportunity without any hesitation. Finally! A chance to look around North Korea!

The next morning we left early around six. Dr. Han drove a Russian car that looked like some monstrosity from a 1950's science fiction movie. The engine was so loud and noxious fumes were coming through the vents. Dr. Han rolled down the windows so we wouldn't suffocate. We drove through the narrow tree lined road that served as an exit and entrance to the university. I was pretty excited about the trip. The roads we took were mostly empty (as usual) with the exception of a couple of army vehicles. We drove by some terraced fields and along a riverbed that seemed to be almost dry. I wondered if North Korea was suffering from a drought.

I remember Dr. Han explaining different things as we drove. He was a nice guy. I always remember him in the fondest way. We drove through some villages and I asked Dr. Han if we could look at one of them. Dr. Han agreed, but warned me to present myself as a Russian because North Koreans were bred to hate Americans and Europeans. We also drove through three checkpoints in a matter of thirty minutes. North Koreans were not playing around. They looked ready for the worst.

We stopped in a village nestle between a stream and some mountains. The rooftops resembled those of the South Korean villages, especially around the ancient capital of Kyongju (Kyongju is in the southern tip of South Korea). The only difference between this village and the one in South Korea was that the roofs were more dilapidated and the walls looked much thinner. I saw many villagers in the fields but none in the center of the village. North Koreans were never allowed to lounge around, that's why you would never see North Koreans just enjoying their lives.

The center of the village was the heart of village government, commerce, and social life (not much of a social life for North Korean peasants). Dr. Han told me that although North Korea officially copied the Maoist and Leninist systems of socialism, Kim IL Sung was intrigued by the Israeli Kibbutz and Moshav systems and tried to copy them. The biggest difference between Israel's Kibbutzim and Moshavim and the North Korean rural system was that the former were not accountable to the government. The Israeli system was never a slave of the Israeli government, therefore the farmers and Kibbutz leaders made all the decisions regarding what and how to grow. Also, the Kibbutzim and Moshavim competed in a capitalist system where their goods were sold, not given, to companies throughout Israel and abroad.

Dr. Han was so proud of the system that I didn't want to bring up the important differences in the two systems. He was a very intelligent person, but he had been stuck in the North Korean bubble. I would soon learn just how insulated the people of North Korea really were. Any news, any source of information, was from the ministry of information. Every book in the library, every magazine, was pro-socialist or North Korea. Information, the driving force behind intellectual freedom, was extremely limited. It started to dawn upon me that I was now living in George Orwell's world.

We stopped and took a walk around the village. Dr. Han took me to the main building where I could see a truck full of cornhusks pulling in. Except for the truck, there were no other mechanical devices to process the corn. It was all being done by hand. As we walked into the building, I could see the shock on the faces of these farmers. I really scared them. The supervisor, who seemed to know Dr. Han, approached us and bowed deeply towards Dr. Han and me. Dr. Han introduced me to the man known as simply "comrade Lee." Many North Koreans referred to each other as comrade. Comrade Lee seemed so happy that we came and insisted that we have lunch with him. We walked for a few blocks towards an unassuming house where comrade Lee's wife greeted us. It was a nice fall day so we sat outside by a table with two benches. Comrade's Lee's wife came out with a couple of dishes that included "Korean Pizza" or *Pajon*, as its known in Korean. It was only eleven in the morning, and already Dr. Han and comrade Lee were putting down some beers.

I sat there listening to Dr. Han and comrade Lee's stories and got the impression that they had known each other for a long time. Both seem to have played an integral role in the founding of North Korea. The two sat there and hashed up old memories of how they helped found this country and the difficulties and triumphs they endured and achieved. One thing I noticed was how each man gave thanks to Kim IL Sung, the "Great Leader." I was only in North Korea for just over a month and I was already sick of hearing his name.

Following lunch, Dr. Han drove me up the beautiful mountains and along the West Coast. We even took a short hike up one mountain, which ended up by an abandoned Buddhist Temple. I asked Dr. Han why it was abandoned. Dr. Han just shook his head with sadness, paused for a moment, then turned to me with a fake smile and said "Religion is the opiate of the people, therefore, we have liberated North Korea from these evils." I could tell Dr. Han did not believe this, but what could he say? In North Korea, everyone is watched. One thing was for sure, that entire day we were not alone. I noticed that on the empty highway, there was always a car behind ours.

We ended the day with a stop in the port city of Nampo where we were treated by another of Dr. Han's friends to a seafood delight. We ate *Haemultang*, which is a hot and spicy soup that contains all types of seafood. It was really delicious. I thought that all those odd sea creatures would not taste good, but they did. I remember working on a deep sea fishing boat one summer when I was in college in San Francisco. We used to go out at night and turn on the lights so that we could see what we were doing. The lights used to attract squid to come right up to our boat. We used to joke about how we wished we could harvest the squid, but then, who would eat it? I'll tell you who, Koreans. They love squid. They eat it as a snack, main meal, or dessert. You name it! This was one of the most memorable days I had in the "Hermit Kingdom."

Chapter 6

MY FIRST CLASS

February 1974

The following week I started my job as a faculty member at Kim IL Sung University. At first, I was delegated to a few translations and editorial duties. The following week, a bunch of camera crews and reporters came to my office to do a special about my defection to the North. I was given a choreographed piece of paper and told to follow it carefully. I tried to explain to the crew that I would be very positive in my interview. None of them even smiled, they just told me to follow my lines. The lines I was told to say were ridiculous. A bunch of nonsense about how I escaped the imperialist South because of the barbaric conditions I had to live under. Of course, it included how grateful I was to Kim IL Sung and faithful to the ideals of *Juche*.

The crew erected a North Korean flag behind me and made me wear a pin with a picture of Kim IL Sung on it. I was going to be the biggest success story for North Korea in decades in terms of propaganda. I was the only mid-ranking American to defect to the North (They made me into a big shot even though I was officially a minimum clearance clerk for the United States government). One of the five Americans to defect period! That night we watched the interview on the only North Korean television channel in Dr. Han's apartment. The producers chimed in some horseshit narration and music that made North Korea look like a utopia that everyone in the world would just die to get into. They mentioned how I was on of the lucky one who managed to make it pass the DMZ. Many more wanted to come, but were shot or executed by the "barbarian Americans and their South Korean puppets. I was already starting to dislike my "host country."

That week I was given my teaching schedule: Advanced English classes in the morning, one beginner class in the afternoon, and an evening class for the University "staff." In between I was suppose to be on office duty. Dr. Han told me that once in a while I would be asked to proofread some reports before they were distributed. Those reports would later amount to many extra hours of work, sometimes keeping me up all night. I was also expected to draw up a syllabus using the materials the university was using.

As soon as I entered on the first day, all the students stood up and greeted my in unison. I asked them to be seated, but they only sat down when one of the students in the front shouted at them. This was one of those things in North Korea. In every level of North Korean society there was at least one leader/snitch who watched the group like a hawk. This leader was usually rewarded with gifts and luxuries that the rest could never afford. Above each leader, there was another man who watched the leaders. This way, the North Korean elite was always on top of things.

February is one of the coldest months all year in North Korea and this was no exception. The classrooms were bare and freezing. The windows had gaps between them where someone had tried to stuff paper in the cracks to keep out the howling wind. The students were freezing because they had to sit still the entire time but they never complained. Complaining, I would soon find out, is a weakness that only the enemies of North Korea are capable of. That was what distinguished North Koreans from the rest of the world in their minds. That was how the regime solidified their control over its people. North Koreans took pride in their level of endurance and the sacrifices they would carry out in the name of Kim IL Sung and *Juche*.

I wasn't given any information regarding the student besides the fact that they were "the top students in North Korea." Being a student most of my life, I was now on the other end and very inexperienced. Dr. Han didn't really give me any tips and I was told to create my own curriculum from scratch. The night before, Eric, the Australian instructor, gave me some pointers and let me look at his lesson plans. He reassured me by saying that what these students really needed was a conversational partner. That was how Eric conducted his classes. Eric's notes were pages and pages of questions he would ask the students. The students had studied English structure, writing, and reading for most of their lives. Their problem was in conversational English. I soon found out what he meant.

The students in my class (mostly men) couldn't speak English very well, yet their grammatical and writing skills were quite good. I realized that the best way to teach them was to assign them readings the day before, then talk about the readings the next day. The first day, I spent introducing the class structure, getting to know the students, introducing myself, etcetera. The next class I had was even worse. I could not get the students to talk at all. It was like pulling teeth. They all stared at me as if I were an alien that had just landed on earth.

That afternoon, I headed over to the library in search of good reading and teaching materials. I was the center of attention at that university. It seemed as if everyone was looking at me with suspicion or curiosity. As I approached the library, a student guard stopped me and began to yell at me to show him my documents. I told him that I didn't have any documents in Korean. He was a little shocked that I could speak Korean. He then pushed me back and pointed in the other direction meaning I could not go into the library.

I went to Dr. Han's office to tell him about my situation. It seemed that news traveled faster than my feet because he already heard about it. He gave me that apologetic smile of his and reached into his desk. He gave me a pass and a gold pin with a picture of Kim IL Sung on it. He told me to wear the pin at all times and carry the pass with me at all times too. He then escorted me to the library. Before he left the office, he picked up a cane he had in the corner of the room. As we approached the library, the same student guard was there. Dr. Han walked right up to him and with brute force hit the student right on the head. The student collapsed and I could see blood coming out of his head. Dr. Han then screamed at him at the top of his lungs "Don't you know who this is? You idiot! Next time you do not respect Dr. David like that, I will put you in an early grave!"(It sounded good in Korean). Dr. Han then calmly proceeded to enter the library with me following closely behind. With a smile, he began to explain about the library and its resources.

When Dr. Han hit that student guard, there were many other students around. To my amazement, no one stopped or even glanced in our direction. Everyone around us just continued to walk to wherever they were going. It was such a rigid culture. No emotions, no outcry. This was my introduction to how things worked in North Korea. Violence in public was a reminder or who was in control in North Korea. To those of you who don't understand how North Koreans can take so much abuse, just wait and see. I'll explain all about it.

The library wasn't much help. Most of the topics on the shelves of the English language sections were about Soviet or Maoist theories and articles. It was all very boring, I assure you, even for my taste. I realized that I would need to write down some of the classic books from my own memory and have the students read them. I didn't know if that was accepted, so I asked Dr. Han's permission. To my surprise, he didn't object. He even told me that he would give me all the supplies I needed. Dr. Han promised to look into acquiring some classics. He also recommended some teaching techniques and resources I could use. For example, translating articles in the North Korean newspapers into English and discussing them with the students.

What a joke those articles turned out to be. Every article dealt with the glories of Kim IL Sung and *Juche* and the evils of America and its puppet, South Korea. The papers were very clear-cut, optimistic jargon about North Korea and negative nonsense about the West. Early on, I began to realize how foolish I was. I used to think that the United States was an oppressor, bent on corrupting the world with capitalism. Now, I was beginning to realize that I was just a spoiled young guy with a very pessimistic view about life in general. Still, deep down I was excited to be in this bizarre world where everything was a learning experience. I brushed the propaganda aside and focused on learning more about North Korea.

The first week of classes was nightmarish. I could not make any considerable headway with any of the classes. Many of my students were scared of me (They grew up hearing nightmares about Americans. The government propaganda machines taught children from an early age that Americans were "bastards" who were bent on killing all Koreans and eating their babies). The second day I made the mistake of touching one of the students, who reflexively turned and put my hand in a lock (most university students were older than those in the United States because they were required first to go to the army for an average of eight years. All of them were trained in the art of combat and especially in Tae Kwon Do: Korean Martial Arts. Touching that student on the shoulder produced a reaction from him that he probably didn't even realize he did. He later apologized to me). At first, I felt more like their psychologist than a teacher. The students were very edgy and nervous. Some were afraid to say anything without the permission of the group leader.

The class materials given to me were humorous but not conducive to learning. Most of the lessons in the English book focused on patriotic conversations regarding North Korea. Most of the words used in the lesson would never be spoken in everyday English. For example one lesson, appropriately called "How Can We Koreans Become More Self Reliant?" used words like "Fatherland," "Diligent," and "Dear Leader." One conversation was between two North Koreans who wanted to do more for the "Fatherland" (referring to the two Kims influence over the country). Suddenly, a young Kim Jong IL comes up to them and gives them a lecture about self-reliance and sacrifice. It is so sad to think that the most spoiled kid in the world is idolized so much.

It was a real introduction to the militaristic style of North Koreans of all ages. The students would march into the class in file with their Mao-style uniforms and the Kim IL Sung pins on their lapels. No one smiled, not even the girls. They responded to any question I had with a chorus of "Yes sir/No sir!" Individuality did not exist in these human robots. Everyone in the room looked as if they wanted to see me dead. When I did ask more specific questions from students, all eyes seemed to turn towards one individual: The group leader.

Koreans, both in the North and the South, were group-oriented. Every social aspect of the culture had groupings with one leader at the helm. The group leader was usually wiser, older, richer, or simply a man. Even the teacher was supposed to direct his or her attention towards the class/group leader. The group leader of my class was a man by the name of "Comrade Cho." He was 31 years old and a senior at the university.

Every class was required to have a student leader, usually chosen for their rank and loyalty to Kim IL Sung (don't ask me how they determine loyalty). Comrade Cho was quiet, dark skinned, and muscular. I later found out that his father was a leading revolutionary during Japanese occupation. His family came from the island of Cheju, the southernmost island in South Korea. After the Japanese were defeated there, his father advocated socialism, but was pushed out by the South Korean-led government. He fled to the mountains where he led an army of pro-North Koreans against the South Korean and American troops.

Comrade Cho later told me more about his father. His father led a very successful guerilla campaign against South Korean forces by attacking the outlying villages at night and erecting North Korean flags all over the island. By daytime, the South Korean forces would move in to recapture the towns. At night, his father would attack again. It took the South Korean government a few years and the cost of one third of the Island's population (around 40,000 people) to defeat the guerillas. His father had managed to smuggle his family a year earlier into North Korea. His father was eventually captured and executed in public in the city of Sogwipo in the southern (rebellious) part of the island.

Because of his father's attempts, his family won instant approval from the North Korean government and therefore was given high priority. In North Korea, that meant an apartment in the best section of Pyongyang, lifetime privileges such as a television, a washing machine, a car, a top job for their children, and entrance into the elite Universities and North Korean honor guard (a selected army unit for the rich and famous in North Korea). All this aside, Comrade Cho was not a bad student leader. I have seen much worse, believe me!

The class dynamics began to materialize due to the help from Comrade Cho, my openness to the students, and their genuine interest to learn English. I had the students role-play situations, debate minor topics (I had to be careful. People were executed for less than that. One Hungarian was allegedly executed for making a joke about Kim IL Sung). As the students became more comfortable around me, they began to ask more questions. Each time, I was very careful not to make the United States seem like a good place. Dr. Han warned me about that the first day I met him.

Day by day, the students seemed to open more and more. I was really starting to enjoy teaching them. At times, I would go too far with my comments, and the students would respond to my frankness with their sudden silence. It was as if they were teaching me about the boundaries that existed in North Korean (which were too many). I also learned a lot about North Korea by asking my students about Juche, North Korean economics, politics, social issues, and history. I had to mentally filter their comments and balance it with what I already knew about North Korea to get the true picture.

It seemed like every week Dr. Han was introducing me to more big shots in the Korean Workers Party, or the official and only political party in North Korea. Dr. Han would stop by my office with one official or another and introduce me to someone who he would later tell me was a big shot that should be respected. I did my rounds of ass kissing and bowing to everyone Dr. Han brought by. I felt like I was an exotic animal in a zoo, but I also realized my special circumstances and deep down I liked the attention.

At the same time, I befriended Eric, the Australian member of the English faculty. Eric really filled me in on all things North Korean. The first few times I met Eric, he would spew the gung ho crap that I heard from the North Koreans. One day into my third week at the university, Eric invited me to drink a few beers in his room. At first, we talked a little about how much we loved North Korea and Eric went on to say how fortunate we were that Kim IL Sung has accepted us in North Korea despite the bad reputation of our countries. Then Eric asked me if I wanted to watch television. Before even waiting for my response, he turned it on full volume. He then pointed around the room and whispered to me that our conversation was being monitored.

Eric pulled a couple of beers from the fridge and we began a very frank conversation about North Korea. Eric told me that he was once young and naive just like me when he first decided to travel to the weird and unknown places around the world. Eric traveled to South America, Eastern Europe, South East Asia, and eventually North Korea. In China, Eric found a guide who was willing (willing because Eric paid him an equivalent of a year's salary) to take Eric to North Korea. He smuggled his way in through China on a tour of Mt. Paekdusan (the highest mountain in North Korea that straddles the border with China. There is a bit of a dispute over the boundaries between the two nations).

Eric was quickly arrested since seeing a white guy in North Korea was extremely rare. Eric spent more than eight months in prison and interrogation. The North Koreans were in fact finally convinced that he was not an Australian spy and delegated him to an English teaching position just like me. Eric didn't really want to stay in North Korea. He wanted to continue to travel. However, leaving North Korea was not an option. North Korea was not playing by anyone's rules and Eric didn't even have a chance to let his family and friends know where he was. If you wanted to be isolated from the world, North Korea was the place to be. Thus, Eric's wander lust hit a dead end.

Eric told me about what to expect living in North Korea. As the token educated white guy, I could expect a very lavish life compared to the other ninety nine percent of the country. We would be treated like royalty, have access to imported goods, and enjoy "freedoms" such as permits to travel around the country and shop at the only department store in the whole damn country. Wow! How exciting! My ears perked up when Eric referred to the choices of prostitutes we would have as well. Although it was very illegal, the elite in North Korea had prostitutes brought in from the countryside and abroad.

The downside was that if we, in any way, voiced our discontent with the regime or Kim IL Sung, we would be exterminated. Eric didn't mince his words. He meant exterminated. Eric told me that he had heard of entire villages and counties that were killed for their "rebellious" tendencies. Executions were almost a daily occurrence in private and public. It was believed that Kim IL Sung wanted everyone, even the elite, to see the consequences of discontent. Kim IL Sung did not climb to the top by being a nice guy (I'll talk more about him later).

Eric told me about the occasional public execution on the university campus. For example, a couple of students were recently executed for their inquiries into Buddhism. The story goes that they were simply interested in researching the relevance of Buddhism in Korean culture. They even tried to find parallels between *Juche* and Buddhism. Buddhism was a religion, and religion was an opiate. The government would never tolerate it. Another student was publicly executed for his views on the dangers of Korean isolationism. He constantly let people know that he didn't agree with "*Juche,*" or North Korean "self reliance." Even his father's high position in the Navy could not save him. Kim Jong IL, Kim IL Sung's favorite son, got hold of this "blasphemy" and ordered him to be executed in the campus quad for all students to see. The entire university was ordered to come and watch the execution. There were no ifs or buts about it. If someone didn't show up, that person was also considered a traitor to the *Juche* ideology.

The worst, according to Eric, was when a sizable group of students held a peaceful march for unification through the campus quad. Rumors have it that a couple of North Korean students who were studying in Beijing, China, met up with their South Korean counterparts. They allegedly decided to hold simultaneous marches on campuses in North and South Korea. I guarantee that if this story was true, the marches went on in South Korea uninterrupted. I witnessed several student demonstrations in South Korean universities and none of the students were arrested. At Kim IL Sung University, however, things were very different. Eric said several plain-clothes agents came out of the woodwork and quickly arrested the marchers. Eric never saw any of them again.

The true insanity of North Korea was beginning to emerge. Eric's hour-long ramblings about the wickedness of the regime took me by surprise. He was especially impressed with the grip of power that Kim IL Sung and his family managed to nurture in North Korea. It was beyond even Stalin or Hitler because of its longevity. This man was now unchallenged in any way. If people did not prove their utmost loyalty to him, they were imprisoned. Not only were they imprisoned, so were their entire families at times. If their families were not imprisoned, they were shunned from society. Eric told me about the Northeast, where entire counties were turned into "security zones." In other words, it would be as if the United States turned New England into a prison.

Accesses to certain parts of North Korea were forbidden to everyone. Pyongyang was a virtual prison itself. Most people needed special permits to get in and out of the city. Most of the outlying city and countryside population were not allowed access into Pyongyang. Within Pyongyang, the elite were delegated to a certain part of the city, which was surrounded by a wall. This was not only to protect the elite, but also to keep a close eye on them. Kim IL Sung believed that the elite had to be watched even more closely than the peasants for they were the first to try to rebel. Kim thought this way because of past historical experiences, including his own rise to power. He was from a well-to-do family, educated, Christian. Now he was completely against the same people he had himself once belong to.

Eric also informed me about the continual downward economic spiral that North Korea was in. Regardless of the ridiculous "five year or seven year plans" by Kim IL Sung to achieve economic self-sufficiency, the country continued to suffer. People were being asked to work harder for the "*Juche*" cause, while sacrificing more. Food rations were decreasing. Simple goods such as radios were harder to come by. The rhetoric and propaganda were increasing. Meanwhile, elaborate construction projects were under way to enhance Kim IL Sung's stature in the world. The most amazing project was the recent completion of a huge statue of him in downtown Pyongyang.

Eric stretched his hands and pointed around the room,

"Look around you!" he said.

"Do you see all these objects around my apartment? These are standard in our countries, but not here. Here, only the top one percent of the people have indoor plumbing, a television set, a stove, and a radio. You haven't seen how the rest lives. They live in a one bedroom shack with absolutely no furniture or appliances. They are lucky if they even have a radio. Just to get water, they have to go to the local well and stand in line. We are so well to do compared to them."

Eric went on to explain about the "special farms" and trade that was privy only the elite in the country. Eric had it on good sources that there were ultra-secret farms where livestock and produce were cultivated especially for the Kim family and his innermost circle of elite. Only the most loyal cadres from the top military brigades were allowed to work and live on these farms. The farms were guarded constantly by elite soldiers. Eric informed me that most North Koreans had never even tasted citrus fruit or eaten a steak. Meanwhile Eric had been to top cadre banquets that offered prime cut meat, lobster, caviar, and the most expensive liquors such as Hennessy and Suntory.

I had no idea at the time about how the rest of North Korea lived. All I knew was that we taught at the best University in all of North Korea. Still, I really believed that socialism had provided North Koreans with more equality than in other countries. I blindly believed that every North Korean, from party leader to corn farmer, lived in similar conditions. I had a lot to learn about this mysterious place.

After leaving Eric's room, I thought deep and hard about the subtle little things I had noticed since arriving in North Korea. I remember how time and punctuality were so important to North Koreans. Not one of my students was ever late, nor was anyone ever wandering the halls or campus during class time. I also noticed the general quietness that surrounded the university almost all the time. KIS was very different from an American university campus. I also thought about the general uneasiness between everyone and the beating Dr. Han gave that poor student guard.

All this was going through my head that night as I tried to get some shuteye. I was also excited because Eric promised that he would show me around Pyongyang the next day. I tried to assess the situation in my head. I had made my decision to defect to North Korea. What did I expect, a quick tour of the country and a ticket home to San Francisco? I should make the best of my situation, learn as much as I could about North Korea, and then try to find a way to visit another country. I didn't want to return to the United States anyway.

The next morning I waited with Eric outside our building for Dr. Han. Eric explained to me that we always needed an escort to go anywhere outside the campus because North Koreans were bred to believe that foreigners were devils. Eric told me that when he snuck across the border from China, he walked into a village and began to take pictures. In no time, the villagers came from the fields with their sticks and farming equipment in hand and hit Eric until he passed out. When he woke up, he found himself in a North Korean army camp.

We drove across one of the only bridges that crossed the Daedong River. At the time, the city center was on the western bank of the river. Nevertheless, I could see that they were busy developing the eastern side as well. Huge cranes were busy building these massive building on the eastern side. At the time, I thought that this was a sign of progress by a socialist state. I thought this was a collective effort that would benefit everyone equally. What an idiot I was!

Dr. Han told me that the Americans destroyed most of the city during the Korean War. Despite the American efforts, no one could keep Koreans down, said Dr. Han. I quickly learned that the woes of North Korea were always due to the United States, Japan, and South Korea. The country acted like a sour kid who found it easier to blame others for his faults. Dr. Han was very proud of the advancements made by North Korea. Still, I did notice the traditional construction methods used while driving by a building. Everything was operated by hand. There were no machines. They even mixed the cement using pine sticks.

Dr. Han was proud of the fact that these massive office and apartment buildings were built in less time than their South Korean counterparts, and, of course, the North Korean apartments were of better value and had more floors than South Korean apartments, according to Dr. Han. The fact was that the poor North Korean people were in a frenzy over making North Korea into a "workers paradise." Dr. Han was also proud of pointing out that everything was free in North Korea. The government provided the people with free apartments, televisions, food, and clothing. All of this, Dr. Han added, was because of the benevolence of the "Great Leader, Kim IL Sung."

The streets in the center of Pyongyang reminded me of what I learned about Napoleon and Paris. Apparently, Napoleon built wide thoroughfares in order to be able to see a rebellion coming a mile away. He could then place a row of cannons on the streets and blast the protesters away. There would very few places they could hide. That was Pyongyang. It was a dark city with extremely wide streets with no real traffic or side streets where people could hide. I think that Kim IL Sung wanted it this way so that everyone was always exposed and could not conspire against him. It also gave the impression that this city was incredibly modern.

We drove to the center of the city, where Dr. Han and I had to go through another checkpoint. This time the guards checked the entire car. Most people know of Korean culture as lopsided in favor of men. However, I saw many women soldiers in Pyongyang, guarding the most important sites around the city. They carried machine guns and looked very serious. Eric told me that they go through tough training just like the men. He also told me that Kim Jong IL surrounded himself with beautiful women bodyguards. It sounded like some James Bond movie.

The center of the city was the gem of North Korea. This was where all the propaganda pictures were taken of Pyongyang. The Mansundae Congress Palace, the Children's Palace (funny that most children in North Korea never had a chance to visit this place that was allegedly built in their honor), the Jae IL Department Store, and the countless statues and monuments to Kim IL Sung and *Juche*. At the time, there was a massive construction project for more absurd buildings and monuments such as the Mansundae Arts Theater (which I would later have a chance to visit) and the *Juche* Tower that apparently was being built by Kim Jong IL as a surprise for his father. This whole country was the Kim's family playground; at their disposal.

Dr. Han stopped the car in front of the riverbank and we walked on the widest sidewalk I had ever seen in my life towards a massive picture of Kim IL Sung. The North Koreans around me looked as if they were in a trance. They gazed at the picture with such awe on their faces. I felt as if I had joined a cult. Charles Manson was a joke compared to Kim. I overheard people around me talking to the picture, almost praying to it. All I could think of was how had they managed to paint this portrayed that stood as high as a five floor building and as wide as a football field.

Dr. Han kept staring at the picture for several minutes, so I eventually lost interest and focused my attention towards the Daedong River. I noticed a group of cranes on the banks of the river. They looked so majestic wading in the water looking for their next meal. They had their backs to the large portrait of the "great leader." The birds were too busy foraging for food to worry about this silly portrait. If only the North Korean people could do the same. Even as early as the 1970's it was obvious that the average North Korean was malnourished. The people were too busy breaking their backs to satisfy a greedy and selfish leader who was more interested in his international standing than on his own people.

After the tour, Dr. Han took me to a hotel (I can't remember the name) where we had a "Western-style" lunch. Dr. Han told me that this was one of the best restaurants where diplomats and party officials dined. Wow! If that was the best restaurant for western food, I was in trouble. The menu only had three choices: Ham, Duck, and Beef. I ordered the duck and Dr. Han ordered the ham. The ham was actually Spam and the duck tasted like rubber. The side orders were French fries and some sort of sauce that hardened up before I could even try it. We were waited on by three different waiters. They turned this simple task into a ritual by doing everything for us besides actually chewing the food. It was ridiculous. I knew that the only good food I would be able to eat in North Korea was Korean food.

After dinner we continued our tour around the city. I did see some families in the afternoon enjoying picnics in the Kim IL Sung Park (Surprise! Everything is named after him and his son). It was the only time I saw ordinary Koreans enjoying their free time in public. Even these "relaxing" picnics looked as if they were arranged by the government. The people crowded around a man playing the guitar and sang in unison. At first sight, it looked like a great gathering anywhere in any park around the world. When I listened to the lyrics of the songs, I caught the words "Kim IL Sung, our great leader" and "we shall fight to the death to protect our rights."

Dr. Han tried to explain to me that because of socialism, people worked in a collective manner and therefore did not have to work so hard. What a load of bull! It was the weekend and the people there were under obligation to show their enthusiasm towards Kim IL Sung by showing up. I later learned that it was only in Pyongyang that these picnics and dance displays were conducted. It was primarily propaganda. Foreigners were taken to these parks and shown what the government wanted them to see. I knew exactly how hard people worked. I saw people leave for work at six in the morning and not come home until eight or nine at night. This situation worsened as the North Korean economy continued to slide in the 1980's and 1990's.

Dr. Han felt obligated to feed me the government line wherever we went. He used more superlatives than I had ever heard from a tour guide. "North Korea has the highest tower," "North Koreans are the most educated and most diligent," "Pyongyang has the lowest death rate." I felt like telling Dr. Han to knock off all the bull and be honest with me. After all, I was not a foreign tourist. I was in North Korea to stay. He didn't have to amuse me. Little did I know that everyone was living this charade. Even if they knew the Emperor was naked, no one dared to say anything about it.

For me, living in North Korea was the biggest lesson of my life: I had to stop criticizing everything if I were to survive. It was the first time in my spoiled life that I could not complain or criticize. I was so accustomed to doing so back home. I don't blame my parents or my teachers; I am just surprised at how far I was allowed to go with my criticism. I mean, I used to argue with my high school teachers about how evil the American government was or how Americans were oppressing others. I used to criticize my mother for being bourgeoisie and my father for being greedy. Here in North Korea I could not even complain about the food. I had to bite my lips for the first time. This was my first lesson in freedom of speech and how precious it was.

The last leg of the tour was the clincher for me. It was the ultimate confirmation of what North Koreans held dear to their hearts (or what the government wanted them to hold dear). The Museum of "Fine Arts" in central Pyongyang was actually another monument to the "Dear Leader." Most of the museum was dedicated to modern *"Juche"* art. The artwork either showed Kim IL Sung himself, or was dedicated to him. I asked Dr. Han whether or not there were any paintings of the ancient dynasties of Korea, such as Choson (Yi) or Paekche. Dr. Han looked at me suspiciously, as if to say: "What? Aren't you interested in you Leader?"

I did finally see one room where ancient art was on display. The paintings were in bad shape and the room was dimly lit. It should not have been a surprise for me. That was the same with the library at the university. Most of the books and essays at that horrible library were either written by Kim IL Sung, or written about him. It was absurd. The only books I did find that were not about that subject were dry books pertaining to science, math, or engineering. Books in the social sciences and literature were obviously a menace because they offered different perspectives.

As night was setting in, Dr. Han drove us around the city making a couple of circles to admire the lighted monuments and statues. Who were the monuments for? You guessed it, Kim IL Sung. They were the only fixtures that were lit up at night. It was as if the city was under a strict curfew, expecting an enemy attack at any minute. In fact, lights were an anomaly in North Korea, even during the apex of North Korea's economy. Even the elite was expected to use only two hours a day of electricity. The only time lights illuminated the city was when important foreign dignitaries visited Pyongyang. Kim IL Sung University was no exception. The only light at night was in the center of the quad, where a statue commemorating Kim IL Sung and *Juche* stood shining.

That reminded me of my first national emergency drill in North Korea. I was accustomed to the monthly drills because I had lived in South Korea. In South Korea, every month, usually in the middle of the month, the sirens rang across the country and everyone had to stop what they were doing and take shelter. One time I was hiking above the mountains of Pusan, a city on the southern coast. As I looked down on one of the roads, I noticed that everything had stopped right in its tracks following the loud sirens I had just heard. Two minutes later, I noticed two jet fighters flying at a low altitude over the city in my direction. I thought that this was an attack from the North, but then I remembered that in my basic training they told us about these drills. Sure enough, the jet fighters were nothing more than a couple of Phantom F4s of the South Korean air force.

The drills in North Korea were more intense. Everyone in North Korea was always on high alert any way. Everywhere you went you saw military installations and checkpoints. There were all sorts of military brigades of all ages and backgrounds on patrol or just positioned somewhere to intimidate others. There were the "Shock Units" (just the title was enough to scare people), young men and women who patrolled the streets or worked as laborers on construction sites (depending on availability).

There were also the "Youth Brigades," groups of youths in training for the army who doubled as informers and "enforcers." They were used in the most manipulative way, to spy on their own parents and family. Since childhood, children learned that Kim IL Sung played a priority to their own family and friends. Therefore, any irregular behavior should be reported to the authorities. It was considered the patriotic to do. Imagine how parents felt around their own children knowing this. This ensured a tight grip on the North Korean people, even in their own homes.

To me, the women were the worst. Kim IL Sung was cunning; I'll give him that. He was one leader (unlike many other dictators throughout history) who saw the value of using women to enforce the regime's rules. Women are fifty percent of the population, yet many governments fail to utilize this power source. Not Kim IL Sung. Women in North Korea served as traffic police, tour guides, community center administrators, monument and museum attendants, and much, much more.

To the unsuspecting tourist, the employment of women might seem like equal rights or gender equality. Bull Shit! These women were used as informants. Their real job was not just to monitor the subway stations and traffic but, more importantly, to monitor people's behaviors. Even at our university, groups of women walked around the campus looking for anything suspicious or out of the ordinary. They were ruthless, and many times I saw them shout at other students or write their names down and warn them about the consequences of their actions.

There was also an entire system of regular informants. The State Security Agency (SSA) assigned its officers to recruit loyal party cadres to inform on their surroundings. Each officer directed 50 informants, who in turn, watched 20 other people. That way even one officer had the capability of watching 1,000 North Koreans. Meanwhile, other organizations such as the Young Workers Brigades (YWB), the Counterintelligence Division (CID), informed on those who informed. Therefore, at several points in every North Korean's life, everyone was being watched and/or watching someone. These organizations resemble the German Third Reich in their efficiency and cruelness.

It was considered an honor in North Korea to be a member of any one of these military organizations. To many, becoming members of these organizations was the only way to climb the North Korean social ladder. It was especially important to the lower classes because it was the only way for them to have a chance to live in Pyongyang and join the Korean Worker's Party. Ironically, the children of the Korean Worker's Party were exempt from such military duties because of their political connections. Only the lower classes had to serve in the armed forces for such an extensive stay.

Chapter 7

SAM, MATT, AND DR. HABIBI

June 1974

Eric, Dr. Han, and I returned to downtown Pyongyang a couple of weeks later, this time in the evening. Eric and Dr. Han were going to show me the only place where foreigners and top brass Koreans mixed. It was a small bar/nightclub located in the basement of the Ryongyang Hotel. The bar did not have a name and barely any lighting. The music was mostly Korean, Russian and English. Surprisingly, the North Koreans knew the English songs well. They seemed to especially like Elvis Presley and the Beatles. The night I was there, there were not more than thirty people in the bar. I could hear Arabic, Russian, English, and Korean.

This was where I first met the two other Americans who lived in North Korea: Sam and Matt. Sam was a former United States Marine stationed in South Korea who defected just like me. Eric told me that Sam was a heavy drinker and was known to get into fights at this bar. He was from a small town in Pennsylvania and was not very bright. He reminded me of the tough Italian or German wrestlers that come from that area of the United States. He looked like the typical burly Marine type and I wondered why would someone like him defect. I would later find out.

Matt was another soldier who defected. Matt was an African American who had a slight Southern accent. He was also very tall. He really stood out in North Korea. Sam seemed more down to earth and reserved. Eric told me that Matt was playing basketball on the Pyongyang team, but was restricted from playing abroad. I don't know whether that was due to the government protecting him from the outside world or whether they were afraid he would flee. Who knows? North Korea was full of mysteries.

Matt was the glue in our group. He agreed with everything everyone said. He just wanted to keep the peace. He felt overwhelmed with the attention he received as a tall black man, yet he kept his smile. The North Koreans treated him very well because of his unique talent and the good publicity he transmitted.

That was the night I also met Dr. Habibi for the first time. Dr. Habibi was an Arabic professor at Kim IL Sung University and lived in the same building with Eric and me, but I never saw him until this night at the bar. Dr. Habibi was a visiting professor from Syria who was actually of Lebanese descent. Dr. Habibi said it was complicated, but that Syria had always played a dominant role in Lebanese affairs. His father, a successful businessman, operated a trading company in Damascus, Syria because he constantly needed the permission of the government for every little business venture. Therefore, it made sense to just live close to the Syrian government and get on their good side.

Dr. Habibi was a Maronite Christian Arab. For those of you not really familiar with that area of the world, not all Arabs are Muslim. As a matter of fact, Lebanon had a sizable Christian population. I learned a lot about the Middle East from Dr. Habibi. He was so happy that I was interested in the area and was thrilled at the chance to explain all about that complex region. He was proud of the fact that he was close friends with such prominent Lebanese leaders as the politician Amin Gemayel and General Michel Aoun. Dr. Habibi was the one man who was good at keeping the bar patrons from isolation. I noticed that he made the rounds between the Arabs, the other foreigners, and the North Koreans. Each time, he would deliberately introduce one person from one group to someone from another group. He also was the glue that kept all the strangers together. If it weren't for him, I think the bar would have been dissected into three parts.

The other noticeable factor of this bar was the constant circulation of bar girls. Unlike in South Korea or elsewhere in the world, these girls were fully dressed. At first, I mistook them for Koreans. I later learned that they were Korean-Japanese and pure Japanese. Eric later told me about the large presence of Korean-Japanese and Japanese who sympathized with socialism in North Korea. This was an odd mix of people who in fact, like me, knew what they were leaving behind in the "capitalist" world. Don't forget, we are talking about the 1970's. People like me thought socialism was a world revolution.

The bar girls were groped, especially by the Arabs and Sam. Sam seemed to have his hands everywhere. The girls just smiled and accepted their fate. It reminded me a lot of the Itaewon district in Seoul. One girl approached me and asked me to buy her a drink. No hello, nice to meet you, just buy me a drink. I bought her a drink and then she would not leave me alone. It wasn't that she was not pretty, I felt that I was new to North Korea and didn't want to screw up. The girl, whose name was Kumi, told me that she knew who I was. Apparently, I had been the talk of the bar for quite some time. She said that she could count on her fingers the number of foreigners in Pyongyang. Nothing about the expatriates in North Korea was a secret (little did she know).

Eric also eventually made his way to a girl and so I felt a little more comfortable talking to Kumi. She told me that she also had a Korean name: So-Hyun. Her husband had been a member of the Japanese Red Army, a terrorist group that was responsible for a number of attacks against any capitalist country in the world. About two years ago, on a mission in Algeria, he was assassinated by the Mossad, the Israeli secret service (The Japanese Red Army worked with Palestinian terrorist groups throughout the 1970's). His face blew into pieces when he answered the telephone in his hotel room. It was in retaliation for the Japanese Red Army's support of Palestinian terrorist groups.

Kumi's family defected to North Korea because of fears for their lives from the Japanese right and rumors that the Israeli Mossad didn't just kill their enemy, but their enemy's family as well. I told Kumi that was far from the truth. If anything, the Japanese Red Army were the ones who considered innocent people's lives unimportant. Although I believed in the socialist cause, I knew that those terrorist groups were only good at killing civilians with booby trap bombs. They were the ones who gave socialism and communism a bad name.

I stopped rambling on about my views on terrorism once I realized where I was. I also noticed that I was talking too fast and above Kumi's comprehension level. I quickly switched topics. I asked Kumi why she was working at a place like this. Kumi just smiled and looked away as if to say: "can't you figure it out?" North Koreans were probably the most xenophobic people in the world. They were bred by their government to truly hate all outsiders, even their allies. The television, radio, newspapers, even my students, were broken records of racial remarks about the "inferior whites," "barbarian Americans," "the Jewish plague," or the "South Korean puppets."

Eric then approached us with another bar girl and asked me if I wanted to go to the "deluxe room" for a private party. The "deluxe room" and "private party" ended up being a place where we could have sex. Kumi and the other girl led us to this dark room after grabbing a bottle of Vodka from the counter. The room just had a Korean traditional mattress on the floor and a small table with four chairs. We sat and drank the vodka. I noticed that Eric was beginning to fondle his girl, while Kumi just kept looking at me with a big smile.

Kumi was a petite Japanese girl with an extremely small waist, but nice round hips and a wholesome pair of breasts. She was definitely my type. I can't say she was very pretty. She had a bunch of crooked teeth, really small eyes, and very pale. Nevertheless, this was the only woman I had even touched since I arrived in North Korea. I could feel my penis swell like I had never felt it swell before. I reached for Kumi's hips and began to kiss her. Meanwhile, Eric was already having full intercourse with his girl. They took up most of the mattress so I decided to have intercourse with Kumi on the table. Kumi seemed very excited. When I went down on her, I could see her clitoris protruding with joy and feel her wet vagina.

We made love twice in several positions. Kumi screamed with joy and definitely gave the impression that she was enjoying herself. Who knows! It could have been part of her act. I mean, she was getting paid to do this. That's why I never really got too excited about sleeping with prostitutes. But after months of no female interaction, I felt grateful for anything. It was the only form of "affection" for me.

After the second time, Eric came over and asked me if I wanted to switch with him. Deep down, I really didn't. Eric had chosen this skinny, low-voiced girl, who just lay there while Eric pounded her (I had glanced at them while having intercourse with Kumi). Still, I wasn't about to say no to my new friend. Eric told me later that he was just trying to get his money's worth. It was customary to switch prostitutes between each other. That seemed to make it even more humiliating. As if they were objects to be traded. Eric graciously paid for the both of us. He probably knew that I had not been paid yet and that I was new to the whole scene.

We drove back to campus around 11:00pm. It was past curfew (All North Koreans had to be off the streets by 11:00), but Dr. Han was no ordinary person. He just waived his identification at the guards at the several check posts and they let us through. Eric later told me that Dr. Han was well connected. If anything ever went wrong, Eric advised me to mention Dr. Han's name and everything would be taken care of.

Chapter 8

HOW DOES HE CONTROL ALL OF THEM?

1974–78

My life was starting to take on some normality in a very bizarre world. I was immersed in my teachings and editorial work, as well as my own research into North Korean history, politics, and culture. It was impossible to come by any unbiased literature regarding anything. As a matter of fact, the lies fabricated by the North Korean regime were hard to swallow even for someone who had no idea about North Korea. This was the biggest question that confronted me: How do the rest of the North Korean population swallow such nonsense? It would take me a few years to completely realize how the North Korean regime (Kim IL Sung in particular) perfected the art of total control.

When I mean the North Koreans "believed" the propaganda coming from the government, I am referring to the ultimate meaning of the word "believe." Just as some messianic leaders throughout human history were able to convince their followers that they were Gods, so did Kim IL Sung. However, I challenge anyone to find another person in history that had managed to hypnotize and terrorize twenty seven million people for his entire life. He is still controlling North Koreans from beyond his grave.

Kim IL Sung was never a favorite among Koreans during and following World War II, just as Stalin was not a favorite to Russians either. What the two leaders possessed was the art of control and deception. Believe it or not, Kim IL Sung combined the two beliefs he knew he could use to influence Koreans: Confucianism and Korean Christianity. These two factors had influenced Korean lifestyles significantly.

The Choson dynasty used the pure form of Confucianism to control the Korean people successfully for over eight hundred years. No other dynasty was ever that successful in Korea. Confucianism is a set of rules laid out by Confucius, which were intended to protect his boss, the emperor of China. The five noble truths of Confucianism focused on keeping order in society. Respect and obedience between the five truths were of the utmost importance. The obedience to the leader by the people, the respect of the parents by the children, the respect for the elders by their juniors, the respect of women towards men, students towards teachers, etcetera.

North Korea was also a stronghold for Christianity. Prior to the end of World War II, Pyongyang was the center for art, education, and Christianity. The people of Pyongyang considered themselves elite by Korean standards and as elites, turned to the West. They adopted Christianity through extremist missionaries stationed there. Their form of Christianity was very orthodox and insisted on a strict following of the scripture. A tradition of almost messianic following of Christianity facilitated an obedient population.

Most importantly, a homegrown Korean practice has always been the "We/Us/Our phenomenon. Koreans are extremely group oriented. Both in South and North Korea individualism is frowned upon. I always attributed this to their unique geographical situation. Korea is a craggy peninsula, over seventy percent mountainous. This meant that since the dawn of civilization there, people have been huddled together in crowded confines. Don't forget, Korea is one of the most densely populated nations in the world.

The most widely used words in the Korean language are We/Us/Our, unlike in America, where I/me/my are more common. Koreans are easily influenced in their groups by the leader. The leader is usually a leader because he possesses one of the Confucian noble truths. Rarely do Koreans question the leader's words or intelligence. This has resulted in some pretty bad decision-making over the years, even in large Korean conglomerates such as Samsung or Hyundai. This lemming mentality was a nightmare waiting to happen and along came Kim IL Sung, a charismatic war hero who possessed all of the 'noble' qualities.

Kim IL Sung, who came from a Christian background, combined all the ingredients I just mentioned and created a manipulative system that answered to no one but him. Kim eliminated his foes with pure violence and therefore had no competition. Even his closest aides were systematically eradicated just to keep everyone else on their toes. Like Stalin, Kim began his career as almost a nobody. Like Stalin, he used violence to climb the ladder. Like Stalin, he killed an unknown number of his own people. Like Stalin, Kim kept a tight grip on the entire population. Unlike Stalin, Kim lived a long and healthy life, ruling North Korean until his death in 1994.

What is most impressive is how Kim IL Sung created a whole personality cult around himself. Just turning on the television, walking on the streets of Pyongyang gave evidence to the cult personality of Kim IL Sung and later his son, Kim Jong IL. Humongous statues and paintings of Kim IL Sung and Kim Jong IL dot every corner of North Korea. Every statement made by a governmental institution, no matter how insignificant it is, must include praise to Kim IL Sung. For example, "Thanks to our Dear Leader Kim IL Sung, our local production of corn in Hamhung Province was able to exceed our expectations for this month." The constant reminder of "the Dear Leader" enforced the fanatical following of Kim IL Sung from birth for the younger Koreans.

The newspapers in North Korea ran constant anecdotes regarding Kim IL Sung and Kim Jong IL. For example, I vaguely remember one article about how Kim IL Sung had always worried about the workers. That was why he made a "long and difficult" trek to a rural factory in the Northeast to show his appreciation of the "hard work" they were all putting in for the good of the nation. The article said that Kim IL Sung got out of the car and walked despite the bitter cold that day to shake the hands of every worker at the plant. He then presented each one with a gift. To a Westerner, it might be brushed off as simply politicking, nothing special. North Koreans have a different interpretation. North Koreans perceived this as an altruistic act from a benevolent leader who truly cared about his people. Actually, this trip was probably fictional, created by the propaganda department.

Imagine growing up and learning that the reason the sun rises every day or the corn tastes sweet was because of one man. Imagine learning as a child that the talented Kim designed new engineering feats and published countless novels that were world successes. I think Kim learned a lot from Christianity and simply over the long term replaced Jesus Christ with Kim IL Sung. The fabricated lies created by the North Korean government concerning the amazing feats that Kim has accomplished would not fly anywhere else in the world. To say that a living human being is God has not worked since the founding of Christianity, Judaism, and Islam.

I remember seeing some of the pictures of Kim IL Sung around Pyongyang and in the cultural centers. In each picture, the artist subliminally informs the viewer of the absolute power Kim holds; while still displaying great compassion for his people. One of my favorite pictures was that of Kim IL Sung sitting on a bench surrounded by young kids who are totally immersed in him. One of the children was wearing his trademark fedora hat. Another child was sitting on his lap and smiling at him. This innocent epitomized for me of the successful propaganda machine in North Korea.

Kim IL Sung was portrayed in that picture as a loving father figure who held the total attention of even young children. As everyone knows, children are easily distracted by anything and it's very hard to get the total attention of every child at the same time. Korean culture revolves around the family and children are the most precious commodities. This picture sent the message that Kim was a kind, thoughtful leader who loved and was loved by all children. Showing Kim with children was a subliminal message to any Korean who might hold reservations about his leadership. In people's minds the title of the portrait would read as follows:

"He is a loving man and has the total loyalty of the Korean population, even the children. Don't try to mess with him because no one will support you!"

That picture reminded me of a picture of Jesus Christ my grandmother had in her dining room. Jesus was sitting in the same position as Kim, holding a child up, with rosy colors in the background. The picture of Kim had almost the same rosy colors and shiny background as my grandmother's picture. This was another example of Kim using his Christian background to his advantage.

Just as there are billboard on American highways urging people to drink Coca-Cola, billboards in North Korea sell Kim IL Sung and *Juche*. It is as if an advertising company joined forces with the government. There were signs all over Korea euphorically advertising life in North Korea. If life were so great there, would the government really need to advertise that fact? Of course not! Thanks to Kim IL Sung's own paranoia, the government continually exhausted its own energy trying to bolster him. It was truly a frightening scene. I don't even think George Orwell could ever imagine such a society.

The most important energy used to bolster his leadership was that of the army. No matter how poor the North Korean people became, the army was always well fed and taken care of. As we can see today, North Korea is suffering from severe draught, malnutrition, and a collapsed economy. Nevertheless, North Korea continues to pour all their money into the military. The North Korean military is still considered the fourth largest in the world.

CHAPTER 9

MY RISE IN THE NORTH KOREAN REGIME

1978–1980

My prominence in North Korean society grew beyond my own expectations. I was becoming a household name throughout the Stalinist state. All of the forms of the media had continued to run front news coverage of my defection to North Korea. The North Korean propaganda machine built me up to a head of state that saw the evils of capitalism and decided to flee the "sinking ship." I was constantly stared at wherever I went and treated with celebrity-like status. For my own "protection," two agents were appointed to watch me when I left the campus. It felt as if I were given a key to a secret dimension that only the elite was allowed to enter.

I was slowly beginning to understand how North Korea operated. Still, I felt that I would need to climb higher to truly know the inner-workings of the regime. Don't forget, my curiosity made me oblivious to anything that resembled a conscious or sincere concern for my fellow humans. During my rise in social standing in North Korea, I continued to party with Eric and others and sleep with many different girls. Matt even convinced me to join some orgies that he had participated in. Those were the ultimate parties: Men sleeping with young girls and boys, one girl having sex with ten men, drinking binges, you name it.

I also managed to meet several high-ranking officials thanks to Dr. Han and Dr. Habibi. Between those two, there was no top official in North Korea who was off limits. Not even Kim IL Sung's own family. Dr. Han was a close friend of Kim IL Sung's son from his second marriage. As you might already have known, Kim IL Sung's first wife died and he later remarried. It was now becoming apparent that there was a struggle for power between Kim's sons. Of course, Kim Jong IL was always his father's favorite.

Meeting these high ranking officials further tainted my rosy colored view of socialism. All of these so-called government officials bragged about the loot they had "earned" being bureaucrats. All they talked about was where to get the best Cognac, or which car was most powerful. I hardly heard any of them discuss the dire need to modernize the agricultural sector or how to improve the healthcare system. One fat government elite once pulled me aside and told me he could fix me up with a virgin.

I attended a few banquets for mostly foreign dignitaries. This was where I made my rounds, usually introduced by either Dr. Han or Dr. Habibi. I was mostly greeted with interest, as I am sure that the majority of the top cadres in North Korea had heard about me. I also think the fact that I spoke Korean so well made a name for myself as well. Every time I began to speak in Korean, I always got a small reaction of surprise from Koreans. I think they thought no foreigner could ever learn Korean. Even the few foreign students in North Korea never really learned Korean that well.

Those banquets were also hornet's nests for all the enemies of the Western world. There were Cubans, Palestinians, guerilla leaders from at least four continents, Communists, Maoists, Anarchists, even a member of Farrakhan's Muslim brotherhood. They all looked shifty-eyed and whispered a lot. I mean, I always wanted to discuss the West's historic domination of the world with other nationals, but these people were scary. I did make the rounds, and to my dismay I found out that these people were worse than anyone in the United States. The guerillas were only in North Korea to get more arms for their cause and to make connections with others who wanted to fight their cause.

Not once did any of the people I met discuss the root causes of imperialism or how to better serve the people of the country they were supposedly interested in helping. For example, the so-called socialist countries representatives had a lot of to say about how evil the United States was, but nothing about how they have used Communism to help educate their people or eradicate diseases in their countries. There were many Palestinians there from so many different factions it was hard to remember their acronyms. The only two that stuck in my head were the PLO and the PLFP. It was the 1970's and these factions were busy raising money for arms to carry out more terrorist attacks throughout the world. To me, they were the most connected. At every meeting, they always worked the floor well. They were charming and people seemed interested in their cause.

Sam told me to be wary of those guys. He thought they were all slimy homosexual baby killers. Good old' Sam. I was beginning to identify with this macho hick. The head of the PLO delegate approached me while I was getting a drink. I forget his name, but not his mannerism or his looks. A fat, sweaty middle-aged man with a moustache and busy hands. At first, I thought that it was simply customary for Arabs to hug and embrace men. But this guy wouldn't let me go. He tried to charm me by saying that "we are all God's children" and that I was so brave for what I had done. At the same time, his slimy hands were making their way towards my crotch. I instinctively grabbed his hand and pushed it aside. He pretended nothing was wrong and continued to smile and talk to me.

One man I met from one of the Communist Palestinian factions by the name of Ahmed, was so full of it. I walked away from him. He had no idea about Marx or Lenin, he only knew about different weapons manufacturers and how much he hated Israel and the United States. When he found out I was from the United States (even though I defected), he attacked me with a barrage of comments, which he phrased as questions. He was one of those narrow minded people who wanted to lecture everyone simply because he came from on "oppressed community." He didn't look "oppressed" to me. He started to make it personal and constantly raised his voice until he was almost spitting. People around the room began to look in our direction, so I eventually just walked away. Sometimes I wish that I had let him have it, right there in that room.

The guilt of deserting my country and having to take so much shit from those who hated the United States was becoming unbearable. Every one of those stupid banquets started and ended with a North Korean delegate mouthing off about the glories of Communism and Kim IL Sung and attacking the United States and its "Puppets." Same old rhetoric, the government couldn't even be original. Every time Americans were referred to as "Imperialist Barbarians" and South Koreans as "Puppets." Sometimes the speeches got personal with name calling, like Nixon the "cannibal" and Park Chung Hee, the "Son of a Bitch." Was I back in Elementary school? How could a government stoop so low?

Still, I swallowed all my feelings and kissed ass. Most of the North Korean elite was very interested in meeting me, but they still had that aristocracy air that was absolutely unbearable. Some of the elite had personal assistants who followed them wherever they went. Once at a banquet, I witnessed one elite member of the party waving to his assistant. The assistant ran over and pulled out a cigarette, put it in his master's mouth, and lit it for him. The assistant then stood there with his hand open while the elite government member flicked his cigarette ashes on his hand, finally putting it out in his hand as well. The assistant didn't even flinch.

Chapter 10

DRUNKEN NIGHTS: KIM IL SUNG'S BIRTHDAY

1970's

My growing frustrations and bubbling anger did not dissipate. I tried to follow a rigid schedule of work and exercise, but I was steadily drinking and partying more. Eric and I hit the foreign nightclub in Pyongyang every weekend as well as drink in his room every other night. Sometimes we would get so drunk in his room we would forget that they were listening to us and talk loudly over the sound of the music playing. I always wondered if they were in fact listening to us and whether they had someone who understood us. I mean, it was hard to find someone who could listen to an English conversation over loud music. When Dr. Han could not drive us down on Saturdays, Eric would get one of the assistants from the office to drive us.

    I also noticed that I was taking my frustrations out in bed. I looked forward to those Saturdays when I could go to the bar, get drunk, and have sex with one of the girls there. Kumi usually knew when I was coming and tried to make herself available. One night, she was talking with another man, so I made my way over to another cutie that I had my eye on for a while. This one was a tall shapely girl who looked like a mixture of Korean and Southeast Asian. She had the sexiest eyes and had always made eye contact with me, even when I was with Kumi.

I bought her some drinks and asked her if we could go get some privacy. She quickly agreed. I noticed out of the corner of my eye that Kumi was looking at us the entire time. I also sensed that she was livid inside. I was beginning to think that she liked me not just as a client, but also as a lover. What can I say; I was always slow in these matters. Nevertheless, the other girl and I went to the back and had sex for over two hours. This girl was just as exciting as Kumi. I was drunk as usual, so I don't really remember as much as I would like to. I do, however, remember Kumi's cold stare when we came out. It was as if she were shooting daggers from her eyes at me. I didn't take it to heart much because I really believed that prostitutes did not have any feelings. I thought that they just had sex for money. I really underestimated Kumi's situation. She became a prostitute because she had no other choice. She was dragged to North Korea to live a life of shame and isolation. She never wanted to be a prostitute. After her husband died, the North Korean government took her apartment from her and made her become a prostitute. She later confided in me how she hated North Korea. She felt so betrayed. They had treated her so well when her husband and she first came to North Korea.

The next weekend at the club I got the cold shoulder from Kumi at first. I finally managed to get her to talk to me. She simply began to cry and yell at me. She was angry at me for sleeping with another girl at the bar and wondered why I would do such a thing. Matt, Eric, and Sam were there and began to heckle us. Sam shouted, "Look at the love birds having a spat." Etcetera. I finally just walked away and went back to drinking. Everything was so strange to me. I was wondering what was happening to me. Here I was in the most reclusive and the weirdest country on earth having a lovers' quarrel with a prostitute.

Dr. Han must have seen what happened because the following Monday during lunch he asked me if I liked that girl, Kumi. I told him that I just liked one thing from her. He understood and just paused. He then asked me if I had any inclination to get married. I told him that I might if the opportunity presented itself. We both paused, and then I turned to Dr. Han and asked him if he thought I should marry. He paused again and then went into his speech about Korean family values and how disappointed he had been that Eric, Victor, and Dr. Habibi had never decided to marry.

I knew he would never have luck with that bunch. Eric loved himself too much to care for someone else. I could tell from day one that Victor preferred the company of men to women. And Dr. Habibi? Well, lets just say that he preferred the company of young boys to women. That odd bunch would never agree to get hitched. The only married foreigner on the staff was Mr. Zhu, who was happily married with five children. Living in North Korea made him immune from the strict laws in China to limit the number of children. Mr. Zhu also liked the unique treatment he received as a foreign lecturer. He told me once that becoming a professor in China was extremely difficult and involved knowing someone in a high position.

Dr. Han felt responsible for the foreign crew at KIS University. It was probably a combination of the tremendous attention the only foreign instructors in North Korea were getting, coupled with a genuine care for us. Dr. Han was not a bad guy. From day one, I felt comfortable around him. He was the only North Korean I truly befriended. Dr. Han, just like most North Koreans I have met, was a very nervous individual. Who could blame him? This country was wearing on everyone, even the elite. I felt that I could probably ease some of his stress by making him believe that I was interested in finding a wife and settling down.

Dr. Han was so happy to hear the news that he started to plan my wedding. I knew it was a mistake, but I just couldn't say no to him. To my surprise, he was thinking of Kumi as my wife. I asked him whether or not that would be acceptable. His response was that it was the only option. North Koreans would not accept one of their own marrying an "outsider," no matter how important he was. Besides, he added, our Amerasian children would be ostracized. This way, we would be a foreign couple and be able to send our kids to the only foreign school in Pyongyang. He already had my life planned out for me. Still, I dragged my feet for another few years before he was able to make me commit.

It was also the first time I was invited to join a party commemorating Kim IL Sung's birthday. This was to be the biggest celebration of the year. We drove to the stadium on the outskirts of Pyongyang where were placed in a VIP section surrounded by glass. When I looked out the window, I saw a stadium full of Koreans. The men wore their best suits, while the women wore *Hanboks*, the traditional Korean dresses. The people outside looked like they were in a frenzied state. They were singing and waving. Some looked overly enthusiastic and it just looked so fake. It reminded me of some of those old Baptist churches down in Alabama or the Appalachians. The whole scene was so strange.

Inside the room, the noise was kept to a minimum. The room consisted of mostly men who stood around and clapped while the announcer on the stadium grounds praised the "Great Leader" for all his achievements. Most of the men in the room with us were high-ranking officials. Some of the military men had rows of medallions on their jackets. The room was catered with food and drinks and everyone was smoking. Outside, I could see that no one was smoking, eating, or drinking. They were just jumping up and down with excitement and singing happy birthday to Kim IL Sung.

Kim IL Sung himself was nowhere to be seen until the end of the ceremonies. He finally appeared on the opposite side of where we were. I could barely make him out. Next to him were Kim Jong IL and other members of his family along with the top brass. One military guy looked so old I thought he might just die right there on the spot. Kim IL Sung stood firm, smiled slightly and waved his hand at the crowd. At that moment, I could hear the rumble of the crowd growing stronger. Some people were going nuts. They looked like happy dogs that haven't seen their master for a while.

Chapter 11

▼

PROFOUND INFLUENCES: SAM AND YOUNG AE

1970's

Out of the handful of foreigners in North Korea, Sam led the most interesting life. As I told you before, Sam was a Marine who deserted like me through the DMZ. Sam was a good ol' country boy who loved to talk hunting, fishing, and girls. He actually sounded like the most normal guy among us sometimes. I always remember Sam with a beer in his hand, raising hell at the foreigner's club. He was mostly interested in getting drunk and having sex. Sam had a serious alcohol problem. He also had a temper that came with the alcohol. Almost every weekend, he found something to fight over. Luckily for him, no one at the club ever leaked out this information about him. It was absolutely illegal in North Korea to behave in that manner.

Sam really hated the Arabs that frequented the club. He told us that they were sick and cowards. He would rail about how they liked to have sex with children, both girls and boys. I would later find out that Sam was a hypocrite. During one of Sam's drinking binges, he revealed to me the reason why he deserted the Marines and ran to the North. One night after a heavy night of drinking in one of those bars surrounding the military bases, Sam went to one of the prostitute's house and raped her eleven-year-old daughter while the prostitute was at work.

Sam knew the girl well. He briefly dated the prostitute and she invited him to her place a couple of times. Sam was convinced the little girl wanted it.

Sam went on to say that he finally met his match because upon finding out that her daughter was raped, the prostitute lost it. She protested outside the Marine base for over two weeks until the South Korean press got hold of the story and published it. It became so big that even Park Chung Hee could not silence the story. South Koreans usually vent their own frustrations by blaming outsiders because they were never allowed to criticize their own government. This story sensationalized the American Army presence and it became obvious that Sam would have to be a sacrificial lamb. Although the United States Army was not legally bound to hand over Sam to the South Korean authorities, Sam was sure they would do it for public relations reasons. While on patrol of the DMZ, Sam decided to make a run for it.

Sam told me he knew the area well and exactly where the mines were planted. The tricky part was to convince the other side that he was not attacking. Those were the only words that Sam still remembered in Korean is "Don't shoot, I surrender, I love Kim IL Sung." Sam was not the adventurous type, interested in learning about another culture as I was. Sam was absolutely drunk when he told me this story. I still think there was more that he was hiding from me, but turns out I would never find out. Sam would not live a long and happy life in North Korea.

Another mystery surrounding Sam's life was his job. What was he currently doing in North Korea? I mean, he wasn't teaching English; he wasn't working for any translation or editing organization. What was he up to? I didn't even know where he was staying. At the bar, Sam never talked about his life. He would usually just talk about hunting and fishing. With me it was different. Sam really felt comfortable around me and finally revealed to me his whole existence in North Korea.

Sam was working for the North Korean film studios that Kim Jong IL himself designed and created. Sam told me it was a whole compound of studios and sets on the outskirts of the city where North Korean films and documentaries were made. Sam said that Kim Jong IL was inspired by Hollywood movies and wanted to create the Asian version of Hollywood to prove to the world how superior Koreans were. Sam had met Kim Jong IL on several occasions. According to Sam, Kim Jong IL really took a fancy to him.

I guess that was why Sam felt invincible. One night, Sam beat a Libyan almost to death in front of everyone in the club. He kept kicking him while he lay unconscious yelling, "what are you going to do about it, huh?" Nothing ever happened to Sam. A couple of "Shock Troopers" showed up and took Sam with them. I saw Sam at the club the very next week. He laughed off the episode the weekend before. That is why I believed Sam's story completely. Only someone that Kim Jong IL really liked could get away with that.

Sam told me a lot about what was going on in those studios. The studios enjoyed deep pockets simply because of Kim Jong IL's fascination with making films. Sam told me that hundreds of North Koreans worked around the clock just to make the place look clean. He told me that the workers even swept the dirt alleys. Besides the fact that the place looked spotless, the movies themselves stunk to high heaven. Sam said that they were so corny they would be laughed at in the West.

Sam's stories about Kim Jong IL's horrible ideas for movies reminded me of the story of "The Emperor's New Clothes." No one at the studios, or in all North Korea for that matter, had the guts to tell Kim that the movies stunk. Therefore, these horrendous movies would be made and distributed all over Korea with full praise from all who saw them. Even the North Korean mouthpiece in Japan would hail the making of a new movie as "superior to all other movies in the world." Unknown to North Koreans, the world didn't even see the movies. If the movies ever did get out, they were probably used as a study of propaganda in some university class.

My interest in Sam's work finally gave him the idea to invite me to the studios. I enthusiastically accepted the offer. Sam used to come to the club with a Korean man that he later introduced to me as Mr. Lee. Mr. Lee was one of the directors at the studios. Sam needed an escort around the city and Mr. Lee was fascinated by anything American. Mr. Lee didn't really try to hide his love of American movies, which made me think that he was also a favorite of Kim Jong IL.

At the other end of the spectrum of my acquaintances was Young Ae. Young Ae was the loveliest person I had ever met in North Korea. She had the nicest smile I had ever seen and it always lifted my spirits. She was an Education student at Kim IL Sung University. Her father was one of the most important party members and businessmen in North Korea. In North Korea business and party member were synonymous. I met Young Ae by chance one day on the campus of Kim IL Sung University.

Whenever I had time, I would make my way to the North End of the campus, away from the hustle and bustle of the crowds. The north end of the campus was a dead end. The government sealed two of the four exits in order to monitor the students and faculty carefully. It almost seemed like prison (but then so did the entire country). The North End was overgrown with tall bamboo reeds, wild bushes, and very old pine trees. It was also the only place where the old architecture could be found. An old wall with an abandoned traditional building in front of it was all that remained.

I would usually sit under one of the pine trees and sketch or read a book. I began sketching in North Korea because wanted to keep some sort of memories of my surroundings. Back in the United States and South Korea I used to carry my camera with me. I lost my camera as soon as I entered North Korea. My interrogators confiscated my camera and most of my belongings. Thus I was left with sketching using the only tools I had: A pencil and paper.

That day I had arrived at my spot earlier than usual because my class was cancelled. A cancellation of a class meant that either the students were needed for some sort of propaganda act or because the university elders were holding a surprise "Self Criticism" meeting. This was another of the brilliant ideas of North Korean socialism. North Koreans were bullied into making confessions in front of their coworkers, neighbors, or fellow students. These "confessions" involved individuals admitting that acted in a selfish manner that harmed the good of the state. It was a great way to ferret out those who were not loyal to the Kim regime.

As I sat and began sketching I heard a young woman's voice behind me.

"That is so beautiful." The young woman said with enthusiasm.

I turned around in astonishment that someone was there with me. It was Young Ae. She towered over me with her long beautiful hair and her stunning looks. She had inquisitive large eyes that seemed to pierce mine. The sun penetrated through the pine branches to reveal parts of Young Ae to my eyes. It was enough to see that she was the most beautiful woman I had ever seen in my life. Even though she wore the usual drab uniform all North Korean students wore, she looked stunning. I was in awe. I really didn't know what to say.

"Thanks!" I answered timidly.

I sat there not knowing what to say next. I thought I was dreaming.

"You really know how to capture the different colors and shades."

Young Ae broke the silence. She spoke in English with barely any accent.

"You speak English so well. How did you learn?" I asked.

"I love languages. I taught myself."

Young Ae sat down next to me as she spoke.

"Just copy what I hear in the television and on the tapes they have at the University. Do you usually come here?"

"Actually I usually come in the afternoon," I answered.

"I love this spot. It reminds me of my grandmother's old home before she moved in with us in Pyongyang."

Young Ae looked up at the pine trees as if reminiscing.

"Where was she from?" I asked.

"From Hwanghaenamdo next to the city of Haeju."

"I have been around there. It is such a beautiful area."

I responded with enthusiasm. Young Ae sat there for what seemed like an eternity talking about so many different subjects. She was such an open person. It was so different than North Koreans I had met so far. We didn't even learn each other's names until we realized it was getting dark and it was time to head back.

That whole week I could not get Young Ae out of my mind. I anticipated our next encounter with such emotions that time seemed to freeze. Every day after our meeting I would run to our favorite spot in hope of seeing Young Ae. Each time I was disappointed. I had also hoped I would see her on campus. I even found out where the Education department building was and tried to hang around there as much as possible in hope of running into Young Ae. No such luck!

Then, as if my wish had come true, Young Ae came to me. She was waiting for me outside the language department office, dawning her famous welcoming smiles. I was filled with such joy at seeing her. I felt like a schoolboy in love for the first time.

"*Anyong Hashimnika Sansengnim!*" (Formal hello to a teacher).

We stood there for an awkward moment before I realized that she wanted me to invite her inside. We headed to my desk. I cleared all my papers from the extra chair beside me and offered her a seat. Dr. Habibi was the only other professor in the office. He looked curiously on as Young Ae followed me to my desk and sat down. She looked even better than the first day I had seen her. She was fairly tall compared to other Koreans and had darker skin than most. I found it very attractive even though I knew most Koreans preferred pale skin. Dark skin signified a rural background because only farmers were exposed to the sun.

"I had brought my sketches just as I promised."

Young Ae reached into her bag and pulled out a roll of papers. I had almost forgotten that she told me she also sketched and that she had promised to show me her paintings. They were beautiful. The pictures varied from people's portraits to landscapes and even abstract objects. Once again I lost track of time as we sat there looking at her pictures and talking about her artwork. Unfortunately, I had to run to my evening class and we left it at that without making any plans to meet again.

That night after class I had to talk to someone about my newfound happiness. I rushed over to Eric's room even before changing my work clothes. Eric was, as usual, already on his second beer and in a relaxed mood. He listened as I told him about Young Ae. I could tell he was becoming impatient as if he really wanted to say something important.

"How old is she?" Eric finally interrupted me.

"Nineteen or twenty, I think." I responded.

"Now how are you?" Eric asked.

I could see where he was going with these questions. Young Ae was much younger than me and she was Korean. I should not expect anything. Eric also added that because she was a student at this school she probably came from a prestigious family. That definitely meant that she was off limits to a "*Oaeguk*" (Foreigner) like me. Once again Eric brought me back to the harsh reality that was North Korea. Eric suggested that I end it before it even starts. Eric thought I should keep away from Young Ae and not give her any hint that I was interested in her.

That was almost impossible to do. Young Ae seemed to be the one salvation I had in this hellhole. Everything else in North Korea was gloomy. The people, the architecture, the rigid rules, the robotic students; it was all just too depressing. I nevertheless heeded Eric's advice. I did not pursue Young Ae and even seemed cold to her the next few times we met. It hurt so much. I felt my heart being torn from the cold shoulder I was giving Young Ae. My apathetic behavior toward Young Ae definitely worked. Young Ae slowly realized that I was not interested in her at all.

The last time we met she gave me a small gift and told me she was going to focus on her final exams for the next few weeks. I knew it wasn't true. The finals were still two months away. We parted in the stairway of the building in which I taught. She looked back at me one last time as she walked down the stairs and out of my view. I opened the gift that night to discover a carved Korean traditional mask from pinewood. She also included a long letter written on rice paper. Even her handwriting was so pretty. Although the letter was personal, I can say that it convinced me that Young Ae was the woman of my life. Under different circumstances I would have married her in a heartbeat.

Chapter 12

THE ONLY TRIP: LAOS, THAILAND, JAPAN

1980

Weeks passed by before I saw Young Ae again. She walked right past me without even saying hello. I just stood there, feeling the same pain I had felt when she walked away from me on that stairway. For some strange reason, seeing her and knowing that she was angry with me alleviated that emptiness I felt. I was doing the right thing. I ensured our survival in a nation that would not accept us as a couple.

Luckily for me, an unexpected assignment left me with little time to think about Young Ae. A week before final examinations, Dr. Han called me into his office. When I arrived, I noticed a square-jawed gentlemen sitting quietly in the corner of the room. He was quite tall and looked in better shape than most North Koreans I was accustomed to seeing. His eyes were cold and piercing. His hairline was receding, but I don't think he was older than forty. He gave me a little smile but did not introduce himself. Dr. Han just introduced him as Mr. Kim (Kim is the most common name in Korea. It could have been an alias). Mr. Kim did not get up. He let Dr. Han do all the talking. Dr. Han started by praising my work and duty to North Korea and its "Great Leader, Kim IL Sung." The praising then switched over to how my loyalty to North Korea had not gone unnoticed by the Party itself. This was supposed to be a great honor.

After the praising, there was silence. It felt as if no one said anything for a long time. Dr. Han looked at Mr. Kim, then at me and popped the question: "How would you like to take a vacation?" A vacation? Sure! Why not? That is what most people would say if their boss offered them the opportunity to take some time off. In my situation, I really didn't know what to think. This was, after all, North Korea. Many thoughts went through my mind. Was this how they got rid of you? Did they want me out of the country? Did they make a deal with the United States government over me? Was I set up? These are the thoughts that first go through the mind of a defector.

I said yes, which made Dr. Han and Mr. Kim very happy. Dr. Han did not waste any time. He pulled out a piece of crumpled paper and began to explain my itinerary. I would be flying to Laos, stay a few nights, then off to Thailand. After a few days in Thailand, I would go to Japan, then back to North Korea. The first question that I blurted out was whether or not I would be safe in those countries. Before Dr. Han could respond to that, Mr. Kim jumped in and assured me that I would be very safe. Laos was a good friend of North Korea, while Thailand and Japan were neutral (I knew that wasn't exactly true. Japan would bend over in favor of the United States and South Korea, while Thailand was aligned with the United States). Mr. Kim also explained that North Korea had many "supporters" in all three of those countries.

I was to leave in three months. Before that, I had to be briefed by Mr. Kim regarding traveling abroad. Of course the whole thing sounded fishy. I mean, I know that I was highly regarded by the top brass, but why was my trip planned so meticulously. Why those three nations? I had never seen this Mr. Kim before and I had met almost all of the top brass with the exception of the two top Kims. No matter! I welcomed the chance for another adventure right away. I have been in North Korea for almost seven years and I was itching to go somewhere new.

For the next several weekends, I attended special seminars at a campground I didn't even know existed right behind the university campus. The whole country was militarized, so I probably didn't even noticed the camp. Mr. Kim greeted me each time and led me to a hanger where I was taught all kinds of techniques. Mr. Kim taught me how to spot someone who was following me. I learned how to dress and behave inconspicuously. I also learned a few survival and hand to hand combat tips. During each lesson Mr. Kim would remind me that this was just precautionary and that I needn't worry about a thing. That was comforting, let me tell you!

I also learned about who might try to do me harm. I was now on the side of the non-aligned states, so I had to fear all capitalist states. Interestingly enough, my worst nightmare was the Israeli secret service: the Mossad. Mr. Kim said that I should not fear the CIA. They were too big and unorganized, plus they could not play dirty because of strict American laws. The Mossad, however, was small, organized, spread out around the world, cunning, and unexpected. The Mossad was also for hire by other capitalist nations, including South Korea. Mr. Kim said several of them used the Mossad before to surprise North Koreans and their allies.

Mr. Kim seemed to admire the Mossad. He focused most of the lesson on that organization. He taught me about how they used women to lure in unsuspecting foes and execute them. The CIA or British MI6 never did that. The Mossad also relied on human intelligence, which, according to Mr. Kim, made them more knowledgeable and dangerous. One story he told me involved an arms deal between North Koreans and nationals from an unnamed Arab country in Tanzania. That night, while they were all meeting in the hotel room, a bomb detonated right under the bed. No one survived. The North Koreans later learned that the stupid Arab whose room it was had invited a beautiful blond up to his room the night before. A lot of money was lost in that deal. It could have only been the work of the Mossad.

Mr. Kim lamented that North Korea was supporting the wrong side. Of all the Arab nations and their allies, not one could ever put an end to that little country of a few million people. Mr. Kim thought it was pathetic. He had no respect for the Arabs. He told me that they were unreliable and could not be trusted. They had all the money and weapons, yet they could not defeat Israel. Not only that, they only used muscle, not brains, in all of their operations. Mr. Kim seemed frustrated with the whole situation. I could tell that he was an important and dangerous man because he was not afraid to let his feelings be known. Most North Koreans never made any commentary about anything, let alone politics.

On the last day of training a group of men and women were brought into the hangar where we were practicing with all sorts of equipment. I was now ready for my makeover. They dyed my hair from dark brown to a sandy brown. I was given a pair of glasses that I was told to wear at all times. The glasses gave the impression that my eyes were lighter than they really were. The most shocking of all the makeover techniques was created by the scar man. Without warning, one the guys cut me with a knife across the cheek. Mr. Kim said that it was to deflect people's attention from my other features. If I had a noticeable scar, people would notice that and not my other features. It was just natural that people would say that I had a scar, but they would not remember any other important features about me.

It was finally time for me to depart for Laos. Dr. Han drove me to Pyongyang airport where Mr. Kim was waiting for me in a room next to the immigration booths. The airport was very small. I hardly saw any passengers there. In the room, I was provided with two suitcases. Mr. Kim told me the week before that I would be provided with travel accessories and clothes, so I should not pack anything. He also warned me about the importance of the two suitcases. The dark blue one was to be handed over to a man I was to meet in Thailand. The black one was to be handed over to another man I was to meet in Japan.

As I reached for the suitcases, Mr. Kim grabbed my wrist and squeezed with a lot of pressure. He looked right at me with his cold eyes and said: "Don't forget! You are not to lose these suitcases." I was really scared of him at that point. I knew that he wasn't playing around. If I were to lose those suitcases, I would probably lose my life. North Korea did not hold people's lives very highly. Everyone was expendable.

I boarded the Air Koryo plane sweating even though it was November. I was now very scared of taking this "vacation." This could be the vacation of death for me. Some vacation! Air Koryo was the only North Korean airline and it only had about five flights a day. The plane was an old Russian model. It looked like it hadn't been used for years, yet there it was. The plane was full of Chinese and North Koreans. The first stop was Beijing. We waited on the tarmac for about three hours, and then took off for Vientiane, Laos. That was when I noticed that there were only six passengers left on the entire plane. Everyone else had gotten off in Beijing. Two men looked like they were security and the other looked like party officials.

We descended into Vientiane a few hours later. The city was tiny; I thought that maybe the airport was far from the city center. The airport itself was very small. It looked like a local airfield in the United States. When we landed, a car was waiting on the tarmac. Two men were standing beside it. One man greeted me and introduced himself as Mr. Wu or Vu, I don't really remember. I do remember the car that took us, however. It was a classic Mercedes Benz from the 1940's. It had a mahogany dashboard and Russian gauges. I thought it was weird at first, but I later figured it out. Laos was a colony of the French. Laos was poor and therefore maintained the European cars the French left behind. They probably improvised with Russian parts from Laos's new ally.

I was right about the city being small. There were absolutely no paved roads and no traffic lights. There were also no office buildings or any modern structures. The city had preserved its the French colonial style. The two story colonial houses that were the trademark of French colonialism could be seen everyone around the city. People also got around either on foot or by bicycle. I could see some beggars on the corners and many people were walking barefoot. The city was dusty from all the dirt kicked up from the streets and there was a funky smell everywhere. I felt like a dignitary driving around in a car in this city.

We pulled up to this big colonial mansion on a tree-lined street. The car waited while a bunch of soldiers opened the gates manually. We drove down a narrow road to the mansion. A butler awaited us on the stairs. I knew he was a butler because he was dressed up in a wrinkled maroon tuxedo. He led us up the stairs to the house, where we were asked to wait in the foyer. A short, dark, graying-haired man approached us with a big smile. I had no idea at the time that this man was the Minister of Foreign Affairs of Laos.

He welcomed me of behalf on the Laotian people and presented me with a gift. I then remembered that Mr. Kim had given me a gift as well to give when I arrived in Laos. I was just in the process of looking for the gift, when the Korean security guy that accompanied me nudged me and handed me the gift. I gave it to the Minister and thanked him for having me. He smiled and led us into the dining room. A feast was awaiting us. In the corner of the room, a couple of beautiful women dressed in the traditional dresses were preparing some kind of dish for us. They were using a rock bowl and an apothecary stone handle that was used to crush pills by pharmacists.

It was some sort of salad, which they then served to us. In total, we were served around six dishes, all of which were very delicious. I sat at the head of the table while the Minister sat opposite me. On our sides sat another ten people who I never got to formally meet. After dinner, I was taken to my quarters right away. I stayed in a bungalow in the back of the presidential palace. As soon as I sat down on the bed, someone knocked on the door. It was the Korean security agent. He reminded me to keep a close watch on both suitcases.

The next morning I was taken on a tour of the city. We went to the beautiful golden temple and this weird sculpture garden that was supposedly created by some Laotian Buddhist monk. I saw many monks dressed up in saffron robes and with shaved heads. Korean monks wore only gray clothes. I had always wondered why the two differed. The highlight of the trip was the newly built Lao Revolutionary museum. It was a miniature replica of the North Korean style museums. It had the same propaganda attacking the French, Japanese, and Americans all in chronological order (The French were the first to colonize Laos, followed by the Japanese).

I learned that more bombs were dropped on Laos by the US military than on Germany in World War II. The reason was that the Ho Chi Min Trail followed the border between Laos and Vietnam. The museum also displayed all the gifts that the president received from around the world. Again, it was a miniature replica of the North Korean museums. As expected from a communist country, the museum used the same combative rhetoric as in North Korean museums. The French were referred to as "Dogs," the Americans as "Barbarians." I always wondered which one was more of an insult. Personally, I liked dogs a lot. The only real barbarians I had ever met came later on in my life.

The next few days were quite relaxing. I was put up the following night at this magnificent villa/hotel in the center of the city. The villa was also a remnant of French colonialism. In fact, my guide had mentioned that Vientiane had some of the best French colonial architecture in the world. Now it was being utilized by the socialist regime that fought so hard to rid of all French influences. The house had a large courtyard with all kinds of exotic fruit trees around. In the center, there was a very large pool that had some etchings on the bottom.

I stayed in Vientiane for three days. The city was nothing like North Korea (or South Korea). It had a very relaxing atmosphere. The weather was nice and balmy. The people always smiled, even the beggars. Nothing seemed to be moving around the city. Time seemed to have stopped. In Pyongyang, there was always a sense of paranoia among the people and everyone was always in a hurry. Here it was exactly the opposite. My guide took me to his friend's café for some breakfast. We sat around for hours just drinking Laotian style coffee (similar to the French café au lait). Very good coffee beans grow in Laos. It was introduced by the French. The grounded beans are put in a tin filter and hot water is poured into it. The brewed coffee then drips into a glass cup with condensed milk in it. Very delicious!

The guide also took me to the local markets, where people from the different tribes came down from the mountains to sell and buy goods. The guide told me that many of the tribes, such as the Hmong people, supported the Americans and Lao monarchy prior to the revolution in 1975. That was why they were forbidden to enter Vientiane. It was "punishment" for their actions. Eric later told me that it was also because there were still guerilla movements in the mountains bent on taking back the capital city. Eric was a wealth of information. His insight into the garbage that we were meant to swallow kept me from becoming a zombie.

Everyone else in these socialist countries were like broken records. You could not reason with any of them.

We also had a scheduled trip to Luang Prabang, the ancient Buddhist capital. However the trip was cancelled at the last minute due to some skirmishes that broke out along the Vientiane-Luang Prabang road. Remnants of the royal family loyalists and Hmong tribesmen were determined to bring down the communist regime. Of course, the guide told me that the attacks on the main road were just a bunch of "bandits" left over from the old regime. Knowing how socialist propaganda worked, I interpreted his remarks as: The government does not have complete control over Laos and they are getting their ass kicked outside the capital. The situation was also tense due to the border skirmishes between Vietnam and China at the time, both socialist allies of Laos. Once again, Laos was a staging ground for foreign conflicts.

On the last day of my stay in Laos, one of the Korean security guards that accompanied me throughout the trip paid me a visit to my room. He reminded me of the mission that Mr. Kim had already told me about dozens of times. I could tell this was very important. He was very serious about it. We went through the steps again. I was given a forged Canadian passport (Canadian passports were evidently easy to forge at the time and would not attract any attention from anyone. Canada was not a threat to anyone. Also, the fact that I spoke and looked like an American could only be associated with a Canadian). My alias was Peter Wendell. I was on vacation in Thailand. The passport showed a Canadian exit visa and a Thai entrance visa.

I was to stay in Bangkok and a small island named Ko Samui for a few days. I was supposed to be an avid scuba diver. I had to suntan for a few days to make it seem as if I was really on vacation. I was to behave as if I didn't have a care in the world. Inside the maroon suitcase was a tote bag. I was to take it out on the last day and claim it as a carry on at the airport. After immigration and inspections, I was to find a seat and put the tote bag on the floor next to me. A man would come and sit next to me with an identical bag. He would then get up and take my bag and I was to take his.

After the drop off, I was to board a plane to Japan. In Tokyo, I was to take a shuttle bus to the Tokyo Train Station. There, I was to buy a Shinkansen ticket to Kokura in Kitakyushu. A man would meet me outside the station and take me to his house where I would hand over the other suitcase. No other information was given to me regarding this "man." During the following week I would go on a sightseeing tour like a regular tourist so as not raise any alarms. After that, I would take another Shinkansen to Tokyo and stay a night by the airport. The next day I would board a plane to Beijing, then board another plane to Pyongyang.

I woke up at three in the morning and got dressed. I was dressed like a tourist: Hawaiian shirt, Bermuda shorts, cabana hat, the whole deal. I looked silly. They assured me that this was how Western tourists dressed in Thailand. An army jeep was waiting outside. We drove through the city streets and then along the Mekong River. We boarded a small traditional fishing boat and headed out towards the other side of the river.

I was surprised to find how easy it was to get into Thailand from Laos. All that separated the two nations was the Mekong River. The Special Forces officer in the boat with me told me that the border between Thailand and Laos was too long to patrol everywhere. He also told me that we were crossing through the infamous "Golden Triangle" area where the majority of the world's opium was grown. I really couldn't make out much because it was dark and foggy. I could, however, hear all kinds of sounds of animals in the forest around us. It sounded like a disorganized symphony.

During our short trip, the officer remarked on the beauty of the Mekong. He told me of gigantic fish that grew as big as crocodiles, and of fresh water Dolphins that lived in the Mekong. I never knew there were freshwater dolphins before that. He noted that most Laotians and Thais believed the dolphins were sacred and therefore not hunted or threatened in any way. I was happy to hear that. Every other animal seemed to be for sale in Laos.

The boat maneuvered its way through some thick reeds before suddenly hitting a bank. The man signaled me to follow him. Another man carried my suitcase off the boat. We jumped off the boat into some slimy water that reached our knees. We waded out of the water and into some shrubs that appeared to have a tunnel in them. It was all too dark to really know what was going on. On the other side of the shrubs were a couple of men with bicycles. The two men with me loaded the suitcases on their bikes and gestured to me to get on the other bike lying beside them. By the time I had picked up the bicycle the men on the boat had already disappeared into the shrubs.

The men on the bikes told me in broken English to follow them. I climbed on the bike and we were on our way. At first, the trail was narrow and I kept hitting some bushes. After a short ride through the bushes the trail ended up at a dirt road. We stopped before reaching the dirt road and the one man signaled me to be quiet. The other guy looked out onto the road then signaled us that it was okay. We made a left turn on the dirt road and began to follow it for a few miles.

It was actually fun riding a bike through the highland jungles of Thailand. It was the first time I was doing something that was fun. In North Korea, people just didn't do anything that I considered fun. The government didn't even allow the people to ride bicycles because Kim IL Sung thought it was too primitive.

The ride was mostly downhill so it wasn't too bad. I remember stopping along the way on a curve. We could see a couple of lights far off in the distance. That night was a moonless night, so it was almost pitch black. I tried to see from their facial expressions whether this was good or bad. The two just looked serious but not too alarmed. We continued to ride for what seemed like a long time. All of a sudden, I noticed that we were cycling through a village. There was suddenly a small clearing in the forest with a field on our right and some huts on the left of the road.

The two guys signaled me to get off the bike and follow them. We walked off the road and onto a small trail that followed a creek. We got to one of the huts where the two stashed their bicycles in the back and then did the same with my bike. We entered the hut as quietly as possible. The two guys put my suitcases in the corner of the room. The whole time we communicated through hand gestures. Not one word was spoken. One of them was trying to gesture to me to lie down on the straw matt and try to get some sleep. I finally got it and followed his suggestion.

Even though I felt exhausted, I couldn't sleep. A million things were going through my mind. I was very worried about my whole mission. What if I got caught, or worse, killed? This whole cloak and dagger stuff was too much for me. I had no experience in it and it was really scaring me. By now I was well aware of how little North Koreans valued human life. Maybe this was a suicide mission? Maybe I was carrying a bomb. I was now in a non-socialist country. What would the Thai authorities do if I revealed my mission? Did I dare even think about it? The North Koreans would surely find me and kill me.

I did manage to get some sleep because I was woken up by one of the guys from the night before. I could finally clearly see his face. He was a short dark-skinned man with a big smile on his face. His eyes told me that I had no reason to fear him. He was probably just paid to guide me, nothing more. He didn't look like a warrior or killer. He led me into the next room where a woman was setting the floor for a meal. She also gave me a nice big smile and signaled me to come and sit down on the floor by the food. It was really delicious. It was a type of coconut green curry stew with green beans, some sort of chestnuts, and leaves in it. There was also steamed rice and a salad as side dishes.

As I was eating, I noticed two kids staring at me from the door. They were both so cute. They just stared at me, occasionally smiling. They were so curious about the stranger that had come to stay with them. I assumed they were this couple's children. The man and I ate while the other members just looked at us. I tried to signal to the kids to come and join us, but they just shook their heads and didn't budge.

After breakfast, I stepped outside to look at my surroundings. I now had a different picture of the village I had ridden into the night before. It was a partly cloudy day with a nice breeze blowing through the trees. I could see several villagers going about their business. In the daytime, this village did not look as menacing as the night before. I started to feel more at ease. There was something about Southeast Asia in general that was so soothing. It was so different from both North and South Korea. I took a walk on the trail to the edge of the stream. Three young boys were fishing on the other side with just a string and some bait. They looked at me with interest, whispered to each other and smiled in my direction.

When I came back to the hut, I saw my guide laboring over this weird looking motorcycle with three wheels. I later found out those machines were called "Tuk Tuks." In Laos they were called "Jumbos" and were a little less sophisticated than a Tuk Tuk. A Tuk Tuk was nothing more than a converted Japanese motorcycle turned taxi. It took my guide a few tries, but he finally managed to get that thing going. He then loaded my suitcases into the back and signaled me to hop on.

That concoction spewed more smoke and made more noise than any motorcycle I'd ever seen. Worst yet, it wasn't that fast. We drove through this peaceful countryside scaring off the birds and oxen in the fields around us. The smoke seemed to blow right into my face. After what seemed like an eternity on that beast, we began to approach a city. My driver pointed at the city and shouted "Chiang Mai, Chiang Mai!"

I checked into a small bungalow/hotel on one of the hills. It was a cozy place, nestled in the touristy section of the city. It was a bit of a culture shock, seeing all those western tourists. There were Germans and Swedes, Americans and Canadians, even Japanese. After several years in North Korea, I was not accustomed to such openness and free spiritedness. I went to a local restaurant and had a nice Thai dinner, Tom Yum Gun, I think it was. The television above the bar was showing a movie, I think it was a police movie with Clint Eastwood. I recognized my hometown right away. Clint was chasing bad guys all over San Francisco. That made me very homesick.

I ordered a couple of beers and struck up a conversation with a Swedish couple next to me. They were avid scuba divers. They wanted to take a break from scuba diving nonetheless and come up to Chiang Mai and experience Thailand's mountains. I asked them where I should go if I wanted to see a nice secluded beach. They immediately recommended this tiny island called Ko Tao (Turtle Island). They told me it was a bit hard to find the place and that the accommodations were not that high class, but that was what they loved about the place.

I went to bed early that night, anticipating another long trek the next day. I took the bus to Bangkok early that morning. From the bus station, I took a taxi to the airport. I deposited the tote bag in a locker and headed back to Sukhumvit Road, one of the famous streets in Bangkok. Sukhumvit was a little less known to foreigners at the time than Khao San Road or Patpong. I wanted to stay clear of Americans, especially servicemen. You just never knew whom you might bump into. Sukhumvit was a bit more classy and quiet. There was one street, Soi Nana, where there was some nightlife. I took a very long walk through the city that day; I even went by the American Embassy. The thought of just walking into the embassy and giving myself up did occur to me. I still thought that if I ever wanted to leave North Korea, they would let me. How naïve of me!

That night I visited one of the quiet bars in the back of Soi Nana, just a couple of blocks from my hotel. I was a bit apprehensive the entire day. I kept thinking about worst-case scenarios. Someone might steal my suitcases. I would be caught by immigration. I kept to myself until an older bar girl sat next to me and asked me my name. I told her my alias and she introduced herself as Jenny. She looked like she was in her late thirties or even early forties. Still, she was extremely attractive to me. I always liked older women. My one experience with an older woman before was incredible. At college, I met this professor's wife at a bar. That night we were having wild sex in her house while her husband was at a rehabilitation center for alcohol abuse. We made love five times that night.

Although I didn't come with the intention of picking up a bar girl, I was now in the mood. Jenny was a dark, full figured woman with sensual eyes and lips. The heat in the city also didn't hurt my libido. I was very eager to get this woman back to my room. We negotiated a price and she followed me back to the room. The nonchalant way of how she described the different prices for different sex acts were a bit surprising. This woman had definitely been around the block a few times. Still, I didn't care. I felt better that she was experienced. I hated to think of those young girls I saw at that bar that were still corruptible. They seemed so innocent and fragile. I wouldn't feel right about it.

With Jenny, I didn't have any regrets. Jenny had the richest long hair and the prettiest eyes. What really stood out was Jenny's pearly white smile and full figured lips. She had a couple of explicit tattoos on her arm and buttocks. Jenny wasn't shy at all. I told her I wanted the works, and by God I got it. She was very good at what she did. She screamed so loudly that I thought the manager might come and complain, but nothing of the sort happened. They were probably used to all that. After that night, I thought about my earlier complaints about how prostitution was wrong and another ill of capitalism. That wasn't true. Prostitution was the oldest profession in the world. It was just as prevalent in North Korea. The only difference was that in North Korea only a privileged group had access to prostitutes.

Jenny hung onto me the next morning asking if I wanted company during the rest of my stay in Thailand. I later heard from a guy I met that the bar girls tried to find a sugar daddy while they were on vacation because it was steady money. The bar scene could be hot or dry for these girls. It was a safer bet to try to get a steady customer. I told Jenny I would think about it. One the one hand, I didn't want to attract too much attention to myself. On the other hand, maybe if I traveled with someone I wouldn't be noticed. Besides, that island I was going to was supposed to be isolated. Maybe I could use some company.

Jenny persisted and I finally agreed to take her with me. She seemed so happy, genuinely happy. I am sure that a chance to get the hell out of that city was a blessing to her. Deep down I was also happy to go with someone I liked. It still pained me to think of Young Ae and I wanted to make sure I would not spend sleepless nights on a beautiful island thinking about her. Mr. Kim gave me plenty of U.S. dollars, so money was not an issue either. Jenny also turned out to be a great guide. Bangkok itself was so confusing, I would not have found the train station if it weren't for her help. We took an overnight train to a small town on the coast of the Gulf of Thailand.

The train made a few stops and every time vendors would come up to the windows and offer us some food or drinks. It was kind of fun. I slept on the top bunk, while Jenny took the lower bunk. When the train made its frequent stops, I always waved my hand out the window to get the vendors' attention. I sampled a bunch of things that night, including this fried banana dessert. This was heaven for me. Don't forget, I had already spent several years in North Korea. Even for someone of my stature, there wasn't much selection in terms of food. You could not even buy an orange in North Korea, let alone papayas or mangoes.

We got off the train early in the morning in this desolate seaside town. Nothing was going on here. It was just a simple fishing village. Jenny asked someone where the docks were and we headed on foot in that location. By the way, I had previously locked the suitcases in the hotel's vault before we left. I really didn't trust anyone around those suitcases. We asked around the docks for a ride to Ko Tao Island and were in luck. Another couple from Denmark was also looking for a ride and the captain of the boat wanted too much for his services. The couple was in their late twenties. The man's name was Toke, and the woman, Dorte. The four of us together were able to come up with his price.

The boat ride took three hours. I kept seeing these islands and thinking they were Ko Tao, but I was mistaken. Finally, a bigger island appeared and the captain yelled out, "Ko Tao." It was a green and lush island, surrounded by what looked like a golden sandy beaches. I was so excited. It was my first time on a tropical island. The Danes were too busy sunning their white skins on the boat's port side to really pay any attention to it. Jenny was busy writing something down in a diary she had brought with her.

I looked over at the island our captain was pointing to. It was magnificent! It really looked like one of those tropical islands I had pictured in the countless books and articles I had read. I could see the white sandy beach surrounding the island. It looked like a white ring around a green rock. The island had a steep mountain that jutted up above the beach. As the boat got closer, I could tell that there was another smaller island that was connected to the main island by a narrow stretch of sand. I was already curious to explore that smaller island and also to climb to the mountaintop.

We docked in a small town in the center of the island. That town also happened to be the "center" of the island. Even the water around the docks was crystal clear. I could see the tropical fish swimming in the water. Jenny asked a local fisherman where we could find a room. The man looked very surprised. He looked at her, then at me, then back at her. Finally, he pointed to the right and Jenny thanked him and signaled me to follow. The Danes tagged along with us. They had come to the island on the same whim that attracted me.

Jenny led us to a house on the edge of the town right on the beachfront. The house was elevated from the beach by wooden beams. It was probably in case of flooding. A man was on the porch smiling and waving to us. He introduced himself as Pete: The one-man show on the island. Pete had the only lodging, the only restaurant, the only store, the only snorkeling and scuba gear, and if you wanted, he could set you up with his daughters. Pete was an ethnic Chinese. Thailand actually had a big community of ethnic Chinese. They usually had the stereotype of being good at business. This guy definitely lived up to the reputation.

Jenny was ruthless, she argued with Pete over the prices of everything the entire time we were there. She even argued with Pete about the ingredients he used in our dinner (Yes, his wife was the cook at the only restaurant around). I have to admit, Jenny was smarter than most women I have ever met. It's strange how life deals the cards to people. Many people do not deserve what they have, while others are under-appreciated. Jenny managed to get a package deal for all of us in the only bungalow Pete had. I was happy we didn't have to stay in his house.

The bungalow was a stone's throw away from the water. It had two bedrooms and a makeshift bathroom. On the porch, there were some chairs and a table and two hammocks. At the time, there were no other guests on the entire island except for some old Italian guy who Pete told us came to there every winter. He was a very nice guy who loved to fish and kept to himself. We only saw him at dinnertime. There was one other bungalow set up on the other side of the island that specialized in Scuba diving, but was more expensive. We were happy where we were.

We stayed with the two Danes. However, we spent our days in different ways. The Danes were avid scuba divers, so Pete arranged it so that they could go scuba diving almost everyday. Jenny and I meanwhile had a rigid routine that we liked to keep. We would wake up early and go swimming. Then, we would have breakfast, go suntan on the beach, have lunch, take a walk on the beach, snorkel a little, then have dinner and read in the evenings. The two Danes had a deck of cards, so we also played cards sometimes.

Jenny also spent some time teaching me Thai. As I mentioned before, I had a knack for languages, so I was able to read headlines of the newspapers by the end of my first week. We had all the time in the world to practice. I mainly practiced with Jenny. Jenny told me that the locals on the island we were on had a strong southern accent and that even she had a difficult time understanding them. Jenny told me she was originally from Issan, the northeastern district of Thailand. It was also one of the poorest regions that produced the highest immigration to Bangkok.

Jenny said she came from a family of six. Her parents were very poor and actually convinced her to go find work in Bangkok. It was normal for women to go to the city and send money back to their family. That's exactly what Jenny did. Unfortunately, the only jobs available were in the sex business. Jenny said she was gangbanged on the first night on the job on purpose. It was a mental weapon to break the new prostitutes' spirits. She told her family back home that she had found a lucrative job as a hotel front desk operator. That way they would not question the amount of money she was sending them. I later learned from Eric that many Thai prostitutes lied to their families about their occupation and that somehow their families often figured out the obvious.

I remember Jenny telling me several times that the women of the Issan region were also the most desired in Thailand because of their beauty, fairer skin, and height. Apparently the women were mixed with Chinese, Vietnamese, Thai, and Laotian, which made them tall and beautiful. The southern Thais, like the ones we saw in Ko Tao were rather short and unattractive. Jenny was an extremely beautiful woman, even for her age. I still remember her face as if it were yesterday. In fact, these are the few fond visuals I still possess. I didn't know what I had until it was too late.

Jenny taught me how shallow I really was. I always felt as if I knew more than the uneducated. I always felt as if they were the reason why the masses suffered under dictators and unjust systems. Jenny and I had lots of talks during our time together and she really knew a lot more about life than I ever imagined a prostitute would. If anything, I could tell that she became more and more disappointed with me. I, of course, was learning more about the world. I was also becoming more and more disappointed at myself. The whole reason for my defection to North Korea was not making sense anymore. I was actually learning less and less about the world by staying inside that "Hermit Kingdom."

The biggest example of my shallowness was when the Danes, over a bottle of hard liquor, suggested that we swap partners. Since we had first arrived, I could tell that Dorte was eyeing me in a very sensual way, while Toke was constantly checking out Jenny. I mean, who wouldn't? Jenny always wore a white bikini over her dark voluptuous body. Sometimes she would just put on a Sarong (Thai skirt) and walk around in her see-through Sarong and bikini top. Her bikini was so small that the tattoo on her ass was very visible. The heat and Jenny's incredible body was a dangerous combination. We had sex several times a day. Jenny was very energetic and I was very attracted to her. We sometimes didn't even get out of our bungalow except to eat and lie on the beach for a while.

Still, I was intrigued by the proposition. I was always interested in couple swapping. Jenny flatly said no to the offer as soon as they brought it up. She later told me that she thought they were a little crazy. I told her that in Denmark people were a little more open about sex and liked to try new things. Still, Jenny didn't like the idea. Of course, I was into the idea. Jenny was nothing to me. I now had the opportunity to be with Dorte, a very attractive woman with the most amazing curves. I used to glance at her every chance I got. She was exactly my type. She had these amazing seductive green eyes and long straight blond hair. I wanted her, even for just a night.

I was pretty drunk that night and blurted out that I thought it was a great idea. Jenny walked out of the room as soon as I said it. I was still too slow to realize that she was beginning to like me. I caught up with her later on the beach and we began a yelling match. I am not sure what I said exactly, but it must not have been nice. I do remember saying something rude regarding how I had paid for her and therefore she "owed" me. She was paid to have sex anyway, so what was the difference? The difference was that Jenny had feelings for me, but I didn't realize it at the time. Jenny finally agreed to our plan, but she behaved very coldly towards me for the rest of the trip.

The following night, after drinking heavily, we began our silly orgy. Of course, everyone was excited except for Jenny. While I was making love to Dorte on the bed, I glanced quickly at Toke and Jenny on the floor. Toke was on top while Jenny had her head turned to the side and was just staring at the wall. At that moment, I saw Jenny in a different way. She was no longer the whore that I paid to accompany me, but a caring individual trapped in a business where emotions are dangerous.

Jenny played the silent game for the rest of the trip. I felt really bad, but I was also relieved that she had learned the truth about me. What was I suppose to do with her anyway? Get married and go live on that island for the rest of our lives? She didn't know the half of me.

The only other thing I remember distinctly is climbing to the top of the mountain alone one day. On the way, I saw one of those large lizards that live on the island. The lizard was so scared when he saw me, he tripped over a pile of rocks while running away. Climbing the narrow trail to the top was not so hard, it was just so humid that I had to stop every few minutes and wipe the sweat off my face.

Coming down the mountain, I suddenly saw a white woman carrying muffins. She stopped and asked me if I wanted to try some. We chatted a little and she told me that she had been living on the island for the past year. She had married a local man while on a trip to the island and never left. She told me they lived on top of the mountain in a small hut. She told me to stop by and say hello to her husband.

I did just that. His name was Wu and he was a very charming young man, probably fifteen years younger that the woman. He was a fisherman by trade, but had the experience of living in Bangkok for half his life. The couple sustained themselves by fishing, raising a small garden and farm animals, and selling their craftwork in Bangkok every couple of months. Wu and I talked for hours. Wu's English was pretty good and he also was very knowledgeable about Southeast Asia.

Coming back down the mountain to the village where we were staying, I noticed a suspicious-looking guy. He was Asian, but definitely not Thai. Thais were mostly dark and not too big. This guy was dark, but a different tone. He was also more broad shouldered and a bit tall. Most importantly, he was not smiling. Thais are famous for their smiles. Thailand is the "Land of Smiles."

The man was sitting at one of the restaurants and pretending to read the paper. He looked too serious for this place. He never looked at me, but I just felt him watching me. Was he a North Korean spy watching me to make sure I was not screwing up? Was he a South Korean spy out to assassinate me? Was he an American CIA or maybe even Mossad? Mr. Kim had turned me into a paranoid freak, especially concerning the Mossad. After talking to him, I thought the Mossad were everywhere and knew everything. I never did find out who that man was.

That trip is still imbedded in my head as if it were yesterday. I wish I could say the same thing about the years I had spent in North Korea. I guess that I consciously remember only the good memories. After we arrived back in Bangkok, Jenny gave me a quick hug and told me to look her up next time I was in town. I knew she didn't mean it. She was disappointed with me. She realized that I was very immature and never was romantically interested in her. It's not that I wasn't interested in her; I just didn't know anything about love. I now realize that she was the best thing that ever happened in my pathetic life.

The night before I was to leave to Japan I went out to the bars again. Not to find women, just to drink. I was so nervous about the mission that was coming up. Mr. Kim and I had gone through the training several times. Mr. Kim wanted to make sure I wouldn't screw it up. Inside the tote bag and the suitcase were two souvenirs of the traditional Thai boats made from a varnished wood. Of course, what was inside the boats was what I could not see. The boats were handmade and sealed naturally so that no one could tell they contained anything inside.

I tried to get a peak at them while I was in my room, but there was no way to find out what was inside without breaking them. I sat at the bar that night wondering what the hell was in those things and why they needed me to transport them. I don't know the answers to this day but I have some theories.

I believe that the North Koreans were selling the famous $100 bill plates they developed a couple of years back. Let's not forget, North Korea was basically an organized crime syndicate, which was only interested in making its "bosses" even richer and stronger. Eric told me during one of our nights of drinking that the government was accused by other nations of dumping fake money around the world in all types of currencies. The biggest launderers were other communist nations and the Middle East.

But why me? Why through Thailand? My only answer to those questions was that no one would suspect a white guy like myself. Maybe the intelligence agencies were expecting a Korean or an Arab to transport the plates through a hostile nation like Laos or North Korea. No one would suspect a Canadian tourist on vacation in Thailand. That is the only explanation I can think of.

The next day I headed to the airport. I was to check the large suitcase and take the tote bag with me. After immigration and inspection, I was to walk over to the phone booth and put the tote bag down on the floor next to me. I was then to just pretend to make a phone call and not pay any attention to the person next to me. While I was on the phone, someone would get on the other phone and put down the exact same type of tote bag as mine. After the call, the person would pick up my bag and I would then take that person's bag.

I was also trained to notice any irregularities that might occur and then abort plan A for plan B. If I felt anything out of the ordinary, I should immediately implement plan B. Without being paranoid, Mr. Kim trained me to notice peculiar behaviors among individuals. For example, someone carrying or reading a newspaper that glances in my direction is definitely suspicious. Any person; man, woman, or even child, who I noticed more than once, was considered suspicious. Plan B would involve aborting the phone booth immediately and going to the bathroom nearest to the phone booth. I would enter the stall and leave the case near me in the stall. Someone in the next stall would replace it with a similar case and leave.

I was sweating bullets at the airport, but it wasn't just from fear. The airport was hot and stuffy. I didn't look suspicious at all. Most of the foreign tourists were sweating. Once I got past immigration, I looked around for the phone booth I was to "make the call" from. I was determined to get a glance at the person who was going to make the switch with me. Mr. Kim was very clear about how I should not do anything that would look suspicious, but I was just so curious.

As I pretended to talk on the phone, I heard someone walk up to the phone next to me. Casually, I veered my eyes over to the person next to me. It was a young, scrawny white man. He was dressed as if he were on vacation. He pretended to make a friendly phone call and even managed to laugh while chatting.

He was speaking French. He then hung up the phone, reached for my bag, and walked off. That was it!

I felt a sense of relief once that tote bag was out of my hand. Now I only had to make one more delivery. I walked over to the gate that read "JAL 005" to Tokyo. I was now off to Japan. On the plane, I thought about Jenny and how sweet she was. It was then that it dawned upon me that she really liked me. I felt a pain inside me, a guilty pain for treating another human being with such contempt and apathy. Who was I to treat her so badly? If I really wanted to do her any good, I would have left right after the first night I had sex with her. That way I could have spared her feelings.

I arrived in Japan in the evening and found my way to the bus depot where I bought a ticket to the Tokyo train station. I now had a chance to brush up on my Japanese. I had studied Japanese for a couple of semesters. The grammar and structure were similar to Korean. The verbs came at the end of the sentences, unlike English and Chinese, where the verbs come in the middle. Japanese was a syllabic language, which made it easy to understand and speak (unlike Korean).

I bought a ticket on the Hikari Shinkansen to Kokura in Kitakyushu. These trains were known as the "bullet" trains because they traveled so damn fast. It was the most comfortable and enjoyable train ride I have ever had. Vendors kept coming by my chair offering all sorts of delicious treats and drinks. Being that I had so much money to spend, I made use of it. I bought several dishes and drinks that were almost impossible to find in North Korea. The Japanese beer was so good. I think I had something like Sapporo Beer. I don't really remember.

I tried to get a glance the Japanese countryside whenever the train came out of the long tunnels. It was the first time I really got to see how much the Japanese really had advanced. It was very different from the Japan I learned about years ago. There were new high-rises everywhere. Big billboards and signs dominated the walls and tops of buildings. People were dressed in colorful clothes and looked happy. A sharp contrast to North Koreans who wore drab colors and looked frightened and depressed. I could also see many cars and electronics everywhere, as well as brightly lit streets and corners. Even the best part of Pyongyang was only dimly lit, sometimes not lit at all.

I was in shock. After several years in North Korea I had begun to forget how different other countries in Asia were. I mean, here I was riding in a bullet train in a country that had also risen from the same ashes as North Korea. The American Air Force had bombed Japan into the Stone Age during World War II. I also had a sense that North Korea was slipping even further into an abyss of technological malfunctions and stunted economic growth. Still, I thought that it was admirable that North Korea was not rapidly industrializing just for the sake of capitalism. I tried to cling on to my stubborn beliefs that capitalism was the ill of the masses.

The train arrived at Kokura station a few hours later. I walked out of the station and looked around for the guide that was supposed to be waiting for me. A short smiling man was standing on the side of the station, looking directly at me. As soon as I began to approach him, he gave me a deep bow and reached for my baggage. He looked at the case I was suppose to deliver to him. He grinned slightly and looked around the station. I thanked him in Japanese and introduced myself. He just nodded and signaled me to follow him. We walked through the train station corridor to another depot where a light rail car was waiting on the tracks. The man handed me a ticket and motioned to me to insert the ticket in the slot.

We hopped on the light rail car and took a seat. It was a cute train consisting of four passenger cars and no engine. It was all electric-powered. We went on a short rail ride to Shingu, a small town along the coast between the cities of Kokura and Fukuoka. Along the way, I could make out the rice paddies and some villages. We got off at Shingu and began to walk. We walked for about fifteen minutes through the town to a small house tucked inside a ravine. I could hear a gurgling creek, but it was too dark to see. There were houses on both sides of the street that meandered up the ravine. We stopped at one of the last houses and the man motioned me to come in.

The house was very cozy. There was a fireplace in the kitchen and *Tatami* mats in every room except the kitchen and bathroom. Suddenly, the man began to talk in Korean. I was a little surprised. However, I was aware of the many Koreans who lived in Japan. He told me to take a seat while he went into the kitchen. I heard a knock on the door and heard a woman's voice in Japanese. She seemed to be older, around that man's age. I then heard some noise in the kitchen as if someone was preparing to cook.

The man came back into the living room with a bottle of whiskey and two glasses. He poured me a glass and sat down next to me. He introduced himself as Mr. Takahashi. He was Korean-Japanese and a member of the *Chochonyon* (also spelled *Chochongryong* and *Chongnyon*).

The *Chochonyon* were the Korean Japanese who supported the North Korean government. In Japanese, they were known as the *Chosen Soren*, after the Choson dynasty name and the name that North Korea has continued to use (Only Western languages refer to both North and South as Korea. The *Koryo* dynasty's openness to the West resulted in the name being recognized among most languages). They were known to use violence and heavy tactics to get their message across to other Korean-Japanese and Japanese as well.

The Korean population in Japan varies between 700,000 to over a million. The Korean community is split in its support for the two Koreas. The Korean organization that supported South Korea was known as *Mindan*. This group was considered smaller at the time and not as powerful. There were some instances where the *Chochonyon* murdered key members of the *Mindan* or any Japanese who criticized North Korea. I read about one Japanese professor who mysteriously vanished after he had given a negative lecture on North Korea.

Interestingly enough, the *Chochonyon* were a Godsend to the North Korean government. During Japanese occupation of the Korean peninsula, many Koreans were forced to move to Japan and work in manual labor and factories. After World War II, many of these Koreans were stuck in Japan, some even wanted to stay. The Koreans in Japan were part of the *Burakumin*, or untouchables. In other words, they were the only people suited to do the dirty jobs Japanese didn't want to do. Some of those jobs included being involved in crime, prostitution, and racketeering. Koreans, always well known for their toughness (during World War II and, the Vietnam War, Korean soldiers were some of the most vicious and feared fighters), pushed their way further into the life of Japanese crime.

A large part of the *Yakuza*, or Japanese mafia, in Japan has a strong Korean connection. One of the largest *Yakuza* groups are predominantly Korean. Most are members of the *Mindan*, however some are *Chochonyon*. Pachinko Parlors, a popular form of Japanese casinos, brothels, nightclubs, and the drug trade are largely owned and controlled by Korean-Japanese. The *Mindan* use some of their funds to support anti-communist groups, while the *Chochonyon* send a large amount of their earnings directly to North Korea. The *Chochonyon* in Japan were nothing more than a criminal gang acting on behalf of the two Kims. The pro-North Korean organization is run by a few greedy men who are drunk with the power that is bestowed upon them by North Korea.

Some people who have spoken out against North Korea and its influence on Japan were threatened or even killed by the *Chochonyon*. Most importantly, the *Chochonyon* serve as the North Korean mouthpiece in Japan and abroad and are an economic lifeline for North Korea. Worst of all, the *Chochonyon* leaders were able to convince a steady stream of unsuspecting Korean-Japanese in the 1950's through the 1970's to take all their belongings and go live in North Korea, the paradise. In 1961 alone, 100,000 Korean Japanese boarded ships in mass exodus to North Korea.

Many of these poor individuals quickly learned the truth about North Korea, but by then it was too late. Quite a few managed to send letters back to Japan warning Korean Japanese not to come. The letters had to be discreet; otherwise the North Korean censors reading the letters would not have permitted them to be delivered. Some of the *Chochonyon* ended up in the internment camps in North Korea. Coming from Japan, they were not accustomed to the harsh living conditions in North Korea. Those who voiced their discontent were imprisoned. Many Korean residents in Japan are blackmailed by North Korea to continue in their financial support, lest they want their relatives in North Korea to experience any "misfortunes."

Mr. Takahashi kept looking at me for a while and then finally blurted out: "So you are the one." I just smiled and said, "yes." At first I didn't know what he meant, but later I realized that he was well aware of who I really was. I had been a big propaganda piece for the North Korea recently. Without revealing too much about my physical measurements, the North Korean propaganda machine used me as a ploy to make all those nonbelievers think that North Korea was indeed a paradise. Why else would these high-ranking Americans risk their lives and defect to the North.

Mr. Takahashi stood up and asked me to follow him. He took me through this long, old house to a narrow staircase that seemed to wind up to a second floor. Instead of going up the stairs, he walked behind the steps and pushed the wall. Suddenly, a secret compartment opened up and another row of stairs appeared leading down into some sort of basement. I followed Mr. Takahashi down the steps into the basement. The walls had all these propaganda pictures and leaflets with Kim IL Sung and Kim Jong IL pictures on them. This was Mr. Takahashi's secret stash of all things North Korean.

There were also all sorts of what seemed to be stolen goods, such as cartons of cigarettes, bottles of liquor, and porno magazines. This guy was up to everything. Mr. Takahashi saw that I was looking at the loot and remarked that that was actually going back with me to North Korea. Mr. Takahashi seemed to be looking for something, then suddenly shouted "ah!" and smiled. He showed me an article in Japanese in what seemed to be a pro-North Korean magazine. I couldn't read Japanese well, so he translated it to say that it was all about me and my escape to the North. I wasn't too surprised. Ever since I arrived in North Korea, I was in this interview or that being hailed as a great success story of how Americans were sick and tired of their imperialist nation and wanted to come live in the socialist paradise that is North Korea.

Mr. Takahashi waived his hand towards me as if to follow him further into the room. At the other end of the room, he unlatched another secret passageway into a smaller room where he lit a candle and the arsenal in the room was suddenly exposed. There were dozens of Kalatchnikovs (AK47), handguns, hand grenades and several knives all lined up on shelves. Mr. Takahashi looked so proud when he showed me this. He had an evil grin that only made me feel more uncomfortable. After a moment of awkward silence, Mr. Takahashi put down the machine gun he was holding.

"We will bring Japan into the power of the great leader, Kim IL Sung." Mr. Takahashi began.

"We Koreans will rule again someday and introduce a new world order. People around the world are starting to see the wisdom behind *Juche* and *Kimilsungism*. You'll see. We already have the tools to disrupt the world order. Once we prove that only chaos can come from capitalism, we will step in to offer an alternative. The suitcase you delivered is the first step."

With that statement, Mr. Takahashi turned around and escorted me out. I remember those words very clearly. Were the *Chochonyon* that confident?

Following the tour of Mr. Takahashi's secret stash, we had dinner. His wife prepared a wonderful noodle dish, *Udon*, I believe. I can still taste that soup. Turns out that the house was not the only house Mr. Takahashi had. Right across the alley was another house he told me was his. That house was even bigger. It was his and his wife's residence. The house we were in now and where I was going to stay in was his "office." Mr. Takahashi's "official" line of work was import/export. He told me he had been to many different countries and spoke Thai, Spanish, Chinese, Korean, and understood a few other languages.

That night Mr. Takahashi took me to a local pub. I loved the coziness of Japan. Everywhere looked small and comfortable. The Japanese really knew how to make the best of space. Gardens, restaurants, everything was so well manicured and maintained. The bar probably could not hold more than twenty people, yet it was very comfortable. The bar owner must have been a jazz lover because the place was decorated with jazz posters and played jazz music the whole time I was there.

I caught the attention of a woman who was looking at my direction and smiling. Mr. Takahashi also noticed it and took the initiative. He invited the girl and her friend to come and drink with us. The two women were in their late twenties and worked in an office in Fukuoka city. They both spoke very little English, which gave me some practice with my Japanese. The woman who was smiling at me was Emi, but I don't remember her friend's name. Being that I was going to stay a few days in Japan, I thought it would be nice to have some company while I was there. One thing about North Korea was that it was very, very difficult to meet women.

Emi was very nice and took a liking to me right away. She took some time off from her job to show me around. I knew that it wasn't such a good idea to get so close to anyone, but I also had the feeling that Emi was a lonely person who just wanted to spend some time with someone that she could feel comfortable with. We took a weeklong trip around the whole island of Kyushu. The train system was so efficient and reached everywhere, even in Kyushu (Kyushu is the southernmost of the four main islands that make up Japan. It was always known to be behind other urban areas such as the Kanto and Kansai regions/prefectures). The train even went up the steep slopes of Mt. Aso and over to the other side of the Island where we spent a night at the famous Beppu Hot Springs.

The motel we stayed in had rooms with personal access to the hot springs. It was the most incredible experience I had ever had. There was a door in the back of our bathroom that led out to the hot springs pool. They diverted the hot spring water from the local creek to the motel rooms and created little pools for each room. Even in the winter people could slip into the hot water and enjoy the view. As I lay in the water, Emi came out wrapped in a towel. As she opened her towel and slipped in I noticed that she was naked. It was customary, she told me, to go in with your birthday suite.

Emi was not the prettiest woman I had ever seen, but she definitely had a great figure. She was fairly tall (for a Japanese person) and had the smallest waist I had ever seen. Yet her hips and behind were nice and round and she had large perky breasts. She was very pale, like most Japanese, and had bad skin. That night we made love about five times. Emi acted as if she hadn't had sex in years. Her legs quivered and her body shook as I caressed her skin and licked her. She screamed as we made love.

"*Kimochi, ahhh…Kimochi, Itaii!*"

I quickly figured out that *Kimochi* meant "It feels good" while *Itaii* meant "It hurts" in a pleasant way. Watching her enjoy the sex so much enhanced my own pleasure as well. I was eager to please her and got off watching her squirm and scream with pleasure. Emi was also very adventurous. We tried several positions and she even let me enter her from behind. She simply enjoyed sex. I had never been with a girl that excited before. It was one of those nights I will never forget.

That week we went through several coastal cities, such as Nagasaki, Oita, Kagoshima, and Miyazaki. All of these cities had their own culture and each city was unique in their own way. I especially liked Kagoshima and Miyazaki. Both cities were subtropical, so there were palm trees on the streets, but the weather was not that hot. I told Emi that I was especially interested in cultural and historical places, so we made some stops in several temples and cultural spots. I really fell in love with Japanese temples. They were different than Korean temples in that they were plain in color, but had superb architecture. Both were beautiful in their own unique way.

I still have a clear picture of one of the temples we discovered on our bike ride through a small town outside Kokura. One temple in particular is still fresh in my mind. It was in a ravine between two small mountains. Emi lived in Kokura and asked me if I would like to see her neighborhood. Kokura itself was not very interesting, but the outlying area was so scenic and relaxing. Emi borrowed a bike from her neighbor for me to use. We rode our bikes through this curvy road that followed a creek for most of the way. On the way, we saw children playing in the river. As they saw us, they waved shyly and gave us a big smile.

Along the way, I noticed a small stairway that was lined with bamboo trees. Through the bamboo trees was a pine forest. There were also a few Japanese maple trees that were in full foliage. The colors were amazing. I felt as if I had discovered paradise. There was something so tranquil about this temple. At the end of the walkway, there was an orange wooden gate. Through the gate was a small temple made entirely from wood. At one end of the courtyard was a well with cute little wooden ladles, which were used to drink with. It was probably just my fond memories, but that water tasted so sweet. I can still taste it.

I have carried these fond memories to this day. Even on my worst days, I would force a smile as I sat thinking about that temple. The inner-peace and serenity I felt sitting at the edge of a bamboo forest. The light breeze, quiet environment, only broken occasionally by the sounds of birds or the swaying bamboo. I think that picture in my mind kept me going when I didn't think I could continue living. Maybe in my next life I can have the honor of being a monk in some remote temple somewhere.

My week's stay in Japan went so fast. I really felt as if I did more in Japan in one week than ten years in North Korea. In North Korea I was a prisoner. On my last day in Japan, I felt very nervous. I was contemplating running away and hiding at one of the temples that I was fantasizing about. What could they do to me? Do they even know where I was? Was someone following?

Since I had arrived in Japan I suspected everyone around me. I was sure that they had someone following me. I had reasons to be. During my trip with Emi to the city of Miyazaki, a policeman began to approach us as we looked at our map.

Suddenly, a man who I had noticed earlier rushed over to the policeman and began to distract him by asking him for help. It was then that I realized that I was in fact being watched the entire time I was there.

I was especially afraid of Mr. Takahashi. He always looked at me with a suspicious look. Even though he was short and quite small, I knew he would do anything to make sure this operation went smoothly. I don't think he trusted anyone. He kept me in the dark the entire time I was there. On the last day he informed me that we were to leave in the middle of the night. I had no prior warning. I didn't know until the last minute that I was going to go back to North Korea by boat.

On my last night in Japan, Mr. Takahashi revealed to me that I would be traveling a clandestine way back to North Korea. I now realized why Mr. Takahashi lived so close to the sea and in such a remote place. That night we took a walk along the coast. Mr. Takahashi made it a habit to take these walks, so no one would ever think it was suspicious. We took a small, steep trail that led through the bushes down to the sea. At one point, Mr. Takahashi and I rappelled down a short cliff by rope. As we walked onto the beach, Mr. Takahashi pulled out a flashlight and clicked it on and off. Suddenly, a light in the distance flickered on and off in response.

We waited for a few minutes until I could see a small rowing boat with two people at the oars. Mr. Takahashi then turned to me and told me that it was time to go. I walked into the water towards the boat. The men helped me in and we were quickly on our way out to sea. Deep down, I hoped that the Japanese coast guard would catch us. I really didn't want to go back. Unfortunately for me, the trip went off without a hitch. Our rowing boat went out to sea for a few miles where we met up with a fishing trawler. The trawler was really a North Korean spy ship, one of the many that North Korea used to terrorize its neighbors.

I spent that calm night looking out at the sea, thinking about the fun I had had on my trip. For a secret mission, I really did enjoy myself. I thought to myself that my life was not as bad as I had thought. I mean, I wanted to explore the unknown, so here it was. I watched the sun set over the East Sea that morning. In the distance I could start to make out the outline of the North Korean shore. I could not stop but think what my future would look like once I returned. Little did I know that my life was going to peak shortly and then go very far downhill.

Chapter 13

▼

WHERE IS SAM?

1984

The apex of my life came with a twist. My mission to Southeast Asia and Japan won the confidence of many party officials, including Kim Jong IL himself. On the downside, I was also made aware of what happens to those who fall out of favor with the top brass in North Korea.

I went back to teaching at KIS University the day after I had arrived from Japan. My students had no idea about my mission except for the fact that I was "on vacation." Most would never even dare to inquire about my whereabouts. An inquisitive mind was a dangerous one. Asking question in North Korea was a sure ticket to prison. The break from teaching really helped. I felt invigorated and ready to teach again. Unbeknownst to me, I would soon have another task in hand.

I met Eric shortly after I came back and we quickly adjourned to our nightly hangout at his apartment. I talked all about my adventures with Eric, who was salivating from my stories. I could tell that he was really ready to travel again. I tried to play down my experiences so as not to make him do something he would regret, like try to escape. Poor Eric, all he ever wanted to do was see the world. Now he was a virtual prisoner, not allowed to leave even the University campus without permission.

Eric was enthusiastic to fill me in on what I had missed. Much had happened while I was gone. He told me about the University and the plan to expand the foreign studies department. He saved the bad news for last. Eric had not seen Sam for the last two weeks at our favorite and only club in Pyongyang. This was highly alarming because Sam never missed a Saturday at the club, never! Eric and I could only speculate on what had happened. Knowing Sam, there could have been several reasons. The one thing we both knew about North Korea was that people "disappeared" all the time. None of them ever reappeared.

I soon learned more about Sam's disappearance. Two weeks after I had returned from my trip, I was surprised to see Mr. Lee, the director from the studios, in Dr. Han's office. Mr. Lee was actually there to see me. I was a little surprised. Was he here to tell me something about Sam? No, North Koreans never had any reason to justify anything. What could he want?

Mr. Lee was very cordial. He took Dr. Han and me out to a restaurant that was a favorite with North Korean party officials. Over a bowl of *kimchi jigye* (stew), Mr. Lee explained to me that the studios were in need of more "Non-Korean" actors. Mr. Lee showered me with praise for my popularity in the "Party" and even as high as Kim Jong IL, the Chairman of the Board at Kim IL Sung Studios. I kept my fake smile and humble reaction to Mr. Lee's praise, but deep inside I was scared. Someone I knew well was gone, I could be next.

Sensing that I was probably curious about my friend Sam's situation, Mr. Lee attempted to ease my worries.

"By the way, Sam sends his regards."

I looked at Mr. Lee with the least bit of shock. I didn't want him to think that I really cared either way.

"Tell him I say hello as well." I responded.

"Sure, you know Sam wanted this job change. I tried to convince him to stay. He was born to act. I guess it was because of you and Eric. He envied you guys. He wanted to be respected professor like you. He now teaches English and Drama at Wonsan Technical College on the East coast."

I knew it was a load of crap from the get go. Sam couldn't teach English, let alone speak it without using profanity and grammatical errors. Unless the students wanted to learn street slang, Sam could not offer much in terms of English instruction. Besides, Sam never liked teaching. He always made fun of Eric and I for being clowns at the university level. He even called me "college boy" on several occasions. Most importantly, Sam hated the countryside. Wonsan was a lot more rural than Pyongyang. My fears that Sam was in big trouble were now confirmed.

Mr. Lee was very enthusiastic about the idea and just kept talking the whole time about the growth and potential worldwide for Kim IL Sung Studios. My duties at the studios would not interfere with my classes and I would be upgraded to a new and bigger apartment. Mr. Lee mentioned that the fact that I was from

California made me a prime candidate for the film industry. I didn't want to break the bad news to him about how Hollywood just so happened to be four hundred miles away from my hometown. To North Koreans, America was the same size as North Korea. The truth was that California alone was bigger than both North and South Korea together. It was no use explaining. North Koreans, even at the top, had no clue about the outside world.

Mr. Lee kept the best news for the grand finale: Kim Jong IL himself had invited me to spend the weekend at his estate. Mr. Lee said that he was very eager to meet me and discuss my future and the future of the studios. It wasn't known to me at the time, but Kim Jong IL was a movie buff. I mean, the guy loved American movies and actors, such as Elizabeth Taylor and Marlon Brando. I didn't know what to say. I was given the opportunity to go see the second in command, Kim IL Sung's favorite son and probably his heir to the throne. I tried to put on an excited face, but deep down I was terrified.

For those of you who don't know why I would be terrified, I suggest that you look at Kim Jong IL's accomplishments, or should I say, the history of his reign of terror. Kim Junior caught his father's attention by taking more violent initiatives than his siblings. Kim Junior planned and carried out several attacks against South Korea. He was also known in domestic circles for his frequent purges of those he thought might not favor his succession to power. Kim Junior also served as head of one of North Korea's infamous security apparatuses. Somewhat like the early Israeli Mossad or East Germany's Stassi; the security service was nameless, operated in complete secrecy, and was never mentioned by North Koreans for fear of reprisal.

The planned meeting with Kim Jong IL was actually not planned at all. All Mr. Lee could tell me was that "Kim was a busy man," and he didn't even know when he would be available. Mr. Lee would let me know as soon as he could regarding our meeting. In North Korea, time stops for the two Kims, not the other way around. Literally, Kim Jong IL has a terrible sleep and work habit that must be catered to by the whole damn country. For example, Kim likes to surprise people by making unexpected, middle of the night visits to factories, schools, and government offices. It is his way of keeping everyone on his or her feet.

That night Eric and I talked about the new turn of events. Eric was jealous of the fact that I had a chance to travel, but not about my prospect of meeting Kim Jong IL. Over a few beers, we tried to write down the pros and cons of being a "celebrity" in North Korea. Our mutual conclusions were that it was never a good thing to be in the spotlight in North Korea, but it sure wasn't good to be a commoner either. Eric and I had an idea of what it was like to be on the lower ends of North Korean society. Some of our students who came from outside Pyongyang confirmed our fears that only the very privileged in Pyongyang enjoyed more than the subsistent existence. For example, one student I had didn't even know what an orange was.

Eric also confided in me about a strange encounter he had made just the other day. Soon after Sam's disappearance, Eric tried to make some inquiries at the club about his whereabouts. On his weekend trip to the campus store, he noticed an older man following him. He thought the man too old to be a student and did not look like the typical Kim IL Sung professor who dawned the Maoist-style clothing. As Eric turned to walk down a corridor of a building the man called out.

"Professor! Aren't you forgetting something?" The strange man asked.

"Your identification card!" The man continued, waving Eric's I.D. card in the air. Eric turned to him and walked over and asked for his Identification Card back. The man just smirked and handed it over to Eric.

"You should keep an eye on your valuables. That includes your mouth!" He continued with a confident grin.

"Where did you find it? Who are you?" Eric demanded.

"For your own sake, you will never have to meet me again. That all depends on you."

With those words, the man turned around and hastily made his way down the long, dark corridor. Eric was still in shock. He had always kept his I.D. card in his front pocket. Surely he would have noticed if someone had tried to steal it. After hearing this story, Eric and I sat there in silence. We didn't know what to make of it. Eric poured me another beer and we just sat there and drank. I know that in my mind I was thinking of the old adage in Asian culture that silence is the best policy. I am sure Eric was thinking the same thing.

CHAPTER 14

▼

KIM JONG IL

Spring, 1984

Two and a half weeks went by before I heard from Mr. Lee again. I was to meet Kim Jong IL the very next day. Everything was arranged. Mr. Lee would pick me up and take me to Kim Jong IL's villa. I was to tell no one of my plans that day and bring nothing with me. Everything would be provided. As you can imagine, I didn't sleep much that night. I was very anxious about the whole trip. One false word could result in my immediate execution. Kim Jong IL had the final say (with the exception for his father) on everything in North Korea.

I woke up early that Saturday morning and waited outside our apartment building. Mr. Lee came by around five a.m. and we were off. As we exited the university campus, I noticed a dark Mercedes on the side of the road. As we passed it, it sped up and began to tail us. It was the armed escort that would follow us all the way to the villa. I didn't exactly know where we were going, but I have always had a good sense of direction and realized that we were heading northwest. In North Korea, there weren't many signs to give anyone any notion where they were or where they were heading. The government figured that the less people knew, the better.

I remember being happy to be on a road trip. I was so curious about the Korean countryside. So far, I hadn't really seen much. We drove through some really beautiful ravines and valleys, surrounded by steep mountains and terraced fields. It was winter, but spring was just around the corner. The snow was melting and filling the small creeks and streams with strong currents. Some parts of the road we were on were flooded due to poor road planning. It was 1980 and I was now in my eighth year in North Korea. I couldn't believe so much time had gone by. I wondered to myself what the future had in store for me.

We had no problems getting past the numerous road checks along the way. After all, I was an invited guest of Kim Jong IL. We made two pit stops along the way: one naptime break and one lunch break. We stopped in a small town and ate at a cooperative restaurant that served as a cafeteria for the factory workers and farmers. At the time, there was nobody there, so we had the entire place to ourselves. The cafeteria hall was decorated with ridiculous communist slogans like: "Let's all meet the challenge!" and "Productivity is our savior." In other words, let's line the pockets of the elite even more. I was already very cynical about the North. It was just my nature to be cynical. It just took a rash defection to an enemy nation to learn this fact about myself.

After lunch, we got right back on the road. I really wanted to look around this quaint little town, but Mr. Lee was on a tight schedule. I still regret not having had better opportunity to explore the countryside of North Korea. Unlike South Korea, North Korea was off limits to almost everyone, including the elite. The two Kims really tried to limit the amount of information anyone had about anything. I guess that was partly why North Korea is still under their control.

After what seemed like an eternity of driving, Mr. Lee made an unexpected sharp right off the main road and onto a dirt road. After about a mile, this uneventful dirt road suddenly came to a well-manicured fortress. Just as we the car turned the bend, there were two tank barrels pointing right in our direction. A high, barbed-wire fence with two tower guards ran across the road and around what seemed to be around a forest. About ten soldiers with machine guns were standing on the road, blocking the entrance to the compound. I could tell from their insignia that they were the special military unit that had the honor of guarding the top ranking officials in North Korea (I had seen them before in Pyongyang).

The guards asked us to get out and checked our car and bodies thoroughly. After that, we were asked to walk into the compound, while one of the guards drove our car inside. We were asked to go into a small room and told to strip our clothes. One guard walked slowly around as we stood there, naked. A few minutes later, we were allowed to get back in the car and drive up to the villa.

What a villa! As we drove up I couldn't believe my eyes. It was three floors high and as wide as a city block. The villa faced the sea and was surrounded by steep mountains. The gardens and fountains in the front of the villa were absolutely stunning. I noticed that someone had brushed away all the snow because there was none around the villa. It reminded me of the Hearst Castle that William Randolph Hearst had built by the Pacific Ocean between Los Angeles and San Francisco. Maybe Kim had that place in mind when it was built. Mr. Lee saw my surprise and just said: "He has seven other villas just like this one." Seven others? So much for socialism and equality for all. What I was about to see would just confirm the fact that North Koreas were far from equal.

As we drove up to the front two men who looked like butlers were waiting for us. It was the royal treatment from then on. The men opened our car doors and escorted us into the house. My shock just continued to grow as we entered the villa. Lavish decorations with incredible chandeliers and spiral staircases awaited us in the main room. As we walked through the main corridor I was shocked at the marble floors, the mahogany furniture, and what looked like gold trimmings around the picture and mirror frames. I also noticed ancient vases that dated back to the Koguryo and Shilla dynasties of Korea all over the mansion. I remember learning about them in one of my Korean culture classes at USC. The place reminded me of an English nobleman's house. I wondered if that was Kim's intention. Did he see himself as nobility? Probably! After all, he and his father were almost Godlike to North Koreans.

The butlers escorted us up to the second floor and down a long passageway to our rooms. My amazement just continued to grow. As we walked through the mansion I saw a large indoor pool through one of the doors and a spa next door to it. My room was bigger than my apartment. It had a mini-bar, a kitchen, a very large bathtub, and a very, very large circular bed. There were mirrors behind and above the bed. I felt as if I was staying in a playboy's pad. The view out of my bedroom balcony overlooked an alcove. I didn't even realize it, but we were not far from the beach.

I didn't have much time to enjoy my extravagant accommodation because of Mr. Lee's call from his room to meet me outside in five minutes. I met him and we headed downstairs to have dinner together. I didn't realize it, but it was already six in the evening. We had been traveling all day. Unlike a Western-style dining room, we ate in a very traditional Korean dining room. The room was covered with rice paper and sliding doors for privacy in each booth. There was one really large booth, but the waiters escorted us to a smaller one. We had to remove our slipper before stepping up to the booth. The floor was made of wood with mats laid on it for our comfort. It was the *Ondol* heating style in which steam heat came from the floor and heated the room.

The low-rise table in the center of the room was covered with all kinds of small dishes with delicious looking food in them. By now, I was familiar with many different Korean dishes, but these were new to me. Mr. Lee told me that many of the dishes contained rare ingredients, including wild mushrooms and exotic sea animals. The main dish was barbequed meat known in Korean as *Bulgogi* and *Galbi*. Our waiter told us the meat was from Kim Jong IL's own ranch. They fed the cows beer and massaged their entire bodies so that the meat would be tender. I have to admit that it was the best meat I have ever tasted. It melted in my mouth.

After dinner, Mr. Lee and I were escorted to a huge den, which looked like a bachelor's dream room. There was a wide screen television, a large bar, two pool tables, a poker table, a stereo system with surround sound, and a few other amenities that slip my mind now. The den had a North American cabin look to it, with all kinds of exotic animals' heads displayed on the wooden walls. I was getting the sense that Kim Jong IL, although a bitter enemy of the United States, actually admired the lifestyle. This double standard of acting as a "brother" of the revolution and living so luxuriously was obviously a betrayal to the North Korean people. You can't imagine my relief in being able to put this down in writing. For years I have lived with this bottled up inside of me.

Nevertheless, I had to be on my best behavior that weekend. Yet, I did not even know what would offend Kim Jong IL. "What should I say? How should I act?" I asked myself over and over again. He was the leader of a "Socialist" state, yet he lived like royalty. I contemplated my behavior over a game of pool with Mr. Lee. Mr. Lee didn't look too comfortable either. He was very nervous. I could tell that Kim Jong IL made everyone nervous, even his closest confidants. That was probably a way to keep them on their toes.

It was well into the night and still no sign of Kim Jong IL. Even Mr. Lee didn't know when he was supposed to come. Kim Jong IL operated on Kim Jong IL time. Time was another element of surprise he liked to impose on everyone. Suddenly, an assistant came running into the den and announced that Kim Jong IL's car had just pulled into the driveway. My heart jumped, I began to sweat almost instantly. Mr. Lee was the same way. We tried to continue playing pool as normal, but neither one of us was really paying attention. I couldn't even hold the pool stick without shaking.

The door opened, and a short man with dark curly hair walked in. It was Kim Jong IL. He was flanked by two beautiful women in miniskirts. One woman was dressed as a nurse; the other seemed to be his "personal assistant." Both were scantily dressed and did not look like their primary jobs were taking notes or administrating medical care. The whole scene reminded me of one of those soft porn novels that are sold everywhere.

"You must be David," he said in broken English. "Are you being entertained?"
"Yes, Mr. Kim, it is an honor to finally meet you."
I responded in a scratchy voice.
He had a big smile on his face and didn't look as scary as I had previously thought. He had the strangest curly hair, which was very unusual for a Korean. He wasn't as tall as he looked in photos and he had a large potbelly that stuck out of his otherwise skinny physique. He was dressed in the usual Mao-style gray suit that I was accustomed to seeing on him in photos, but he was also wearing really nice Italian leather shoes. I tried to wipe my sweaty hands off on the pool table before I shook his hand, but I remember that I still had some perspiration on it.
"You don't have to be so nervous, I am not a bad fellow."
Kim switched to Korean.
"I'm sorry! It's just that I have been so excited to meet you."
I responded in Korean.
"Wow! Your Korean is very good! You even have that Pyongyang proper accent."
He chuckled with amusement.
There was an awkward moment where I didn't know whether to continue bowing or offer my handshake again. Looking back, I feel so terrible for kissing his ass so much. At the time, I felt that it was for my own survival to be very nice to him. I was extremely careful not to anger him or do anything out of the ordinary. Mr. Kim then turned to Mr. Lee and greeted him with a simple "Anyong" (hello in Korean) and then turned back to me.
"David! We have lot to talk for,"
He said in broken English.
Kim reached for a button in the wall and pressed it. An assistant came running in and bowed deeply to Kim. Kim ordered the man to bring in some refreshments and turn on the television. Kim then sat down and signaled to me to sit next to him. Kim Jong IL was always shrouded in mystery. This was the first time I found out he spoke some English. In the biographies of him I read at the university's library, it never mentioned his English proficiency. It did, however, mention that Kim excelled at everything he did. Still, he insisted on talking mostly in Korean because he felt it was "patriotic."
"David, what do you know about making movies?"
He asked.
I told him that although I was from California, I only had a brief experience in high school acting in a school play (I was a terrible actor). Kim wasn't really listening to me and just continued to talk. He went on and on about his dream to

turn North Korea into the Asian Hollywood. He rambled on about how Asia was fast outpacing the Western world and would do so by the year 2000 it would compete directly with Hollywood movies.

Competition was the key issue. Kim wanted to be the first to prepare North Korea for the world of film. He admired the Japanese for trying with their "Godzilla" films, but thought that they lacked passion and originality. Kim believed that an evolution of film was on the way in the developing world and that North Korea was going to be at the helm because of Kim's insight into the field.

Kim had directed several movies in North Korea that resembled the Japanese-style Godzilla movies. I had seen one of them at one of the only movie theaters in all of North Korea. It was overacted and missed the suspense climaxes critical to a scary movie. The acting resembled the anchormen and anchorwomen on the state run television. They acted as if they had just found God. None of it was believable by any international standard.

One thing I was warned about was interrupting Kim. No one interrupted him or became distracted while he was in the room. He commanded full attention. I had no choice but to sit there and listen to his babble about movies. Some of what he was saying didn't sound so bad; I just did not understand how bad his films really were yet. At least we were all getting nice and pickled from the constant supply of booze that Kim insisted we have. He was a heavy drinker. He loved hard liquor, especially whiskey and *Sake* (a Japanese liquor, similar to Korean *Soju*).

After an hour or so of Kim's ranting and raving about film, he abruptly stopped, pushed the button, and an assistant came running in again. Kim ordered him to bring in the "entertainment." After a few minutes a harem of girls came into the room in a single file and lined up right next to where we were sitting. It was truly an international array of women. There were Asian, Black, White, and what seemed as either Hispanic or Middle Eastern. Kim had lined up all the colors of the rainbow for me.

"Choose what you want" Kim said.

I was stunned. I was asked to choose a girl/s to be with for the night from this lineup of beautiful girls. Each one of them was scantily dressed in either micro-mini or bikinis. I felt as if I was a judge as the Ms. World Competition. One girl in particular attracted my attention. She was black, tall, and very attractive. She had inquisitive eyes and the smoothest skin I have ever seen. She was pitch-black and very curvy. She had a beautiful smile with pearly white teeth. I pointed to her and Kim just nodded his head.

"Take her with you. We'll talk later."

Kim rose, motioned to one of the girls to follow him, and walked out of the room. I stood up and gave my hand to her. She took my hand and we walked out. As I turned around before leaving the room, I saw a couple of the girls stay with Mr. Lee while the rest exited the room.

I led her to my room in complete silence. It was an awkward moment. I didn't even ask her name. I felt empowered to just take her and make wild love to her without finding out a single thing about her. Yet, at the same time, I chose her because of her inquisitive and sharp look. I just had this sense about her that she was as smart as she was beautiful. I really wanted someone to talk to. I was surrounded thus far in my life by women who were paid to be with me. I just wanted someone who wanted to be with me for who I was.

"Do you speak English?" I remember asking her.

"Yes, of course! I am from Uganda. We learn to speak English from an early age,"

I could tell from the minute I met her that she was sharp. She had began to undress when I stopped her and asked her to sit down on the bed next to me. I asked her about her background. I mean, it's really not normal for a black woman to be living in North Korea. Her name was Yolanda, but here everyone called her by her English name Helene. For some reason she trusted me. She told me that she was one of Idi Amin's nieces. Idi Amin, the absolute ruler of Uganda, gave her as a "gift" to Kim Jong IL. She was just part of Idi Amin's property. She said it wasn't too bad; she could have ended up sleeping with her own uncle if she had stayed. She was only sixteen when she left Uganda for North Korea. She had been in North Korea for the last three years, which would have made her only nineteen years old.

She had very fond memories of growing up in Uganda. She missed her family very much (with the exception of her uncle) and wanted to escape the horrors of North Korea. She told me Kim Jong IL was intimidated by her. She was probably too big for him. He didn't know what to do with her. Just like Eric used to do, she turned on the music and whispered while she recanted the strange experiences she had undergone. Kim was a heavy drinker who loved to push the boundaries of what was considered voyeurism. She thought that the reason he probably liked weird sex was because he could not perform well in bed and needed to stimulate his libido.

Kim used to have wild parties that usually ended in orgies or sex shows. He really liked to watch as well as participate. He had one room where he kept all his sex toys that were imported from Europe. Kim was the first man in her life and an experience she didn't want to remember. Kim had her participate in orgies where she was forced to do all kinds of sex acts sometimes with an entire audience of dirty old men from the party. Because she was black, Kim liked it when she dressed up in her leopard bikini and acted like a savage. Yet most of the time, she didn't have to do much; he had an army of women at his service and actually preferred blonds and Asians.

Helene was very mature for a nineteen-years-old. She realized that once she got older, she would be of no use to Kim and eliminated. There was no retirement plan for his young harem. She told me that Kim already did not find any interest in her. He was interested in young virgins and found pleasure in corrupting them. Some of the girls I had seen at his compound looked like they had just reached puberty. For the first time I had noticed the futility in this beautiful girl. All she had ever wanted was to travel and see the world. As a girl, she loved reading books in English and French (she also spoke French). She especially wanted to visit Europe and live in a big city like Paris or London.

We talked for what seemed to be an eternity. We talked about every subject possible while sipping our wine. It was as if I had found my long lost best friend. That night seemed to be a hazy dream, which I had not wanted to wake up from. I don't remember what exactly happened, but I just remember waking up and seeing Kim Jong IL standing over me. I panicked. Was he going to kill me? Did he hear what Helene and I were talking about? I looked over to my right and saw that Helene was gone. It all felt like a dream. I sprang out of bed and bowed deeply to show my respect. Kim just looked at me for a few seconds, and then spoke.

"I want you to see this movie with me."

He spoke while continuing to stare at me.

"You know, I have the biggest private collection of movies in the world. Fifteen thousand."

I looked at the clock. It was four in the morning. Of course, I acted enthusiastic and followed him. I still felt drunk and dreamy. We walked into a large cinema with a wide screen at one end. The front row seats were reclining chairs, equipped with tray holders on each side. The cinema walls and curtains reminded me of the old movie theaters built across the United States in the 1940's and 1950's. A couple of scantily dressed women stood next to the chairs and bowed deeply as we walked towards them. Kim signaled me to sit next to him. He ordered the two girls to bring us refreshments.

"You see American movie Godfather?" Kim asked.

I told him that I had not.

"That movie is about my father and me." Kim was convinced that the movie, "The Godfather" was modeled after his family. I'm not exactly sure if he meant that the director was inspired by his family, or that the storyline simply had a resemblance to his life. He probably meant the latter. Either way, Kim loved the movie.

"I see it as a psychological and physical power struggle. It is a natural battle that even the most sophisticated people experience. I believe that no matter how far we advance in science, technology, and general living, we are still animalistic inside. What do you think?"

He suddenly turned to and waited for my response. I knew that if I didn't contribute, I would lose my standing with him. That could seriously affect my whole existence. I also felt confident enough to disagree with Kim without any repercussions. I answered that what he argued was compelling and explained a lot about human behavior. However, humans have evolved in their behavior and have learned to become competitive in other ways. Modern societies are still competitive socially and economically, but find that physical competition is obsolete. Men do not fight to the death over their women, as do lions or monkeys.

After I answered this difficult question, Kim sat silently for a minute, without any expression on his face. After a few seconds, he smirked and began his soliloquy.

"Humans are indeed as physically competitive, just not in such an obvious way that people would imagine."

Kim countered my viewpoint.

"Humans…" He continued, "still fought wars and behaved just like animals just for the sake of opposite sex companionship. It was just not that obvious because of the gradual complicated life people lead. To me, cities were still just 'urban jungles.' An extension of primitive life."

He went on for what seemed like an eternity, using Machiavellian reasoning to convince me of the anarchic nature of the world. I have to admit that this stimulating conversation was a good change of pace. Here I was, with the man who supposedly was in charge of maintaining the dogmatic jargon that spewed out of North Korean people's mouths, yet he was far more complex that what he enforced. I guess it had to do with the luxury of being at the top. He did not have to watch what he said. He was the only "free" person in North Korea.

We finally watched the movie, "The Godfather." Kim would stop the movie once in a while to tell me his thoughts about the scene. He believed the movie showed the next step he must take as the next generation of North Korea. The

"Godfather," played by Marlone Brando, was his father. Michael Corleone, played by Al Pacino, was Kim Jong IL.

In the movie Michael had asserted his control over the failing family influence by using violence and weeding out those within his own family who were betraying the organization. Kim paused the movie during the scene where Michael has his brother-in-law Carlo killed. He turned to me with those hollow eyes of his and said:

"You cannot trust even members of your own family, especially if they are not blood relatives."

What a prophetic line. Kim Jr. would later take care of his own family members in a similar way. This was the first time I had ever seen the movie. I must say, there were some interesting resemblances. I am sure that Kim Jong IL especially liked the fact that both Corleone Jr. and Sr. used violence and intimidation as a way to grasp and retain power.

The most interesting part was how Michael Corleone used more violence than his father had to retain his family's control. Was this what Kim Jong IL was intending to do? It seemed more than possible at the time. By the early 1980's, Kim Jong IL had already built up a reputation of being ruthless and in control. His father, Kim IL Sung, seemed to take his son's actions in stride and with full approval. It seemed as if the stage was being set for transformation of power. This was like the scene when Corleone Sr. sits quietly in the back of the room while his son, Michael, begins his power consolidation. Michael Corleone's execution of the family's rivals and untrustworthy rivals was a sign of things to come from Kim Jong IL.

Kim Jong IL was a big fan of Francis Ford Coppola, the director of "The Godfather." He stopped the movie to tell me that he had also seen "Apocalypse Now." He was pleased to see what he believed was the first true portrayal American blunders. Once again Kim found metaphorical significance that seemed to reflect American attitudes towards North Korea. I told Kim that I hadn't seen the movie. He looked at me with surprise. I reminded him that I had been living in North Korea for the last decade and did not have access to foreign movies.

Kim was so shocked that he asked me to stay another night. It was already morning by the time we finished "The Godfather" (because of the constant interruptions by Kim). Kim looked very tired, as did I. I did not dare yawn or fain interest. Kim was like a spoiled kid. He was accustomed to having the floor at all times. He called in his "assistants" and commanded them to prepare his bed. He turned to me and told me to get some rest and that tomorrow we would watch "Apocalypse Now." I thanked him for his hospitality and headed to my room.

I laid in bed thinking about all that had happened so far. My whole life seemed surreal at this point. It was a decade ago that I had decided to defect to North Korea. I was curious about the unknown and idealistic. Now, in my thirties, I realized the stupidity of my actions and felt utterly useless. My whole point in coming to North Korea was hopefully to make a difference. Now, I was a slave, a lackey of a methodological mass killer.

I thought about just putting an end to Kim Jong IL's life. What if I just killed the bastard while he and I were alone watching the movie? Kim had a collection of different knives and swords in the hallway. What if I were to take the smaller knife and stab him when we were alone in the cinema? Were they watching us even in there? I doubt it. Kim liked his privacy. What would the world be like without him? His father would most likely just train one of the other sons to be just like Kim Jong IL. It was probably useless. Still, deep down I felt the evilness in this man. He was delusional with power. He was a sick man who enjoyed watching others suffer.

The next morning I woke up to the sounds of knocking at my door. It was Mr. Lee. He asked me if I wanted breakfast. It was nine in the morning, but it felt as if I hadn't had any sleep at all. I joined Mr. Lee for breakfast. Once again it was just the two of us, waited on by several people regarding any need we might have. It was the first time since arriving in North Korea that I had an American style breakfast: bacon, eggs, muffins, pancakes, real maple syrup from Canada, and fresh fruit. I had not tasted oranges or grapefruits since arriving in North Korea. What a treat. I still remember the taste. My hangover seemed to diminish after eating a couple of oranges and a grapefruit.

After breakfast, Mr. Lee asked me to look at a movie script Kim Jong IL had written. I quickly leafed through it while he explained the plot. It involved a heroic Korean figure living in Europe. The hero tries to make sense of life over there. I don't believe Kim wrote the actual script. It was common practice for everything in North Korea to be credited to Kim IL Sung and Kim Jong IL. From poetry to the engineering of a bridge, it was all done by the pure genius of this father and son duo. The sad part was that most North Koreans actually believed it. It was the whole magical aura that surrounded the godlike status of these two men.

I took a walk that afternoon on the heavily guarded beach just outside the villa. Everywhere I walked, I felt as if a million eyes were watching me. There were two patrol boats permanently docked by the shore and several guard posts on the beach and surrounding cliffs. Several other soldiers walked in pairs along the beach at all times. Two other soldiers were assigned to watch me while I took my walk. I walked along the shore. Although it was a bit chilly that day, I took off my shoes and walked in the surf. I used to love to do that growing up in San Francisco.

As a Kid, I always had fond memories of going down to either Ocean Beach or Baker Beach with my parents. I would take my shoes off as soon as we reached the beach. The feeling of bare feet in the sand and surf was nostalgic to me. I felt goose bumps on that beach in North Korea, even though I was surrounded by soldiers, staring at me at all times. For a while, I felt at peace. I felt as if time had reversed itself and I was back in San Francisco as a kid again. I yearned for the security of my parents. The two people in my life who always looked out for me and wanted only the best for me.

I walked up a small embankment at the end of the beach, which ended in a small forest. Those familiar pine trees covered the area from the beach up to the surrounding mountains. Pine trees were so resilient. They grew under any circumstance. They didn't seem to mind that they were patrolled by soldiers and in such close proximity to the salty air. I sat down under one of the pine trees overlooking the sea. This weekend was supposed to be a huge step upward for me, yet I could only think about how much I missed home. I felt a deep pain in me that could have only been due to homesickness.

That evening was a repetition of the last. Mr. Lee and I dined alone again. After dinner, we retired once more to the den. This time, we were both exhausted from the charade and stress of being at Kim Jong IL's villa. We were both very apprehensive. Who wouldn't be? We were the guests of the unpredictable ruler's son's house. Who knows what could happen?

Once again, Kim showed up late. Kim asked us if we were taken care of. He had the girls come back and line up in front of us. This time he wanted to have an orgy. He chose a couple of women, then asked me to choose a couple more. I chose Helene again and another Korean girl. His idea of an orgy was a scripted act, which seemed very rehearsed. At first we watched the girls kiss each other, then Kim took a dildo and inserted it in each girl's vagina and behind. He was like a little sick boy who was given access to girls. The whole thing was pretty sad. These girls just had to follow his every whim. At one point, he took his fist and stuck it right into one of the girl's vaginas.

Kim then took the one blond and began to have sex with her on the floor (which was in the Japanese *Tatami* style). Mr. Lee then jumped on one of the Korean girls. Now I was the only one not with someone. I looked at Helene, who was giving me a warm smile and took her hand. Unlike the two other couples,

Helene and I had a very passionate experience. We kissed sensually for a long time before I entered her. I could tell that she really enjoyed it, as did I. Helene was the best sexual encounter I had ever experienced in my life (I realize that I have not had that many experiences, but nevertheless Helene was wonderful). It was passionate as much as it was lustful.

Although I never saw Helene again after that night, I will never forget her. I can still picture her warm smile and beautiful eyes. I don't dare imagine what became of her. It most certainly is not a pretty picture. Just like a kid's toys, Kim's women are discarded when they are no longer desirable. I later dreamt that like a knight in shining armor, I rescued Helene from Kim's "evil castle" and we lived happily ever after. I believe dreams are the only escape for people from their mistakes and repressive environments. In reality, most humans are too afraid to follow their dreams and are bound by social responsibilities.

After this bizarre orgy, Kim ordered us to the cinema. This time, Mr. Lee was invited to join us for the screening of "Apocalypse Now." Watching this movie, I noticed Coppola's borrowing from one of my favorite books by Joseph Conrad, "Heart of Darkness." I also started to understand why Kim liked this movie. The movie showed the absurdity of American influence on the world and the uselessness of hegemony. By now, I was starting to believe that the United States was right in its hostility towards North Korea. The best thing that could happen to North Korea was the assassinations of the two Kims and party officials. Boy! How much I had changed in the last decade!

Kim told me after the movie that he understood Colonel Kurtz. He was assigned by the United States to win a war. Yet the United States did not agree with his methods and turned against him. Kim believed that pure force was the ultimate control over people. Kim even believed that if the United States followed Colonel Kurtz's example, they would have won the war in Vietnam. Oddly enough, he believed that the United States' ultimate demise will come from it's own freedoms. He thought that it was absurd that the power of the people led to mass protests and a pullout from Vietnam. To him that was a sign of weakness.

These were all good signs of things to come. Kim Jr. would most likely continue his father's legacy of absolute control over North Korea. If anything, things were going to get worse before they got better. I wanted to tell Kim about Joseph Conrad's true intentions when he wrote "Heart of Darkness" and how delirious people were. Leaders who were blindly followed by their people lived a lonely life and ultimately met with a very early death. Of course I didn't say anything. I was too afraid. What possible change could I inflict on this man? Besides, his father so far was living a long and healthy life as a ruthless dictator. Maybe I was wrong. Maybe people were that desperate to be led by an absolute ruler.

I now had a glimpse into the mind of the future leader of North Korea and it scared me. Kim Jr. thought his father was too soft. Too soft? I could not imagine at the time someone more ruthless than his father. Unfortunately for me, that day would come (Of all the places I had to choose to protest American hegemony over the world, I chose the one place where the despot could have recommended a vicious system that the United States could use to eradicate its enemies). If North Korea under Kim Jong IL had the power the United States possessed, the world would have been a dark place.

That night we did not stay up as late as the night before. Kim, seeming restless following the movie, just got up and disappeared. Mr. Lee told me later that he just did things like that. He once walked out for no reason from an important general assembly meeting. He was an anarchic figure in a world of his own order. He answered to no one and did as he wished, yet all had to follow his every command. Mr. Lee and I left early Monday morning. I mostly slept the entire way. I looked back at the villa one more time as our car drove away. I thought about the whole weekend and guessed that it would always be memorable to me.

I thought about what would be the future for Helene. She seemed like such a wonderful person. I would have loved to get to know her better. She could have been a great friend. It's so sad what cards we are dealt in life. I had many choices in life, yet I chose to come to such a dark and depressing place. Helene dreamed of going to places such as Paris or New York, yet was forced to come to North Korea. I'm sure she thought I was a bit of a fool to choose to come to North Korea. I was beginning to see her point.

Chapter 15

RUMORS AND TOURS: SAM AND PAEKDU MOUNTAIN

1984

"Big Brother not only watches, but also acts."

Eric was so happy to see me the next day on campus. I could tell that if it weren't for me, he would have gone nuts. Eric was a smart guy, but he did not have patience for the stupidity that confronted him on a daily basis in North Korean. He really enjoyed taking out his frustrations with his students by talking to me. I have to admit, my patience was wearing thin as well, but I somehow managed to contain it. I chose exercise as a form of stress release. Eric chose alcohol. My almost daily ritual of climbing the university's rolling hills or going for a jog really kept my nerves together. I even used the miserable gym the school had three or four times a week. Eric just brooded in his room, drinking all night sometimes. Eric would pop a *Soju* (Korean liquor) or beer bottle as soon as he got back from his classes. I tried to get him to exercise with me. He did for the first few weeks, but then went right back to his old routine.

    That night in Eric's room, over a bottle of beer, Eric dropped the bombshell. He had found out what might have happened to Sam. One of Eric's students was the son of a warden in a "Re-education Camp" (basically a prison). He had heard news from a fellow warden at a different camp about a foreigner who was executed recently. The foreigner and a group of television crewmen were accused of making pornographic movies and distributing them in North Korea and Japan. The student also told Eric that the foreigner was definitely American. He screamed "America" over and over before he died. The foreigner defied his captor up until his execution by spitting on the warden. The warden was so angry that he blurted out what had happened at the camp to anyone who would listen.

That was surely Sam's M.O. Sam had a terrible temper and a total disregard for authority. Sam would never go out quietly. It was a surprise he lasted this long in the most authoritarian state in the world. Like I had said before, authoritarian regimes were most likely to give a lot of leeway for someone who was high ranking. Up till this point, Sam was protected by the top. However, not even the top could save him from what he had done. I still believe to this day that the pornography was not the reason why Sam and the others were killed.

In North Korea, there was always a struggle between top elite factions regarding who could skim more off the top. Most likely, Sam was on the losing side this time. I even think Mr. Lee pulled this one. Mr. Lee was probably trying to rid of his competition at Kim Jong IL Studios. It was common sense even in North Korea that the government made money any way it could.

In Japan, there is a huge market for sick porno that shows everything from rape scenes, to torture, to little girls. Some of the films were distributed by the *Yakuza*, who received their shipments from the *Chochonyon*. Why was it then that all of a sudden these films came under the investigation of the internal police? Almost always the answer came back to a rivalry between two greedy members of the politburo or some government faction. The winner was the one who was able to bribe the police to arrest the other. Mr. Lee was not the head-honcho at the studios, yet now he was personally taking me to meet Kim Jong IL. Coincidence? Not in North Korea.

Usually, Eric was the master of conspiracies, yet this time it was I who explained this revelation. Eric was convinced as well. We both knew that Sam was well protected and had gotten away with murder, literally (Sam told us one night in his drunken stupor that he killed one of those "damn Arabs" and made it look like an accident). As usual, Eric took this story and wove it around to include Kim Jong IL's own involvement in trying to get rid of his familial competition. You see, Kim Jong IL was not the only person who had the right to take over after his father died. Kim had a younger brother from Kim IL Sung's second wife. Although Confucian tradition stipulated that the eldest ascend to the throne (literally), it was not uncommon for a younger sibling to physically take over. I never went as far as Eric did in terms of conspiracies, but I did know that anything was possible in North Korea.

I never did see Sam again. I can safely say that the foreigner killed that day in the re-education camp was Sam. Sam lived his life in the fast lane. That kind of lifestyle was not a match for North Korea. I am truly surprised he lasted this long. All I could think about was my desire to go back to the United States and tell his family about his life in North Korea. I am sure that would have made them feel better.

It was at that minute that it dawned upon me that my own parents were probably in the same boat. What were they thinking? How were they holding out? I had tried to suppress my feelings towards them from the minute I defected to North Korea. Alas, there is just so much a person can suppress before it comes back up and hits you like a ton of bricks. I really missed my parents the night I heard Sam died. Death shook me by the shoulders and reminded me of my true feelings.

The television, the radio, even posters in North Korea, all advocated hatred of all "outsiders," especially Americans. Reports such as: "Americans are disguised beasts. The imperialistic intention of the United States will doom Korea. The Americans and their capitalists puppets want to kill our children and destroy everything we hold dear to us." With this kind of propaganda, it was only a matter of time before some North Korean who saw me would think I was his enemy. That was another reason why we were always escorted and followed every time we went outside the University. Even within the University campus, a student leader or faculty member was assigned to watch us at all times.

My first violent encounter with North Koreans happened on a tour to Paekdusan (san is mountain in Korean). Dr. Han had arranged for Eric, Victor, Dr. Habibi and me to go on a trip for the summer to Paekdu Mountain. Mr. Zhu, the Chinese professor, did not join us. He lived with his family and pretty much hung out with them whenever he could. On occasions, he would join us for a drink at the club, but that was about it. It was the first time that Dr. Han planned a trip for all of us. Was he loosening up or were the North Koreans just giving him more leeway with us? I had to believe the latter because I felt as if I knew Dr. Han well enough to understand that he really wanted the best for us. At the time, I thought that my trip to see Kim Jong IL went well and in return Kim Jong IL passed it on that we should have more freedoms and be well taken care of. Little did I know what would happen next.

It was the middle of August, the official "break time" for North Koreans. Too bad most North Koreans did not have the luxury of time or permission to go anywhere special. Since I had arrived in North Korea, the only trips we took were day trips to local sites or the ritualistic weekend trips to the club in Pyongyang. I don't count the trip I took to Kim Jong IL's mansion because it wasn't really sightseeing and I didn't get much of a chance to see the "real" North Korea. This time, we were to spend a whole week exploring the Northern area. I was genuinely excited about getting out of the Pyongyang area.

For the last few years at KIS University, I had felt the noose of North Korean oppression tighten around myself. I was becoming very depressed and moody. I lost my temper with my students on several occasions. Luckily for me, it was the norm. Professors ruled the classrooms with autocratic powers. I was allowed to physically harm my students, but never allowed to give an opinion other than the standard state sponsored jargon. I was looking forward to both getting out of the city and the prospects of working at Kim Jong IL studios. In a country where everyone felt trapped, it felt like a new lease on life to change jobs or travel.

Paekdusan was the highest mountain on the Korean Peninsula and a Mecca for all Koreans. The mountain bordered both North Korea and China. Of course, North Koreans claimed that China "occupied" the other half following the Japanese surrender in World War II. I am sure the Chinese have their own version of the story. The trip to Paekdusan from Pyongyang, although not that far for Americans, was a journey for North Koreans. Just to get through all the red tape to get permission to leave Pyongyang was an incredible ordeal. Then, traveling by train, then car, would take two days. Being that it was August, the only airline, Koryo Air, was booked by high party officials (Most of the airplanes were old Russian Tupelov models that were very unreliable anyway). From my own experience flying Koryo Airlines, we were better off taking the train.

A university van drove us to the train station early Saturday morning. Unlike the rest of Pyongyang, the train stations were immaculate. High ceilings with grand architectural designs suggested a train station that looked as if it should be busy. The reality was that most of the locomotives were in disrepair and rusting behind a wall that was erected just to hide this shame (North Koreans were fixated with making their nation look good to outsiders, therefore they tried to hide the many "blemishes" that existed).

Our train looked like it belonged with the rest of the junk I saw behind the wall. It reminded me of those trains I saw in the old western movies with a touch of a communist look to it. It was most likely made somewhere in Eastern Europe or the former Soviet Union, but like everything in North Korea, had a Korean sign that read "Made in the DPRK." To instill pride in North Koreans, the government relabeled products to show a North Korean origin. To some extent, South Korea did the same thing. Early South Korean cars and electronics were actually Japanese imports.

The train had more than three different levels of travel. So much for the idea that 'everyone is equal.' The first car we walked by was second-class. The chairs looked very small and worn out. I could already see people running to catch a seat. I thought to myself, if that is second-class, what does the third class looks like? Do people sit on the floor? Fortunately for us, we were considered VIPs. We were escorted by a train attendant to the first class seating. I had heard that working as a subway or train attendant was considered prestigious for women. That was why only pretty young women were given the job. Maybe I was blind, but I did not find these women very attractive. They made them wear these horrible uniforms and silly hats. Most of them looked worn out and in need of a good night's sleep, but then again, so did the rest of the country.

The first class seating was much better than second class. We had our own little room with chairs facing each other and two bunk beds above us in case someone wanted to sleep. Dr. Han also informed us that an attendant would come by later with snacks and beverages. I felt so bad for the rest of the passengers, but then again I was getting used to the special treatment I had been getting in North Korea over the years. To be honest, I now resembled the biggest hypocrite on the face of the earth. My entire young adult life in San Francisco I had protested against the disparities between the classes and embraced socialism. Now I was in a "socialist nation" and living like a bourgeoisie compared to the average North Korea.

Just like a kid, I grabbed one of the window seats so that I would have a good view of the Korean countryside. All those years in North Korea, and I still had not gotten a chance to really see the rural part of North Korea. Was there something the government was trying to hide? Of course! Even in the repressive "Hermit Kingdom" not all was well. There were several rumors of widespread rebellions and demonstrations, especially in the rural areas. Eric believed that there was worse to come with all the natural disasters and deep decline in the North Korean economy. He thought that there would even be a civil war in North Korea in the next few years. Eric was a sensationalist, so I took everything he said with a grain of salt.

The train finally started crawling along after almost an hour of waiting. It was only eight in the morning, but it felt like it was late because we were up so early. The first sights I got to see were of rail yards and walls with barbed wire around them. I finally got a glimpse of some of Pyongyang's suburbs as the train began to pick up speed. I could see tall gray apartments on both sides with signs on them praising *Juche* and socialism. These signs were suppose to encourage the tired workers as they came home after a long workday. As the train got farther from central Pyongyang, the housing units looked worse and worse. Although this might be a common scene in the United States, it should not have been the case in a "socialist" nation such as North Korea.

Once the train completely left the outskirts of the city, the natural beauty of North Korea began to reveal itself. Terraced fields surrounded by craggy mountains, clear creeks and rivers and spectacular forests dotted the journey to Paekdusan. Although I was very tired, I didn't want to miss any of the scenery. Eric and the others were coming in and out of naps while I stayed awake the whole way.

Victor was trying to teach Dr. Han chess, but was having communication problems. Victor himself did not know many of the words in English and Dr. Han did not speak Russian. Eric and I chatted for a while along the trip about the University. Even when we were away from there, we couldn't stop talking about it. It was largely because we were afraid to talk about something too serious in the train and also due to the fact that we didn't have much of a life outside of the university.

Eric did ask me about Kumi, but I kept it brief because I was secretly losing interest in her. The only fun that I felt I was having in North Korea was my daily walks around the university and the Saturday night trips to the club in downtown Pyongyang. Every time I got there, Kumi wanted to spend all her time with me and I didn't get much of a chance to hang out anymore. My own selfish reasons included the fact that I wanted to meet some of the other bargirls on a more intimate level. Kumi was becoming a nuisance to me. I know now that I was very lucky to have someone like Kumi, but back then I didn't care about anyone but myself. The whole reason I even defected was to draw attention to myself.

The train made frequent stops, usually to change locomotives or pick up and drop off passengers. I tried to get a good glimpse of the towns we stopped in, but most were out of view of the train tracks. I did, however, see some of the locals. At one station, I was surprised to see beggars on the platform. It was absolutely against the law to beg in Pyongyang. I heard about the poverty-stricken countryside, but I still could not believe begging was allowed. One beggar was absolutely covered from head to toe with rags. At first, I thought it was a young child because of the small body frame. As the beggar looked up into our window, I was horrified. The beggar was an adult who was obviously suffering from severe malnutrition. His sunken eyes and skeletal face looked at me with the same horror I was projecting. I guess we both surprised each other with our peculiar appearances.

The beggar began to make some strange noises as he looked at me and then slowly stood up and began to approach our window. By now, Eric also noticed the beggar and let out a "Holy Shit, what the hell is that?" cry. The beggar was now right at our window and letting out shrieks at the top of his tiny lungs. He was so thin. He looked exactly like the Jews in the Nazi concentration camps that I had seen in documentaries. At this point, his strange high-pitched screams drew enough attention to alert the guards stationed on opposite sides of the platforms. They rushed over and without thinking twice butted the beggar with the tips of their rifles.

The beggar went down instantly. His screams vanished as soon as the guards hit him (Actually, I'm not even sure if it were a man or a woman. The beggar was in such bad shape, it could well have been a woman). The guards looked furious. As soon as the beggar was down and motionless, one guard looked at me with disdain, as if it were my fault the beggar was a nuisance. Dr. Han, seeing that the guard was eyeing me, yelled at him, "what are you looking at, you dog? Do you know who I am? I could have you in the re-education camp by sundown if you do not get out of here right now!"

Re-education camps! The old communist adage of "reforming" those who "strayed off" the path of good communism. As in other communist countries, this served as a convenient way of dispensing with people who were a threat to the regime or those who simply might be a threat. In North Korea it was well known in every circle that few ever left the re-education camps in one piece. Even if they did leave, their lives were destroyed. Their families were most often humiliated and punished as well. When they were released, they were forced to go to remote parts of North Korea where they had to work under the worst conditions.

Eric heard from a student that most were worked to death in labor camps. After a hard day's work, the prisoners were forced to spend the evenings self-evaluating their lives and what they did wrong to end up in the camps in the first place. The worst of it all was that they had to memorize entire speeches given by the two Kims and recite them in front of the guards. If they made a mistake, they would end up in solitary confinement for weeks. I was beginning to believe Eric and his students. Before, I took everything Eric said with a grain of salt. Now, he was the only one I really trusted in the Hermit Kingdom.

The train pulled into a small station where we got off and waited for a bus to transport us to the base of the mountain. There was a small souvenir shop at the entrance to the National Park. Among the normal items one might find at a tourist shop were all kinds of Kim memorabilia. According to North Korean history, Kim Jong IL was born on this mountain while his father was a revolutionary leader fending off the Japanese colonialists. Most accurate accounts put Kim Jong IL's birth in a top-notch hospital in Moscow. The invention of history has always served as an amazing propaganda tool.

In any event, the welcome wagon at the Paekdusan National Park was arranged just for us that day. Not many tourists made it to Paekdusan back then. Today I hear that there are even plans to bring South Koreans on group tours there. We climbed back to the bus with a couple of guides who were going to accompany us the rest of the way. One of the guides was a lovely young woman who seemed to be very excited about our trip up the mountain. Another was a stoic looking man who most definitely was not in the hospitality and tourism business. He was most likely an agent assigned to watch our every move.

It was too late to try to hike to the top that day. The bus went a couple of kilometers further into the park to a small restaurant/inn. In South Korea, this was also known as a *Minbak*, or country inn. In North Korea, the placard read "The Workers Rest Home." Don't even ask! All the signs and propaganda never made any sense. A middle aged gentlemen and a younger woman were waiting for us at the entrance. They greeted us with "*Oso oshipshiyo!*" or "welcome" in Korean. The inn was built entirely out of the unique trees that grew on Paekdusan. It had the motif of some Swiss Chalet with a hint of traditional Korean flavor (Korean roof tiles and bricks). It was actually not a bad combination.

We each had our own room. This *Minbak* was definitely fancier than any South Korean one. It had private bathrooms, queen sized beds, a large dining room, and a recreation room equipped with a television and bar. By North or South Korean standards of the 1980's, this place was top of the line. After we put our bags in the rooms, we adjourned to the dining room where a lavish lunch was awaiting us. My favorite, *Neng Myong*! This was the North Korean delicacy of cold noodle soup served with sliced beef, cucumber, soy sauce, and buckwheat noodles. I know it doesn't sound like the best thing under the sun, but it is an acquired taste. After lunch, we were forced to listen to a rehearsed speech by the jovial female guide about the history and significance of Mt. Paekdusan.

The drive up to the base of the hiking trail was steep and windy. Nevertheless, it had spectacular views. We could see the forested area giving way its to alpine terrain. The trees kept on getting shorter and shorter until they were just little stubs in the ground. There were some amazing views along the way of the mountain ranges and the valleys below. There were three guard posts on the way up. We were now close to the border with China. Although China was North Korea's closest ally, the border was heavily monitored. The North Koreans were more concerned with internal than international issues. It was becoming more and more common for North Koreans to try to escape via China. Something was rotten in the state of the Kims and many people wanted out.

We arrived at the hiking trailhead around eleven in the morning. Even though the weather was hot down in the valley, I could already feel the cool mountain air. A light fog was drifting in and out of the trees. It was beautiful. I took in the fresh mountain air as a relief from living in the smoggy city of Pyongyang. North Koreans still lived in the dark ages where coal was the principle form of energy and the environment was trashed for the sake of "progress." (I know, Seoul isn't the cleanest place either). I wanted to bottle up the air and take it back with me.

We hiked continuously except for a few pit stops scheduled by our guides. The guides had to show us where Kim IL Sung did this or that. I just ignored the bullshit, closed my eyes, and tried to listen for the sounds of the forest. I remember the guide giving me an evil stare when I opened my eyes. I guess getting to know her better was out of the question. That was fine by me. I was becoming more and more spiteful of the North Koreans and their endless propaganda. My anger outweighed my sexual desires with most women I met in North Korea. That was one of my bad habits. I remember one of my friends in college telling me I would never be able to keep a girlfriend because of my super-critical attitude.

We reached a small clearing by the bend of the trail where we stopped to have lunch. The inn prepared the traditional Korean picnic lunch known as *Kimbap*. *Kimbap* is steamed rice with vegetables, scrambled slices of egg, rolled inside dried seaweed. Sometimes meat or seafood is added (especially in South Korea). It is still one of my favorite Korean dishes. After lunch, we didn't waste time because we still had to climb another hour or so to the crater. Everyone was doing well except for Dr. Habibi, who was a heavy smoker and was always short of breath.

After about thirty minutes of hiking, I started to make out the rocky top of the crater. It was breathtaking. The wind was constantly pushing the fog at the top so that we could get short glimpses of the crater. By now the air was cold and we all put on our jackets and sweaters. There were two guard posts in view, but I am sure there were many more out of our sight. North Koreans were good at camouflage.

We all posed for pictures at the top while our guide explained that Paekdusan was originally entirely in the hands of Korea before the Chinese took half of it over. That was Korean pride for you. They hated each other but also found time to hate their neighbors too. South Koreans had the same problem with Japan over a bunch of rocks in the East Sea (The name 'Sea of Japan' is an insult to Koreans). The guide also informed us that three separate rivers had their origins in this mountain.

The trip back down was rewarding because we could now see below us. We made several stops to take more pictures of the valley below. We got back to the inn around four or five and devoured our dinner soon after. We were rewarded with a dinner that contained all sorts of wild plants and mushrooms that grew around the area. I still remember the taste of those side dishes. The atmosphere also helped. The dining area was built in the traditional Korean style of an elevated room with rice paper walls and doors and *Tatami* floors. After dinner, we adjourned to the recreation room where we began to drink. One of the biggest pastimes in North Korea was drinking. Not much else was allowed and life was pretty miserable for most people.

The next morning, recovering from the usual hangover (North Korean alcohol contains all sorts of chemicals for a cheap and quick distilling process. The hangovers from this were some of the worst I have ever experienced) we embarked on our long journey home. This trip was one of the last positive memories I have about my stay in North Korea. I mean, I knew that life was not getting any better for me, but I could not have expected what would happen next.

Chapter 16

KIM JONG IL STUDIOS: HOLLYWOOD AND SOCIALISM

"A Truly Militarized Nation"

1980's

One month after my trip to Paekdusan, Mr. Lee from the studios came to visit me. After not hearing from him for a while, he suddenly came back into my life with strict orders from the top brass to involve me in the studios. Every question I posed to him was answered in a roundabout way. I think he was already frustrated with the fact that I was so inquisitive. He was used to ordering people around, not taking questions. After several questions, Mr. Lee suddenly got up from his chair and waved his hands at me as if to say: "this interview is over."

He grabbed me by the shoulder, as is the tradition for men in Korea, and led me to his chauffeured car that was waiting outside. As I got into the car, Mr. Lee bent over and spoke in a low voice:

"You know, in Korea it is rude to ask so many questions. Just a little advice."

The car sped off almost running down a couple of students. We drove a few miles northwest to a place I had never been before. It must have been ten miles out of Pyongyang proper. This was home to the Kim Jong IL studios, the only motion picture studio in North Korea. We passed two separate checkpoints just to get to the gates of the studio. The place was immaculate. I saw one worker sweeping an already clean sidewalk. The buildings really looked like those studios I had seen on my trips to Los Angeles. I would not be surprised if Kim Jong IL had requested that they be built like that. The only difference was that this studio was hardly as busy as the ones I had seen on tours in Hollywood. In fact, it looked deserted.

We pulled into what seemed to be the main offices. As usual, two large photos of Kim IL Sung and Kim Jong IL hung on the wall. Two receptionists greeted us and escorted us into a windowless room in the back of the office. Two men, Mr. Cha and Mr. Nam greeted us with a cheery smile. I was surprised to see the lax atmosphere that existed in these studios. I was becoming accustomed to the tense environment that existed everywhere else in Korea, even at my University. Both men seemed elated to meet me. I felt as if I was some amazing discovery for them.

As is customary in North Korea, we sat down for some tea and a smoke before we began to discuss business. Mr. Lee dominated the conversation while the other two just smiled and agreed with him. Once again, Confucianism preached that the elder or boss must be in total control and the rest must obey. Mr. Lee was in total control. He rambled on about the future of KJI Studios and the dream of Kim Jong IL to become a world leader in filmmaking. Part of the *Juche* or "Self Reliance" ideology in North Korea required the world to know about it in order for it to work. North Korean movies and television shows were the best way to show how far North Korea had come and the value of their ideology.

So what was my role in all of this? Quite simple, I was to be the token foreign actor at the studios who would usually play an evil American or European, whatever the script asked for. It was obvious that I would be replacing Sam. According to Mr. Lee, I had a "typical" American look and I was, after all, from California. Most North Koreans thought San Francisco was a suburb of Hollywood. It was fruitless to explain to them that California was bigger than North and South Korea put together.

I would not star in any major role for a while, but I would play an extra and in smaller roles when needed. The matters of money or whether or not I would even accept the job were not even mentioned. Mr. Lee made up his mind and nobody except for Kim Jong IL disagreed with him. I would continue to teach at KIS U. but might have to cut back on my hours when there was a big project at the studios. To be honest, I was excited at the time. How often does someone get to be a star anywhere in the world? I finally thought I would get the recognition I deserved. Looking back on it now, I realize that I was an egotistical brat who just wanted attention. The whole purpose of my defection was related to this weakness.

After the meeting, we all went out to a high-end restaurant in the heart of Pyongyang. I never even knew this place existed until that day. It was a nameless place with a shabby entrance. Across the street from the restaurant and on each corner were armed soldiers standing guard. From the insignia on their shoulders I could tell that they were from the elite shock unit. They were only around if someone important needed protection. The restaurant was packed with people, all of whom looked liked big shots in the regime. Mr. Lee made his rounds of each table, greeting everyone. In some respect, I guess he resembled a movie producer from any country. His job was to make connections and to entertain people.

This restaurant was different from any other restaurant I had ever been to. Pretty waitresses in miniskirts served us raw steaks and caviar while cabaret singers performed on stage. Most of the people eating there were men and I felt as if I were in the midst of a pedophile convention. There were old men everywhere, fondling the young waitresses and hostesses. It was the apex of decadence. Had the North Koreans even read Marx or Lenin's work? They resembled everything Marx and Lenis hated. I got a lot of unhappy stares that night from the diners around me. Even though I was with Mr. Lee, I could see the hatred in the eyes of these North Korean elite. They too believed in all the propaganda that they were spewing. One North Korean once told me: "The only good American was a dead American."

Speaking of propaganda, I think it is important to understand this aspect of North Korea. Without propaganda, the Nazis would not have been able to achieve as much. Still, the Nazis did not last as long as North Korea. Of course, it has to do with who the Nazis invaded and how many people they exterminated. Yet, it is also important to see how powerful the propaganda machine really is in North Korea. I am sure that now that reports are leaking out about the famine in North Korea people around the world wonder why the people do not do anything to change the situation. I had already explained about the security apparatus. However, I have not explained about the propaganda machine in detail.

Propaganda was spoon fed to North Koreans as soon as they are born. Every baby was supposed to be a blessing by Kim IL Sung. Once a year, the regime gave a birthday gift to babies in North Korea as a token of their "struggle for *Juche*."

The gift was always due to the "benevolence of Kim IL Sung, the great leader." In school, Children were taught about Kim IL Sung and *Juche* before they even learned how to write. Children were taught to hate, hate those who were constantly trying to destroy North Korea. Hate the Americans and their allies, hate South Korea and Japan and loathe all capitalists. Even China and Russia were taunted as "sellouts" and morally weak nations that had not accepted *Juche*. Children were prepared to fight as young as five years old. Students practice war drills. They built bunkers in their schools and communities.

The entire country was bunkerized, militarized, everything! Even the subway was built deep in case of an air strike. The North Korean regime brainwashed its citizens to believe in the devil: The outside world. Every piece of news was false and always showed the evils of capitalism and the preparation by American to attack North Korea. North Korean children memorized Kim IL Sung and Kim Jung IL speeches in school and recited them word for word. Those who made mistakes were chastised as "unpatriotic." High school students learned how to fight and used their school time marching in unison and chanting patriotic songs. Propaganda was used everywhere. North Korean press always hailed the frequent attacks by North Korean infiltrators in the South as "freedom fighters who were trying to topple the oppressive South Korean government."

Similar to the way some people ask how were the Nazis able to get away with such cruelty, the North Korean regime continues to hold a tight grip on all of North Korea. When I think of it now, I realize that Kim IL Sung was an evil genius just like Hitler. I just wonder how long the Kim dynasty will be able to hold on. When the Nazis were defeated, the world truly learned the horrors that occurred within their conquered borders. Although North Korea did not conquer any other nation, there are many secret horrors yet to be uncovered within its borders.

After lunch, Mr. Lee took me back to the University. As I got out of the car, Mr. Lee called me over:

"I'm putting all my trust in you. Don't disappoint me like your friend did."

Before I could even respond, he shut his door and the car sped off. It was a not so subtle hint of what could happen to me if I messed up. In North Korea, people who did not perform up to the expectations of the ruling class were made examples of immediately. The sole purpose of these examples was to warn everyone else. That was how the two Kims kept a tight grip on the country. The whole reason for the "Re-education" camps was not really to rehabilitate those people, but to remind the rest of the country of the consequences of disobedience and noncompliance.

That night I wondered what direction my bizarre life was leading to now. At the time I was excited, just like the time when I first arrived in the North. I thought that I would finally get the recognition I was seeking. I also believed that once I was a star, I would be immune from the growing uncertainty that was North Korea. The economy was starting to rapidly fall apart while North Korea's allies were beginning to change and distance themselves from the reclusive nation. One did not have to be an economist to realize that something wasn't right. Food rations were becoming smaller and forcing people to turn to illegal methods in order to survive. The successive droughts did not help either. It was a time of uncertainty and I was selfishly worried about my own future in the North.

Chapter 17

DR. HAN IS REPLACED/ STRUGGLE FOR LEADERSHIP

1986

The 1980's were just the beginning of the really bad years for North Korea and its people. Although the government tried to put on an air of normalcy, it was obvious that there were some serious problems in the system. The government blamed the usual suspects: Foreign Devils, the weather, and internal spies who were trying to sabotage the Socialist utopia. By now, I had a pretty good rapport with enough of my students to have them trust me and confide in me. Because all the students at KIS University came from the privileged class, they sometimes knew what was really going on.

Every week or so, a group of my favorite students and I would make time to have lunch or a picnic together. Sometimes we even had a couple of beers together back at my place. I kept these to a minimum because I knew that the campus spies would report us to the internal security apparatus. My students were becoming increasingly concerned with the state of affairs in North Korea. Things were going from bad to worse. Supplies, even in Pyongyang, were reduced. Rations were not always delivered to the countryside, making the people start to look for food themselves.

For those who are not familiar with Socialist and Communist systems, there were hardly any stores or supermarkets where people buy their food and goods (with the exception of the ruling elite and foreign dignitaries, who have access to the only department store in North Korea). People receive food rations from the government at their local community centers. Every family supposedly received an equal amount of food and supplies. The reality was that those higher ups received a hell of a lot more than those at the bottom.

My students were very worried about the future. I tried to console them but deep down I was also losing hope. I didn't need the students' information to realize that things were getting worse. Materials at the university were running low. Cafeteria portions were smaller and less diverse. If we at KIS were suffering just a little, that meant that the rest of the country was much worse off.

On the other hand, my new job at the studio was going very well. I played a couple of small roles in documentaries and one drama, always as the bad Westerner. In one of the documentaries I played a "dirty Frenchmen" who robbed the sacred Paekche tombs in the nineteenth century. They put dirt on my face and told me not to shave for a few days so that I could get that "Frenchman" look. North Koreans considered all Westerners dirty and untrustworthy. It reminded me of those horrible documentaries the Nazis had made of their image of the Jews and Gypsies.

Everyone at the studios was treating me very well. It was like a different world there. There was even one Russian and a South Korean couple who were supposedly pretty famous (The man was a director and the woman an actress) back in their native country. I later learned that the couple were kidnapped during their vacation somewhere in Asia and brought to North Korea at Kim Jong IL's request. Supposedly, he liked their work so much that he just had to have them. Kim Jong IL was a television and movie buff. He was also powerful so he had his needs met no matter how absurd they seemed. To what extent the couple held against their will I never knew. We got along very well because they were the only people who knew what life was like in the United States. We had a lot to talk about.

I was invited to big parties and mingled with the elite of North Korea. It was as decadent as the Pre-French Revolution must have been. Wild private orgies, gateways at private estates, and the most delicious food I had ever tasted in my ten years in North Korea. I always had Eric come with me because I didn't want to feel like the only foreigner there. Usually, Eric and I were the only foreigners there. We were now among the most powerful people in North Korea. We both felt like big shots. The reality was that we were actually with the relatives and children of the elite more often than with the top party members. Party members lived extremely secretive lives. One nephew of a party cadre once confided to me that party officials lived in extreme fear of being purged by the two Kims. The best way to stay on top was to stay out of trouble. The best way to stay out of trouble was to avoid these wild parties we attended.

These parties were officially illegal and punishable by death, but Korean traditions were stronger than the law. Korean culture has always had a weakness towards family members. Parents and relatives spoiled their kin beyond any Western standard. The Confucian ideas of "family before anything else" made it so that the elite' children were exempt from any wrongdoing. We were partying with these spoiled brats and we knew that no matter what happened at these parties, nobody would be in trouble. That made for some interesting parties. One party a naked girl came running out of one of the rooms with blood all over her. Apparently, some of the drunken guys had a go at her and had gone too far with their violent sex acts. The party went on as if nothing happened and the girl was escorted out by some security guys.

Unfortunately for Eric and me, not everything was going well. In North Korea, time was always extreme. Either plots took forever to materialize or they happened overnight. Usually, both had the same source, the Kim clan. It took years for Kim IL Sung to tighten his grip other over powers. He murdered those who were close to him before they knew what was happening. That was the secret to his success. It was not time for his son to consolidate power. Kim IL Sung was getting along in age and needed an heir apparent. For the last few years, Kim Jong IL was trying to suck up to his dad in order to be chosen as the successor. He was competing with Kim IL Sung's second wife's children. Unfortunately for them, Kim Jong IL was faster and more cunning. He was slowly making his presence known and, in so doing, eliminating anyone who was not in his camp.

Dr. Han, a respected scholar in North Korea, was not in Kim Jong IL's camp. Dr. Han was a good friend with the top advisor to Kim IL Sung's other son. Like lightening, Dr. Han mysteriously disappeared one day. No explanation, no reason, not even a trace of where he could have gone. This scared the hell out of Eric and I. Before we could even start to think about what might have happened to Dr. Han, a new director was already occupying his office. Literally, the next morning we were summoned in to meet with the new director.

Dr. Koo asked the whole department in for a meeting that same morning. He began by simply stating that Dr. Han was assigned to do research abroad. Of course, nobody believed this. Then Dr. Koo told us that from now on, every detail of every class must be reported directly to him. We now had more paperwork to do and more meetings to attend. The meeting lasted no more than twenty minutes. Dr. Koo abruptly asked us to leave. As we were leaving, Dr. Koo asked me to stay for a minute. He told me that he didn't care how much of a star I was; my acting career should not interfere with my teaching. As with everything in North Korea, I never quite knew why Dr. Koo hated us so much. In North Korea, most questions and mysteries went unanswered and unsolved.

As soon as Dr. Koo took over, my life became very complicated. Before, Dr. Han had cut back my hours so that I could have a break before I went to the studios. Dr. Koo now made me teach more and warned me that he would be watching me carefully. He said the same thing to all of us, but I could tell that he just didn't trust Eric and me. Now that I think about it, under the circumstances, Dr. Han was very flexible with us. Dr. Koo was on a warpath. It was as if he were sent there specifically to watch us. Was there a spy amongst us? Probably! After all, the North Korean regime survived due to spies and informants. You couldn't even trust your own children in North Korea.

It was very difficult for me to teach and work at the studios, especially when there were lots of scenes to shoot. I was now working sixteen-hour days, six days a week. I knew that the only way to put a stop to this was to let Mr. Lee at the studios know what was going on. Of course, I didn't really think that getting Mr. Lee involved was the best way, but I just couldn't work that much. Mr. Lee sat there quietly while I told him how hard I was working at the university. After I was done, he just continued to sit there quietly. Then he jumped up from his chair and just told me not to worry. He grabbed my shoulder and led me out of the room.

Talking to Mr. Lee was good and bad. Dr. Koo cut my hours, but intensified his torture of both Eric and me. We were now not allowed to leave the campus, nor were we allowed to invite more than two people to our rooms. If we wanted to visit each other, we needed Dr. Koo's permission. We were also forced to hold longer office hours. Eric was really furious with Dr. Koo. I have always respected Eric for his dignity. After all, I defected to North Korea while Eric was forced to be there against his will. Eric definitely had more pride than me. He began his own campaign to get Dr. Koo off our backs. Eric was convinced that if the faculty acted together, we could all overrule Dr. Koo's authority.

At first, we simply ignored Dr. Koo's orders by going over to each other's rooms without asking for permission. Then, Eric would hold large parties in his room just to piss off Dr. Koo. Losing face in Korean society was the most humiliating insult one could bear. Dr. Koo saw Eric's parties as a personal insult to his authority. I warned Eric not to push our luck, but Eric was on a set course and could not be diverted. Over the years, I had noticed Eric's physical and mental condition deteriorating. When I first met him, he was in great physical condition and had a vivacious personality. By now, Eric was a heavy drinker with a beer gut and a big bald spot. He also looked as if he had aged thirty years.

The most disturbing thing about Eric was that he was also becoming very cynical about everything. He used to not care so much and just let things slide. Now, everything offended him. He had a personal vendetta with every kind of establishment. I seemed to handle things better because I have always been cynical anyway and considered myself a stranger all throughout my life. North Korea was just another place for me to act as a loner; someone who just didn't fit in. For Eric, it was the beginning of the end.

Chapter 18

BREAKING THE MYTHS: REAL TOUR OF PYONGYANG

1987

Korean New Year, known as "Sol Nal" (Solar Calendar) began for me with a ceremonial trip to a new College on the outskirts of Pyongyang. The college was built in one of the new massive development neighborhoods of western Pyongyang. North Korea's competitive nature was spiraling out of control. Construction workers were pushed to build humungous apartment building to rival those in South Korea. The end result was these thirty floors-high and one kilometer wide apartment buildings. The other reason for these enormous buildings had to do with military defense. The apartments were built so that the military could install surface to air missiles in case of an attack. North Korea always played dirty. Kim IL Sung and his son would do anything to protect their regime, even hide weapons behind innocent civilians.

For the first time ever, Eric and I were taking the trip on our own. No one was available to tag along with us. Nevertheless, I could tell we were being followed. We took the shuttle to the nearest subway and boarded the subway. The subways were either completely empty or completely full. That was because every worked on the same schedule. Obviously, the two other people on the subway were the two agents assigned to follow us (Agents in North Korea were not that clandestine. The government did not have to explain why they had people followed).

The college was at the last stop of the subway line, right below a hill. It was much smaller than KIS U., yet had its charm.

The college was the first of its kind, a Foreign Language University dedicated to immersing top students in foreign languages. Rumor had it that it was one of the first big projects carried out by Kim Jong IL and symbolic of the subtle change of power from father to son. Kim Jong IL was reclusive, weird, even a bit sick, but he was progressive compared to the old skeletons that still held top positions in the Korean Workers Party. It was rumored that Kim Jong IL wanted to bring North Korea slowly out of isolation without losing grip on power.

The inauguration of the new college was an extravagant celebration with hundreds of Korean women dancers in traditional Korean dresses (*Hanbok*) and a live band. Kim Jong IL showed up late in his Mercedes Benz limo. As usual, his hair was frizzy and he looked as if he had just woken up. He got up to the podium and spoke for over two hours about everything and nothing. My role in this inauguration was to put on a smile as they announced me as the head of the English department. I found out about my role the night before. I had no idea how I could spread my time any more, but I knew they would find a way.

After the ceremony, confusion set in and the organizers of the events began running around trying to see what we were supposed to do next. Eric and I saw this opportunity as a chance to split without anyone noticing. We pretended to go use the restrooms and then just walked past the restrooms to a back alley. At the end of the alley were a main thoroughfare and a bus stop. We waited for a while until a bus came. As we got on the bus, we got the most astounded stares from the passengers and bus driver. I am most definitely sure we were the first foreigners they had seen. I asked the bus driver how much the fare was in Korean, which shocked him even more. A foreigner who spoke Korean? I had to calm him down and reassure him that we were not spies or "devils" but simply respected professors from the university out to explore Pyongyang.

As we sat down and looked at the passing apartment buildings, I realized that this was the first time since I had arrived in North Korea that I was unescorted by a North Korean. Eric and I were actually on our own for the first time. I looked back at Eric. He looked excited, like a kid on his way to a carnival. It was the first time I had seen him smiling in a long time. The bus took us through some suburbs before entering Pyongyang. For the first time, it dawned upon me that Pyongyang was like the Oz in the Wizard of Oz. The big buildings, high rises, clean streets, statues, all a farce. If one looked behind the apartment buildings, one would discover the real Pyongyang. They would have seen shantytowns with small alleys meandering through them. This was where the real people of Pyongyang lived.

We got off in the perimeter of central Pyongyang with the intention of walking a few kilometers until we reached the subway line that would take us back to KIS University. On the way, we passed through some very narrow unpaved roads where micro-markets were bustling with people. This was the North Korea no one was meant to see. Old women with almost ninety degree hunched backs selling what looked like tree leaves and plant roots. One vendor was selling toilet paper and wood. Even deeper into one market we saw a man selling Japanese chewing gum, combs, and Chinese cigarettes. I asked him how much one pack of gum was: "10 Won." Ten Won was a week's work for most North Koreans. One apple was 50 won, while the average monthly salary was 70 won. Food is a luxury.

North Korean law strictly forbade any form of free market because of fears of losing control. All items had to be purchased through the central store with government coupons. The reason why these markets existed and were growing in numbers was because the North Korean central government was extremely corrupt and was neglecting common North Koreans. Those with connections or at the top received new televisions, cars, exotic fruit, and imported foods. The rest of the population, about ninety percent of North Koreans, could not even afford the basics like meat, rice, soap, and toilet paper. Not only had my socialist ideals and values disappeared long ago, I now believed that no centralized government could ever be efficient.

After wandering through some of the more shabby areas, we crossed the river into an entirely different neighborhood. The exclusive neighborhoods in Pyongyang looked like impenetrable fortresses. High brick walls surrounded the neighborhoods and armed soldiers stood at the entrances to "protect" the area. I think they not only kept the common North Korean from seeing how well the rich lived, but also kept tabs on the elite and reported back to the dreaded North Korean security apparatus. Both Kims never trusted anyone, especially the party elite. That was why Kim IL Sung frequently purged party leaders.

These neighborhoods looked familiar to me because these were the places where North Korean propaganda films were shot. The footage was used as "external propaganda." In other words, it was sent for the outside world so that people would think North Korea was some sort of socialist utopia. Surprisingly enough, the guards did not even raise an eyebrow when we walked right through the gates. I guess we were not the first foreigners they had seen enter those gates. Inside, every other car was a Volvo or Mercedes Benz. I had heard that the top cadres were given Mercedes Benz, while those underneath them received Volvos. Those underneath them were stuck driving the unpopular Russian made cars with a North Korean logo on the hood as if it were made in North Korea.

The apartment building had playgrounds with swings and slides for the children, tennis courts and a pool for the adults. There was even a building in the center of the apartment complex that looked like a community building. An army of sweepers was sweeping an already clean street. Many housewives were sitting on the benches and chatting with each other, while their children were playing in the park. The whole place sickened both Eric and me. I was reminded of one of my favorite books growing up: "Animal Farm" by George Orwell. The elite were living like the two pigs: Napoleon and Squealer. They had adopted all the ugly mannerisms of the previous tyrant, Mr. Jones. Orwell's critique of Socialism gone mad was analogous to North Korean "socialism."

If anything from what I write down in this memo comes out, it should be the gluttonous lifestyles the elite enjoy here. It is worse than many capitalist nations in the world. Everything, from medical care to produce differed dramatically between the elite and the rest of the nation. The elite lived similarly to those in Europe and America, while the average North Koreans were dying of malnutrition. Highly trained physicians treated the elite, while the poor died from simple colds. The elite stayed in the exclusive Rongyong Hotel, gambled at high rolling casinos, while the average North Korean had to share one room with six people. Since I had arrived in North Korea, the gap between the elite and the rest of North Korea had continued to grow.

The worse was yet to come. At the other side of the apartment complex was central Pyongyang. Across the street from the rich neighborhood was the First Department Store. For lack of a better name, it literally was the first department store in all of Korea. The only problem was that less than a fraction of the population could even afford the cheapest item in the store. It was built with the intention of showing to the world that North Korea was a modern nation and in anticipation of a growing tourist market. The tourists were slow to come, but the elite used the department store even through the worst food crises in the history of the Korean peninsula.

I looked at the window displays of the department store. It was a crude example of American department stores. The clothes looked drab and wrinkled. The lighting in the store was dim at best and the whole store looked deserted. Just like everywhere in North Korea, there were no information signs on the buildings or streets. People were not supposed to know anything. The less people knew, the better. Even though it was midday Sunday, the store looked closed. As an American, I could not believe a department store would be closed on a Sunday.

One thing both Eric and I noticed that two inconspicuous men were following us. At first, I didn't take much notice. After we entered the exclusive neighborhood, Eric nudged me and pointed to the two men behind us. They must have been watching us very closely at the ceremony because I thought we sneaked out without notice. Even though we thought that we were finally on our own, we were being closely watched. By whom? Did Dr. Koo send them, or were they just there to follow anything unusual? My hunch was the latter. One was never alone in North Korea. The Kim dynasty held on to power by building a massive secret service apparatus. Children, housewives, family members, coworkers, lovers, all were encouraged to spy on one another.

After looking at the pathetic excuse for a downtown, we decided to get on the subway and head back home. This was the third time I had been on the subway. The subway was built in the same lavish style as the subways in other communist countries. It was built deep in the ground to serve as a shelter and troop transport in case of a war. Eric told me that the entire city of Pyongyang was like a honeycomb. The city was built for war. The walls and ceilings of each station were painted with detailed pictures of all sorts of socialist motifs. Crystal chandeliers and gold lettering lined the ceiling of the main subway stations. Once again, North Korea was trying to put on the air of a modern nation. One day, this Wizard will be exposed.

Chapter 19

DISILLUSIONMENT AND THE 1988 YOUTH FESTIVAL

1988

"Irony: Far from a socialist paradise, our boss just 'inherited' a new Mercedes Benz. North Korea is the most corrupt nation on earth." Eric jotted down these words while we were sitting in one of those boring lectures Dr. Koo had always gave. Dr. Koo kept us busy with silly paperwork and continuous training sessions. One thing he had no clue about was his job or how to run a school. He supposedly studied English during his mysterious posting at the North Korean embassy in Libya. Most North Korean embassies served as black market centers for all the shady businesses North Korea was involved in.

Like many North Koreans, Dr. Koo learned English, but entirely missed all the nuances and common expressions that make it so complicated. He once yelled at me for responding to a student with "Not too bad." Dr. Koo thought I was telling the student that I was not doing well, thus giving a negative impression to the most "prestigious school in the world." When I tried to explain to him that "Not too bad" actually meant "good," he became even more infuriated. The fact that I would correct his English skills in front of other students was the biggest insult he had ever experienced. Under Confucianism, I was not supposed to correct someone older than me, let alone my boss.

I did my best to ignore Dr. Koo's insults. Deep down, I spent most nights plotting how I would kill him. I could not believe the anger I felt towards him. Every night I thought about the hideous way I would slowly kill Dr. Koo. The anxiety and frustration prevented me from getting any sleep, even though I was exhausted from my two jobs. I knew that if I were to survive, I would need to give up my acting job at the studios and focus on teaching. I knew Dr. Koo would never let me leave the teaching job.

If it were up to me, I would have left the university job and worked full time at the studios. The university looked less and less like a bastion of education and more like a circus. Rich students at the university learned that their money and power could buy everything, including university degrees. Those students at the top used money to get whatever they needed, while the rest just tried to survive: Literally! Most of my students barely show up for class. Some of the poor students who were fortunate enough to get into the school took illegal jobs just to survive. Everything around me seemed to depress me even further.

For the last decade, I had seen the country tumble, and tumble, and tumble. What is amazing is that no one has yet to exposed that the emperor is naked. People continue to starve while the government puts on the impression that the country is advancing. The Government stopped supplying food entirely to the people to support the youth festival in 1988. It was just the beginning of the dismal situation North Korea was heading towards.

It was not only in the countryside that the people suffered anymore. Pyongyang, the gem of North Korea, now felt the dire situation. Schools didn't have windows. Most of the people on the street were suffering from malnutrition. They were so thin and small. The growth of most of the children had been stunted. Factories put on the image that they were producing when they were not. Kim IL Sung and Kim Jong IL visited the same old factories every year, but those at the top knew that those factories have not been in use for the last few years.

I thought things could not get any worse in this "Hell-Hole." Slowly but surely, things got much worse. The government continued to blame "Outsiders" and the weather for the nation's failures. Food rations continued to dwindle, even on campus. There were more drunks everywhere, publicly displaying their anger despite the harsh repercussions. Even the elite young looked depressed, yet they still found time to look down at the rest of the people in North Korea. If things are this bad in the city, I can just imagine how bad they are in the countryside and other cities. Before he "disappeared," Dr. Han confided in me that it is believed that the Northern part of the country is "enemy territory." Kim Jong IL does not trust the people up there and has turned it into a "security zone." That could only mean one thing: Grief for anyone who lives up there.

Although security was still strict, it seemed as if by the late 1980's the government began to turn a blind eye to some minor illegal doings. For example, local markets were now prevalent everywhere, moving from the back alleys to the center of the communities. Drunks and beggars now appeared on every corner. Most of the time, the police did not arrest them or beat them as they once did. The only places that were monitored heavily were the national monuments, museums, and government areas. It was all like a Hollywood movie set. To us viewers, the city looked serene and majestic, but behind the set was utter despair and poverty.

During one of my trips from the university to the studios, I came across an altercation in one of the alleys around the bus stop that was most convenient to get to the studios. It looked like a gang of young kids had ganged up on an older man. The older man was completely red in the face and seemed to be drunk. He kept yelling at the kids to leave him alone and that he had "earned it himself." The kids were all half his size but were using their numbers by making a circle around him. Each time one boy would hit him; he would turn to that boy in response. As soon as he turned, two or three boys from the other side hit him from behind. The kids just continued to beat him with a viciousness I had never seen before. I stood there in surprise, watching the fight.

Then suddenly, one of the boys noticed me and ran up to me. He asked me if I were a "Yankee Bar[...]. When I told him who I was, he didn't care much. I don't think these k[...] ever seen television. He just wanted to know if I had something to e[...] told him no, he got angry and ran back to his friends. At this point I [worri]ed that I might be next, so I started to walk away. As I turned back to look down the alley one more time, I saw the man lying still on the ground and the gang of kids rummaging through his pockets. I could only imagine that they were looking for food and money. After that day, I took the main streets from the bus station to the studios.

The spring and summer of 1988 were the busiest ever. The entire faculty at Kim IL Sung were given a task to perform to facilitate the "World Youth Festival" to be held in Pyongyang that year. It was suppose to be a gathering of the world's youth for a couple of weeks of events. The festival was meant to signify the importance of young minds and talent around the world. It was just a selfish promotion by Kim IL Sung to try and grab some of the attention form the Olympics to be held that summer in Seoul, South Korea. This immature reaction by a paranoid regime just infuriated me more. I had very few illusion of grandeur by now regarding the altruistic intentions of North Korea.

The preparations that were taking place resembled a Hollywood studio set of a Wild West Town. One the exterior, it looked real. A thin, weak structure was propping up this make-believe environment. Everywhere I went, I saw youngsters frantically preparing their marches and dances to be performed at the event. The University students were exhausted as well. It was the only time they slept in class. Everyone had to pitch in to help bolster Kim IL Sung and Kim Jong IL's standing in the world. It was shameful.

Dr. Koo warned us several times to be on our best behavior when the "guests" arrived. Any sign of discontent would be handled with severe punishment. He even went as far as mention the mysterious disappearances of our friend, Sam, and our mentor, Dr. Han. That was his character. Dr. Han was a little man physically and mentally. His insecurities bred into hurting those around him.

The "dignitaries" from around the world hardly represented their respective nations. Many nationals of poor countries arrived simply because it was a paid vacation by the North Korean government. Very few Westerners arrived, yet the spotlight shined on them. It was *De Ja Vous* for me. I saw the same propaganda on the state run television for the Americans and Europeans that had arrived as I did when I had first defected. Most of the Westerners represented obscure Communist parties or curious youngsters who wanted to see what all the fuss was about.

I met a few of the visitors at our campus. It was the most frustrating experience in my life. One Brazilian kept on commenting about the wonderful and warm treatment he was receiving in Pyongyang. The man was so impressed with *Juche* and how everyone in North Korea seemed to be benefiting from this "Socialist Paradise." He turned to me and remarked how he had wished other nations would learn from North Korea and how he would spread the message to his countrymen. I just looked him straight in the eyes and smiled. In my mind I was thinking: "You dumb son-of-a-bitch! You have no idea!"

Chapter 20

ERIC DISAPPEARS

1989

The gang of kids I saw that day was part of the growing number of beggars, especially *Kotjebis*, or young orphans in North Korea. As more and more North Koreans were dying from malnutrition, curable diseases, or simply "disappearing," more people, especially children were roaming the streets. Rations were also being squeezed. Some of my students told me that in the countryside, people were having a tough time getting essentials. Meat was now very rare to come by, even in Pyongyang. One student had even told me that people in his hometown were dying from simple diseases because they did not have access to proper medical care. The only reason Eric and I were still eating well was because of our well-connected students and my job at the studios.

At the time, I really didn't know how severe the situation was around the country. It wasn't until I escaped into China that I began to hear reports on the real state of affairs in North Korea. It just goes to show how well run the North Korean government apparatus was and still is today. Honestly, I don't think anyone besides Kim Jong IL himself, really knows what the real situation was in North Korea. This is due to the immense concentration of the North Korean regime on domestic intelligence gathering. Everyone was spying on everyone.

Unfortunately for Eric, he had a first-hand experience with the North Korean security apparatus. Like Hitler's "Brownshirts" or SS, North Korea recruited young and vicious personnel with *Carte Blanche* to spy and harass anyone who even looked "unpatriotic." This was just another band of hoodlums the regime created to spy on the other bands of hoodlums. The idea was to divide and conquer. Let every North Korean, from the simple farmer to the top party cadre sweat over anyone they met and keep their comments to themselves or face the consequences. Even within our classes, there were spies. Eric was beginning to criticize the University's policies openly in his classes. Eric always believed he had a good rapport with his students. He really thought that because they liked him, he could say anything to them. He forgot this was North Korea.

In fact, there was at least one student, if not more, who reported everything that transpired in Eric's class to the "Young Worker's Party Association." This was a student organization that was supposed to emulate the largest and only political party in North Korea. The group included the elite students in the school and those who commanded the most respect. The University students, like the rest of North Korea, were divided into cells, or groups. These cells always had a very strong leader who shaped the rest of the group. The leader was usually considered the most patriotic, therefore the most suitable for the position.

One particularly cold October night in 1989, Eric disappeared from campus. It wasn't the first time I had noticed someone disappearing from the University, except this time it was someone very close to me. Eric was my best friend in North Korea. I had known him since the day I had arrived on campus. He was the first to really open up to me and show me the ropes. He was the only person who I could really trust and confide in. Now he was gone.

That morning I realized that Eric was not at the cafeteria. He never missed the opportunity to meet me there and have our daily ritual of bland coffee and a bowl of soup. Even when he was sick, he made the effort to come down and meet me in the cafeteria. After that, we usually went for our daily walk around the wooded area of the university's perimeter. Even though Eric began to drink heavily, he always made it for breakfast. That day, I went around frantically searching for him. His room, his class, the faculty lounge, even the gymnasium.

Eric disappeared as if he had never existed. Dr. Koo became angry when I asked him for the second time whether or not he knew where Eric was.

"Why you ask? What is your problem?"

Dr. Koo yelled at me.

"I think your friend play roulette with life. He like danger."

He yelled as I walked out of his office.

Dr. Koo had waited for this moment. He never liked us and blamed his hatred of foreigners on us. I never understood why he had majored in English if he hated Westerners so much. That was a very common characteristic of Koreans, both from the North and South. Because Koreans are a homogenous society, they see life through group identity. Every Korean that had approached me had some comment regarding what foreigners, Westerners or Americans, were like. I spent countless hours trying to explain to Koreans that countries like the United States are eclectic and therefore hard to generalize. Most did not understand me. Some were intrigued and found a non-homogeneous society "dangerous."

How could different kinds of people live together without problems? How were the day-to-day operations conducted with so many different ethnic groups? These were some of the questions students raised. I had to be very careful how I answered their questions. I could not defend the United States, nor could I explain in a positive way how a capitalist nation operates. I was therefore forced to agree with my narrow-minded students and say that the United States in fact was a barbaric system that does not work. This frustration accentuated the fact that I had always taken for granted how free Americans really were. When I was in school, all we did was criticize American foreign and domestic policy.

For the first time in many years I became very concerned about my own well being. Up till this point, I thought I was immune from persecution because of my fame and connections. Now I realized no one was safe in North Korea. I mean, it was never safe for anyone; not even the top brass. Nevertheless, I always felt needed, therefore untouchable. After all, it was I who taught the top students in North Korea, it was I who gave the regime all the information I had about the United States Armed Forces in South Korea and more. It was I who taught the top spies in North Korea about American and Western mannerisms. And it was I who North Koreans saw on their television and movie screens portraying the "Western Devil." Why should I have anything to fear?

Of course, that question was irrelevant in North Korea. I was just ignorant of the fact that even I had to fear for my life. It was now becoming clear to me that I was in a struggle for my life and that the only way I could win was by getting out of North Korea. Eric didn't just go for a long forgetful walk, he was sent to those "rehabilitation centers" everyone knew but didn't talk about. I had seen lots of people "disappear" since I defected to North Korea. I just didn't think it would be someone so close to me and in the same position I held. Eric was popular, important, so I thought. All it took was for one asshole like Dr. Koo to make false claims about him and poof! He was gone.

I gave up looking for Eric the following day and began working on an escape plan. One of the production staff at Kim Jong IL Studios made several trips a year by special permission of Kim Jong IL's Executive office in search of the necessary equipment needed for running a film studio. Dong Hak (he liked it when I called him by his first name) was part of the North Korean government's illegal operations. It was no secret that North Korea dealt in counterfeiting and illegal drug manufacturing and distribution. This was how they paid for the Kim dynasty's ridiculous needs and desires.

Dong Hak was one of the few North Koreans I felt comfortable around. He had a lot of experience with foreigners because he had served in a joint military unit of North Korean and then Soviet Union soldiers. Dong Hak told me the unit was so secretive that no one in North Korea or Russia would admit to its existence. They trained in the Eastern part of Russia and even made reconnaissance operations into "unfriendly" nations. Dong Hak spoke Russian, Chinese, English, and some Japanese.

The fact that Dong Hak confided in me and was so friendly with me made me believe that I could trust him. I also thought that his experience would help with my plans to escape. Not to mention the fact that he made so many trips to China. Still, I had to be careful with everyone. I would have to indirectly bring up my wishes to leave North Korea.

The opportunity to broach the subject came during our usual all night binge drinking. As I had mentioned before, drinking was the only way people in North Korea loosened up. We usually drank after long days of shooting and editing at the studios. Many of the staff, including Dong Hak, lived in a small apartment complex a few blocks from the studios. Dong Hak's bachelors place had no food, but plenty of bootlegged alcohol. There was Chinese beer, Russian vodka, Japanese sake, and even Californian wine. During these drinking binges, I would usually stay at Dong Hak's place along with Eric. I always brought Eric along. This was the first time without him.

The next morning, over a cup of instant coffee, I asked Dong Hak if I could accompany him on one of his trips to China.

"Are you serious?"

Dong Hak looked stunned.

"Sure! Why not? I replied.

"Do you know how hard it is just for me to go there?"

"I just want to travel. I always wanted to see China"

"David! What did you think when you came to North Korea? It would be a vacation place? That you would get to travel and do as you want? Do you forget where you are?"

"Come on, Dong Hak! You can do what you want because you know the right people and know your way around things."

Dong Hak stood up abruptly and put his hand on my mouth. He then signaled me to be quiet with his finger while he insinuated with his eyes that there were listening devices around the room.

"I don't know what you are talking about." Dong Hak retorted.

Dong Hak turned on his radio, sat right beside me, and leaned over until we were almost touching.

"I found a listening device a few months ago. Even here! In my own apartment! I think that was the only one, but you never know. Kim likes to know everything about his studio staff. He is suspicious of everyone and especially of those closest to him."

Dong Hak paused for a moment. For the first time I had sensed fear in a man I had always thought was invincible.

"You know better than anyone that travel is an anomaly here. Only outsiders really know what that word means. I know what you really want. Do you think all those years of training in espionage haven't taught me anything? I have been trained in the art of observation and what I have observed about you is that you are disappointed. I have watched you from the first day you came to the studios with your naïve optimism and innocence. I also see you now with your solemn face and broken spirit. Your problem is that you are not from here. You know what is out there. You have seen the outside and you can't help compare it to your life here. You thought your fame in North Korea would bring you happiness, but it has done nothing of the sort. Do you know why? Because nobody is happy here, not even the elite. People live in fear and fear begets unhappiness. Now you want me to help you escape this unhappy place."

It was as if Dong Hak knew my innermost feelings. But in fact I was so miserable that it was not too hard to figure it out. What really bothered me about what Dong Hak was saying was that it was the harsh truth of my whole existence. It was becoming apparent to me that the whole reason I defected in the first place was to get recognition. Just like a spoiled kid, I wanted people to pay attention to me. I wanted people to follow me. Instead, I was becoming like Colonel Kurtz in Joseph Conrad's novel, "Heart of Darkness." I had illusions of grandeur. I was blind with the circus-like attention I was receiving in a nation where nothing seemed real.

Angered by the piercing analysis of my life I sat there in silence for a while. Finally, I blurted out that whether or not he helped me, I would travel to China.

"I could get you into China, but you would need papers once you were in China. What if you were stopped on the streets by Chinese policemen?"

Dong Hak finally spoke. I was so happy that he would help me. We decided to meet the following weekend at Dong Hak's place and plan our trip. In the meantime, Dong Hak would plan everything, from the forged papers I would need to the safe house I could stay in Yanbian, the Korean autonomous region in China bordering North Korea. After that, I was on my own.

For the next few days I did not hear from Dong Hak at all. I didn't even see him at the studios. A week later Dong Hak appeared at my apartment at the University at six in the morning. Dong Hak pushed his way in as soon as I opened the door. Koreans would customarily wait to be invited in, but Dong Hak was not anxious to be seen talking to me. Dong Hak looked around my room, headed over to the radio, and turned it on.

"Every security apparatus has its window of opportunity. Six to seven in the morning is the time when the intelligence officers usually switch shifts. During this time, nobody is really listening in. I know this because I was once part of that division."

"Are you ready to leave as soon as tomorrow?"

Dong Hak asked.

"Of course" I answered in a daze.

"You better be sure! Lots of people can get hurt if this doesn't work," Dong Hak warned.

"We need to leave now while the river is still frozen. I already have passes to get to the border as well as a forged Armenian passport. Lots of Armenian engineers are working on a dam by the Tumen River, so they will not suspect you. If you carried a larger nation's passport, the Chinese might suspect you for being a spy. Not many foreigners venture into the border area."

I needed two passes for North Korea and China. That was especially why I relied on Dong Hak. No one in North Korea, with the exception of people like Dong Hak, could travel from province to province. Dong Hak had that permission from Kim Jong IL himself to buy necessary materials for the studio such as reels of films and camera equipment. Still, even Dong Hak's equipment was given a quick check by the Chinese guards on the other side. This was why I would need to make my own way across the river. I also needed documents once I was in China. Chinese authorities were very vigilant in the Yanbian border region with North Korea for obvious reasons. This autonomous region on the border had over two million Korean-Chinese. The Chinese government wanted to make sure none were helping the growing number of escapees. I would also need a passport if I were to leave China.

The North Koreans were experts at forging documents. Heck! They even printed the best-forged U.S. Dollars ever. It is believed that most of the forged one hundred dollar bills and other documents had their origin in North Korea. In the underground markets in North Korea I once saw fake dollar bills being sold for a fraction of their value. I also saw fake artifacts that were supposed to resemble authentic Chinese, Korean, and especially ancient Japanese artifacts. The *Chochonyon* (Korean-Japanese) would come to North Korea to purchase these artifacts and then sell them abroad. These artifacts went through painstaking processes to look authentic. For example, Chinese porcelain vases would be rubbed in the exact same dirt that would be found in China for weeks to give it that used look as if it were uncovered at an excavation site.

The next morning I was all set: a little food, some warm clothes, home made gloves made from socks, and my documents in my shoes. Dong Hak was waiting for me on the other side of the campus so as not to raise any suspicion among those who knew me. One strange thing about Dong Hak was that he didn't smoke. Most North Koreans smoked. I always wondered about that. Most of that morning I rode up front with Dong Hak as if I were just accompanying him on a fact-finding mission for the next filming project we had. I presented my travel documents as we headed north from one province to another.

After three hours of driving, we arrived at our first destination. It was a small city where Dong Hak had to pick up and drop off some bags. The city looked like a planned city built by the North Koreans in the 1970's to show the world what a great country they had. Dong Hak suddenly pulled over to the side of the road, put the car in park, turned to me and asked:

"Are you sure about this, I mean, you don't have any second thoughts about it?"

I was a little surprised by his question and paused for a little before nodding my head affirmably. Dong Hak put the car in gear and we were off into the city. We stopped at what looked like a government building. As usual, there were no signs in front or anywhere else.

"Do you mind helping me with some of these bags?"

I picked up two of the bags and followed him inside. The building seemed abandoned. There was nothing in the main room or any of the other rooms. I followed Dong Hak down the hallway to a door with a stairway that seemed to lead deep into the pits of hell. I usually do not suffer from vertigo, but these stairs were incredibly steep and endless. The only light guiding us down was the light from the top of the stairs and from the bottom of the stairs. As we continued our descent I noticed a shadow to my side. I turned my head back to the top of the stairs and there was a man standing at the entrance. This was the first person we had seen since we entered the building.

As I stepped off the last step I did not even have time to look around before I felt a sharp blow to my head. I don't know how long I was out, but I bet only for a few minutes. A large jawed man slapped me back to consciousness while a smaller man next to him was yelling at me to wake up. My hands were tied to the back of the chair I was sitting in. I felt the warm blood slowly making its way down my head where I was struck earlier.

"Yankee dog! Son of a foreigner!"

The smaller man kept yelling. Being called a son of a foreigner was one of the worst insults a North Korean could utter.

"We know everything about you. We always knew. We have been watching you since you first came here. You idiot!"

The smaller man continued to yell in Korean.

"You have betrayed our 'Dear Leader.' You have let him down. Now you will pay for your selfish act. You foreigners only care about yourselves, you never care about anyone but yourselves."

The little guy continued to yell at me while the large jawed monster slapped and punched me. It was very obvious by now that Dong Hak had set me up. I wasn't mad at these two guys, I was mad at the fact that I was so alone in this God forsaken country. The last vestiges of trust left me that moment. I had no one I could confide in and that hurt more than all the beatings these guys could give me. I was so angry I jumped up with my chair, screamed at the top of my lungs, and ran straight into the little guy who was yelling at me. I hit him so hard that I knocked him into the wall. Next thing I knew was that I lost all control of myself. Even though I took a direct hit from the wall myself, I managed to turn around in a split second and lunge at the big-jawed guy. He, however, was ready for me and pulled an easy Tae Kwon Do move using my own momentum to trip me over and knock me down. Once again I felt a tremendous thump on my head and passed out immediately.

I was brought back to consciousness by a violent surge up my left arm. They had tied two wires to my thumb. They were electrocuting me. It was the most painful sensation I had ever experienced. I can't even describe it. In between volts of electricity, the two brutes asked me all sorts of questions. I could not understand half of them. It was as if I had forgotten my Korean. That only made things worse and they continued to shock me. I finally passed out again.

Chapter 21

IMPRISONMENT

1991

When I came around this time I found myself on the floor of a dirty truck driving on what seemed a very bumpy road. At the end of the benches of the truck were two stone-faced guards. They didn't seem to care that I had awoken. I felt the back of my head, the blood had crusted in my hair and helped stopped the bleeding naturally. I could still smell my singed hair from the electrocutions. I laid there for what seemed like hours before the truck finally stopped. The guards stood up, picked me up, and forced me out of the truck. My immediate reaction to my surroundings was that I was in a detention camp.

There were a series of hastily constructed long shacks everywhere. In the distance, I could see high fences and groups of single uniformed people walking quickly from one place to another. Above where the truck had stopped was a guard tower with what looked like an M60-style machine gun. The guards led me into a smaller shack and made me kneel down all the way to the ground. They were trying to make me bow the most respectful Korean bow usually only reserved for special occasions like weddings or New Years. When I rose from my bow, a pudgy-faced man was smiling at me.

"Mr. Walker, so nice to finally meet you."

The man said in a British accent. He was dressed in a very clean, well-pressed uniform. He had so many medals on his uniform. Of course, he had Kim Jong IL's and Kim IL Sung's pins proudly displayed at the top.

"I have seen many of your films. You would think that you were some famous Hollywood star."

The man was referring to the North Korean propaganda films I had been in. Over the years I had starred in almost fifty propaganda films.

"Where are my manners, please sit down. Can I get you something to drink? Oh! By the way, my name is Commandant Lee."

Commandant Lee motioned for me to sit down while he hovered over his large mahogany desk, smiling the entire time.

"There are very serious allegations by the people against you. You have betrayed your host country after all that was done for you. Is there anything you would like to say in your defense?"

I knew that I had to begin my pleading and try to cajole the warden to take it easy on me. I knew better than to deny the charges. Living in North Korea for such a long time had taught me that going against the wishes of the state only made things more difficult.

"Commandant Lee, I wish to express my sincere apologies for the troubles I have caused and for the shameful behavior I have brought upon this great land and most honorable leader, Kim IL Sung. As you might be aware, the 'Dear Leader' and I have a very cordial relationship and the last thing I would want to do is hurt those magnificent interactions."

I groveled. Bowing deeply and not making eye contact with Commandant Lee.

"Then you should be aware of the fact that the only reason you are still alive right now is because of that special relationship you hold with the 'Dear Leader'."

Commandant Lee interrupted.

"The 'Dear Leader' has most graciously spared your life so that you can reflect on your wrongdoings and correct them. In this facility you will have plenty of time to do just that. We are counting on you to do your best and follow the rules. I would hate to see one of my favorite actors stray even further off the path of righteousness. I will personally inspect your progress and report back to Pyongyang. Now, if you don't mind, I am a very busy man."

Commandant Lee yelled to the guards in an angry tone to take me away. Two guards grabbed me and led me out of the building and across a courtyard. Commandant Lee's office was the last glimpse I would have of "civilization" for a long time. The prison looked like the concentration camps the Nazis built to exterminate the Jews. Everything was gray, even the sky. There were rows and rows of poorly constructed tin shacks and what seemed to be a factory at the end of the complex. Nothing seemed to grow anywhere in the camp. The ground was muddy and there was a horrific smell that filled the air. The only colorful objects in the camp were the pictures of Kim IL Sung and Kim Jong IL, which adorned the entrance to every building in the prison.

The guards took me to the entrance of one of the shacks and led me into a room. A short stocky man with a deep scar on his cheek was there to greet me. He handed me a pair of gray pants and a shirt and told me to get dressed. I was given a comb, one blanket, and a tin bowl. He then pointed to the second door and told me to go through it. As I turned to go through the door I felt a sharp blow to my head. The stocky man had used the cane he was carrying to hit me.

"What? No thank you? You better learn to thank me every time you see me, you American dog!"

The man screamed in Korean. He was so angry his entire face turned red. I got right back up and thanked him.

"*Komapsummida!*"

I thanked him in the most respectful way the Korean language allowed. I swallowed my pride and took the beating as a lesson. This was the only way to survive from now on. I would learn quickly that this man was the equivalent of the dean of students or vice president of a school. It was his job to take care of all the disciplinary situations and he seemed to enjoy this job too much. His name was Mr. Kwon and he was the reason why everyone in the camp suffered so cruelly.

The guards led me through the second door and pointed to the empty bed on the right among a row of bunk beds. At the entrance of the room were two pictures, one of Kim IL Sung, the other of Kim Jong IL. This would be the last two faces I would see before going to sleep and after waking up for the next few years. I was told to stand there and wait until it was time for dinner. I stood there for what seemed like hours until I heard a horn blare. A few minutes later several men came marching into the room in file. They walked in an orderly file towards their bunk beds. I noticed that several of them were foreigners like me. A couple of them were white, one looked Middle Eastern, and the rest were Asian. Each one grabbed their bowl from their beds and waited.

One guard came in shortly after and commanded us to go. I followed the men with my bowl to another complex. This complex was the cafeteria. The line to where they were serving food was long. As I was waiting, I noticed a familiar face sitting at one of the tables. It was one of my old students, Min Ki. He was looking at me as well. He looked so different. He used to be such a vivacious character. He always made everyone laugh. He had lost so much weight. His eyes were sunken and expressed a fear in them that I will never forget. He finally turned away and wolfed down the rest of his soup.

The soup was just lukewarm salt water with a piece of radish, some corn and beans in it. It tasted awful. It was amazing how quickly I would adjust to this food. That is what happens when hunger consumes a person. We were only given a few minutes to eat. After dinner we were led back to our dorms where we set our bowls by our beds. We were then led to another complex where the Kim memorabilia surrounded the entire room. This was the "Self-Analysis Room." A place where we were expected to get up in front of everyone and confess our crimes against the state and the principles of *"Juche"* or Self-Reliance.

Several prisoners stood up and gave a song and dance about their past sins and how they had "shamed" the state and the "Dear Leader." I felt as if I were in one of those revival tents in the Deep South. The prisoners shouted back at those who were standing, some acknowledging their mistakes, others accusing them of hurting the state and the principles of *Juche*. It all seemed like a dream.

It was very late by the time we all headed back to our bunks. Nobody said a word the whole time. In no time, we all fell asleep from exhaustion. All except for one.

"Pssst! Hey!"

Just as I felt myself falling asleep I heard the guy in the next bunk call me.

"Hey! New guy! Where you from?"

The guy had a thick Russian accent.

"Pyongyang" I replied.

"No! Idiot! Where you from originally?"

"America."

"East or West Coast."

"West, from San Francisco."

"Ohhh! San Francisco, the city by the bay, Golden Gate Bridge. I want to see this city. I think it's like my hometown Vladivostok."

"I heard they are similar." I replied.

"Shhhh!" Whispered the guy above my bunk.

"Do you want to get us in trouble?"

The Russian guy ignored him and continued to ask me questions.

"Why you here?"

"For the same reasons we are all here." I answered.

I knew better than to give too much subjective information. The North Korean regime continued to exist thanks to the basic idea that there were spies and informers among the entire population even in detention camps. Anything I said could go right back to the Warden.

"Don't worry so much! I am here long time. I will show you how to survive. This like Russian Gulag. I know much information on Gulag. Just follow me."

"Thank you." I replied.

I then fell into a deep sleep only to be awakened by that horrible siren. It was still dark outside. I followed the rest of the prisoners across to the cafeteria again where we were served the same soup from the day before. After breakfast we were given a few minutes to wash our faces and use the bathrooms. The bathrooms were disgusting. It was one big hole in the middle of the room and everyone would urinate and defecate around the same hole. At first, the smell was revolting. I quickly adjusted to this as well.

After a very short bathroom break, I followed the rest of my bunkmates in a quick pace to another unassuming building on the outskirts of the camp. This time, there were two guards at the door. I also noticed a very large radar installation on the roof of the building. Inside the building were rows of desks and what seemed like an endless supply of papers stacked up high. On some of the desks were antiquated radio transistors. There were no windows or any dividers. All my bunkmates quickly assumed their positions and began work immediately. Not knowing what to do, I just stood there waiting for an order.

"Ya! Iriwa!"

A man shouted to me in Korean from the other end of the room. I walked quickly to the other side of the room were a Korean was sitting at the front desk facing all the other workers' desks.

"You know what to do?"

"No Sir" I answered.

"What? Nobody told you?" The man was aggravated by the fact that he had to teach me the ropes. The man was known as Mr. Lim. He was our supervisor.

"We give you documents, you translate. And, you listen to radio and translate important information. If I catch you making mistakes, you will be punished severely. Ask your comrades. Now go there and start your work."

He pointed to an empty desk with a pile of newspapers on it. For sixteen hours that day I had to translate newspapers into Korean. I read all kinds of newspapers, from the International Herald Tribune to the Los Angeles Times. It is very difficult to translate newspapers from English to Korean, but I did as I was told.

The whole day we were not even given one break. At one point, I couldn't hold myself and urinated in my pants. I knew better than to ask for a bathroom break. If the old-timers around me were not asking for a break, then there was a reason for that. The smell of the urine did not irritate anyone around me; the entire camp had the most awful smell all the time. Another bad odor in the mix did not make a difference.

I noticed that Mr. Lim had a pile of rocks on his desk. The mystery of the rocks did not take long to solve. Working all those hours without a break led me to nod off while at my desk. I must have been extremely tired because I didn't even remember falling asleep. Suddenly I felt a sharp, but small blow to my forehead. I lifted my head just in time to dodge another rock Mr. Lim had just chucked at me. Mr. Lim used those rocks to keep us awake at the job.

That night I ate voraciously and fell asleep as soon as I hit the bunk bed. It is amazing how quickly one adjusts to the most uncomfortable surroundings. The next day it was the same routine. This time Peter, the Russian guy, sat next to me at dinnertime and we talked a bit.

"You work at KIS before, right?"

"Yeah!"

"You know there is one more professor from KIS in the camp. His name Eric."

"Eric? Eric is here? Where?" I asked nervously.

"In the cages on the other side of camp."

"What are the cages?" I asked.

"The cages are where bad workers go. Eric talk back to Mr. Kwon. Listen, you make sure you are good with Mr. Kwon. He likes you, you are okay. He doesn't like you, you will die soon."

Comforting advice. I was still shocked to find out that Eric was okay. Peter's advice was secondary in my thoughts. Cages? What were these cages? What kind of punishment was Eric enduring? That night Peter told me a little more about these cages. Apparently, they were like animal cages used to punish prisoners. It was no more than three feet high and so narrow that sitting down or standing fully erect were out of the question. All a person could do is squat the entire time. Prisoners were not let out for any reason. They even had to defecate and urinate in their cages. Some prisoners were left to die in these cages, while others were released. I was hoping Eric would come out soon.

That night I had also told Peter why I was sent to the camp. I told him how I had trusted Dong Hak and believed in him.

"Ha!" Peter interrupted.

"What, you think there is trust in North Korea? You are so…how you say in English…Stupid! You trust no one here, not even me. That is how system work so good. Everyone here watching everyone. Even the man who cleans Kim Jong IL's ass is being watched by government person. That man betray you because he is watched always. No choice! Stalin used same system. No one trusted anyone so no problems and leader stay in power. You Americans are so innocent. You think everyone has freedom. Freedom this, freedom that! What stupid!"

"Shhhh...*Choyong hee hae*!" (be quiet!)

Takahiro, the Japanese prisoner in the bunk above me, whispered to us in Korean. Peter was getting too excited and risking us all. If we were caught talking at night, we would be tortured then sent to the cages.

A couple of weeks went by with the same routine every day. I work all day translating useless documents and papers. We at the same soup, and attend the two-hour self-criticism classes every night. Then we got up and did the same thing. During this time, I got to know the other bunkmates a little. Takahiro was a Japanese interpreter who claimed to be pure Japanese, not Korean-Japanese. Peter told me later that Takahiro was one of the many Japanese the North Korean commandos kidnapped in Japan and brought to North Korea. Takahiro was quiet and revealed hardly anything about his past. The only thing he would talk about was the great nightlife he once enjoyed in Japan. He also fantasized about Japanese food and sports. He loved playing soccer and watching baseball.

Another prisoner was Raseem, a Palestinian from Syria. Unlike Takahiro, Raseem was quick to protest his innocence and the unjust treatment he had received in North Korea. Raseem came with a "delegation" of Palestinians by the request of the North Korean government. They were here to learn about North Korean education and public administration, as well as about the unique North Korean system of *Juche*. Next thing he knew, he was imprisoned and sent here.

Peter later told me a very different version of the story. The North Korean government invited Raseem and the other Palestinians. They were here to learn military techniques and train with North Korean commandoes. Peter thought they were probably members of the Syrian-Palestinian faction of Abu Nidal. He recently read in the Russian Pravda magazine he was given daily to translate that North Korea protested to the Syrian government regarding late payments for weapons purchased by the Palestinian factions in Syria. Peter had seen other Middle Eastern looking men at the camp earlier. He therefore concluded that the North Korean government was holding these men as ransom until the Syrian government and Palestinian factions paid them their dues. One day, he noticed all the Arab men were gone, all except for Raseem.

So why was Raseem still there? Peter had a theory about that as well. Either Raseem had fallen out of favor with the Palestinian faction and been left to rot in North Korea or Raseem had done something to piss off the North Koreans. Peter didn't like Raseem. He felt that Raseem had some dark past to that was haunting him. That thought took me back to the Middle Eastern men I met in the club in Pyongyang. Was Raseem one of them? I couldn't remember.

After a few weeks at the camp I began to lose track of the days. We didn't get any days off so I didn't know what day it was. Then, as if out of the sky, Eric was in our bunkroom as we returned from our self-criticism session one evening. He looked so much older. His hair was almost entirely gray, his body was as frail as a young boy's, and his gaunt face and sunken eyes were almost unrecognizable. As the guards left our room, I tiptoed over to his bunk and gave him a big hug. He looked up at me with a forced smile and a sparkle in his eyes.

"You decided to join me." Eric snickered.

I just smiled and held his scrawny hand. He looked like a helpless infant in need of desperate care. I held back my tears. For the first time since arriving in this awful country I felt like crying. I was always sad, but I never felt like crying like I did that moment. All that was wrong with this place was expressed in Eric. They had taken the best of humanity and destroyed it. Eric was not the happy-go-lucky adventure seeker I once knew.

That night Eric told me about how he was taken in the middle of the night from his apartment to an interrogation room. Dr. Koo was there. He took pleasure in watching Eric being tortured. Dr. Koo had made up accusations against Eric. The interrogators asked him to confess to it. They had attached wires to his genitals and shocked him; they had beaten him so badly that he suffered broken bones and internal bleeding for months. He showed me his crooked arm where the bone had not set properly. After confessing to the false charges. They left him in a cell for days. They then brought him to this prison.

Eric told me Mr. Kwon was always giving him a hard time. Eric thought that Dr. Koo somehow had asked the prison supervisor to harass him because Mr. Kwon had it in for Eric. Every day Mr. Kwon would find a reason to beat him. Then one day, Eric hit back. While Mr. Kwon swung at Eric with his stick, Eric managed to grab the stick and pull it out of his hands. Eric then took the stick and threw it over the fence. Mr. Kwon felt so insulted that he instructed the guards to throw Eric in the Cages. Mr. Kwon would come by from time to time with a new stick and jab Eric in the cage, daring Eric to try and grab his stick again.

Eric told me how he survived in the cage. He was only given one meal, a bowl of salted water mixed with corn and cabbage. An occasional bug would mistakenly come in reach of Eric's cage and Eric would eat it up. After about the third day in the cage Eric had no problems eating bugs. It was a question of hunger and survival. He was so weak and tired that he would go into hour-long hallucinations. To pass the time, He would reminisce about his childhood in Australia and what he would do when he got back home. He also tried to keep a mental diary of his experience thus far. Thinking was what saved him from all that ailed him.

Eric came back to work with us the next day. His desk was right behind mine. We now shared the English documents and radio messages. Eric focused on the British-speaking world, while I focused on the American. It wasn't such a harsh prison term if you think about it. I passed the day translating NPR News, Voice of America, and the American Forces Korea Network (AFKN). I say this because I would soon learn more about how other prisoners were being treated around North Korea.

Kim IL Sung and later Kim Jong IL had survived this long by being suspicious, thus careful, of any dissent among the North Korean population. Even the slightest dissatisfaction by a North Korean wound up in harsh imprisonment not only for that person, but also for the person's family. There were two types of prisons in North Korea, those for political prisoners and those for their family members. Of course, the North Koreans did not call them prisoners, rather "subversives." The prisons were called "re-education centers" so that people would believe that there was a way to reform oneself.

Worst yet, by the time I had reached this "re-education" camp in the early 1990's, the situation had deteriorated even further. Through reading American newspapers and listening to American radio, especially AFKN, I learned about the chaotic situation around the country. In some Northeastern provinces, entire North Korean battalions and villages were attacked by the regular army for fomenting food riots and anger among the local population. I knew the situation must be desperate if the docile North Koreans were protesting. I also realized that those people must have paid a heavy price for their dissention.

I was right! The newspapers and radio covered some reports that entire Northern provinces were branded "hostile" by the North Korean regime and turned into virtual prisons. It was hard enough to travel during the seventies and eighties, now it was almost impossible. This further isolated the North Korean people on all sides. Kim IL Sung punished those areas by cutting off food shipments. The closure of the areas was a security measure so that no information could come in or out of the region. That was why Koreans in other parts of the country were oblivious to the dire food shortages and abuses that those regions were enduring. This closed off area in the Northeast was also known as the "Security Zone" and the area where we were most likely being held.

The prison camps had no names, they were known simply by numbers. Our camp was number 12. It was one of the most heavily guarded camps because of our operations there. Peter seemed to think that we were the best off because we had an important skill to offer. Most Korean prisoners ended up in the Gulags, or work camps, where many were worked to death. One story going around our bunk was about a gulag in an old mining area in the Northwest. Apparently, most of the coal had already been exploited from the mine. The camp held people of short stature and children. They were selected because they were small enough to reach into the deepest crevasses of the caves and retrieve coal and other stones and metals.

The camp that held people of short stature was a whole other story. There were also rumors (valid ones, I might point out) that Kim IL Sung was trying to eradicate the physically and mentally handicapped population in North Korea. The same thing Adolph Hitler and the Nazis attempted to do. The ironic, better yet, tragic part of it was the fact that Kim IL Sung's own son, Kim Jong IL, was very short and did everything to seem taller. Even when I met him, I remember noticing his platform slippers, which added several inches to his height. Was his father ashamed of him?

During the next few weeks at the camp Eric seemed to be getting his strength back. His back, however, remained crooked, and he still looked as if he had aged twenty years. Mr. Kwon continued to harass Eric and me. I think Eric was right about Dr. Koo. Either Dr. Koo had paid him off to nail our asses to the wall or Mr. Kwon simply hated both of us. He was cruel to all the prisoners, but extra cruel to us. Peter and Raseem would kiss his ass just to get away with a limited number of beatings. Takahiro was a quiet man who seemed resolved to accept any fate given to him. Mr. Kwon and the other guards barely even noticed his existence.

I could tell that all those weeks Eric spent in the cages had not broken his pride. He was determined to defy Mr. Kwon by standing erect and staring right into his eyes as Mr. Kwon dealt the physical blows to Eric's body. Eric pretended not to care but he did. After Mr. Kwon would leave, Eric would collapse and one of us would have to carry him back to his bunk bed. Sometimes, Mr. Kwon would make us stand outside in the freezing rain all night for no reason. He always tried to find something to blame us for. He didn't want to just kill us; he wanted us to suffer first.

The beatings and humiliations were not the worst things I experienced at camp number 12. The worst thing was the primitive condition human could devolve into if forced to such limits. My fellow prisoners scared me more than Mr. Kwon and the guards. Among every group there were informers. Those were the prisoners who were given an extra bowl of soup or less punishment for squealing on other prisoners. Raseem was definitely a squealer. I had my suspicions about Peter, but I never was sure. In this hell hole Takahiro could have been a squealer too. The lure of food to a hungry soul is stronger than most moral convictions.

I had witnessed prisoners fighting over morsels of food while guards just looked on with amusement. Once I had encountered a group of Korean prisoners kill another prisoner in the restroom, then throw him into the septic tank. When they saw me, one of them motioned me to come over. He told me that the prisoner was a Christian and was always getting them in trouble. The guards thought that the whole group was Christian and therefore they were constantly tortured. Killing the Christian would win them favors with the guards, they thought. When the Christian did not show up for roll call, the entire group was blamed and sent to the cages. How ironic!

Eric shared my disgust with the level of depravation human beings could sink to. However, by the time I arrived at the camp, he was already physically and mentally broken. He had accepted his fate and decided to go out fighting. One night, during our usual session of berating by Mr. Kwon, Eric snapped. He had smuggled a broken antenna out of the workroom. Mr. Kwon was standing in Eric's face and hitting his side with his stick. Eric pulled out the antenna with the broken part facing outward and began stabbing Mr. Kwon with it. He exploded with such anger and ferocity that I did not know him capable of. I thought the antenna was too flimsy to penetrate Mr. Kwon, but I was wrong. Eric continuously stabbed Mr. Kwon with short and powerful thrusts to his stomach and neck area so that in an instant there was blood everywhere.

Mr. Kwon let out a couple of shrieks like a little girl or a yelping dog. In those few seconds, his vulnerable side came out in true form. I could see in his eyes the fear and shock that had overcome his constant self-assurance. I have to say that as horrified as I was, I rejoiced in his pain. Somehow I knew Eric was gone. The untamed, cornered animal in Eric had taken over.

Everything happened so quickly. Eric was still on top of Mr. Kwon when the guards ran up and began beating Eric with their rifles. I stood there, frozen, while they beat Eric senseless. Eric probably passed out from the first few hits, but they continued to beat him just the same. I stood there because I wanted to live. My desire to live was still strong. I did not spent weeks in a small cage or suffer the blows of Mr. Kwon as much as Eric. I still had hope.

Weeks passed before I would see Eric again. It was also the last. Eric had severely hurt Mr. Kwon and rumors had it that Mr. Kwon was actually killed by the doctors in the infirmary. Peter believed that Commandant Lee wanted the whole incident done with. If Mr. Kwon were still alive, he would serve as an example to the prisoners of the vulnerability of the system. That was how things were dealt with in North Korea. Violence was the ultimate solution.

In the middle of our work routine, we were ordered to come out to the quad at the North end of the camp. There must have been thousands of prisoners there. These prisoners looked worse off than we foreigners. Some looked so young either because they were young or because of malnutrition. I really could not tell. Some were so skinny I could clearly see their bones. They also had a very sick color to their skin, as if they were walking corpses. In front of us were some poles in the ground and immediately in front of us were piles and piles of rocks.

As we waited, several guards marched out, dragging Eric with them. Eric looked dead already. His body was limp. The guards had to lift him up and tie his hands to the back of the pole. As soon as he was tied, Commandant Lee and an entourage of guards came out to the front of the crowd. One of the guards carrying a small wooden platform put it down in front of Eric. Commandant Lee stood on the platform and gave a short speech regarding the sins Eric has committed. He accused Eric of acts of terrorism against the state and *Juche*. Eric was a spy, a traitor, and a criminal.

After the speech, Commandant Lee left and the guards began shouting at the prisoners to pick up the stones and throw them at Eric. The prisoners at the front began to throw the stones at Eric and then moved to the sides, while the next row threw stones, and then the row behind them. The guards stayed at the front and made sure everyone threw a stone. If one prisoner was too slow or missed Eric, he was hit with the rifle. Most of the prisoners seemed apathetic. Some even seemed to be releasing their frustration by throwing the stones at Eric. It was gruesome to watch.

When my row came up, I chose the smallest rock and intentionally missed Eric. I was beaten for this. By the time many of the prisoners were done, there was not much left of Eric. We were forced to keep our eyes on Eric. Anyone who looked down or away was beaten. I watched my only friend in this hellhole die slowly and I could not do anything. I couldn't even cry. I felt so weak and dehydrated that no tears came out. Eric's body had no recognizable form anymore. His body looked like a red-soaked bag that was coming apart at the seams.

As soon as all of the prisoners were done, we were ordered to get back to work. I didn't even have time to contemplate what I had seen that day. That night Peter told me that we foreigners had been sheltered from this style of execution up to this point. Peter had witnessed the Korean prisoners marching to the North quad on several occasions. It was now obvious why. I sat in my bunk and just listened while Peter went on and on about the different torture methods, executions, and other cruelties that were committed in the camps. The whole time I kept thinking about Eric. Eric was the last bastion of decency in this land of evil. I had decided that I would get out of here or die trying.

Chapter 22

"CAMP OF NO RETURN"

October 1993

As though life wasn't hard enough, it was about to get harder. Eric's vicious attack on Mr. Kwon made the camp's leaders uneasy. They were especially concerned about the message it was portraying to the rest of the camp. What if all the prisoners got the idea of going out fighting. For once, prisoners experienced first-hand a prisoner successfully killing a supervisor. Maybe they even thought of the Warsaw Ghetto incident in which the remaining Jews fought valiantly against the Nazis. Not only would the guards be in harm's way, they would have to answer to Pyongyang. Either way, there was a good chance they would encounter violence.

This, I'm sure, was Commandant Lee's number one concern. That was why he would now make all of our lives a living hell. Two days after the execution we were selectively ordered into the interrogation room where we were beaten until we said what they wanted us to say. When my turn came, Commandant Lee was there along with my supervisor, Mr. Lim. Commandant Lee was as cool as ever. He had that same smirk he had when I first met him. This time, his left eye seemed to be twitching uncontrollably. He was probably stressed over the incident with Eric. Peter and I came to the conclusion that Eric's bold move was a first in this particular camp. Korean prisoners were indoctrinated since childhood and less likely to rebel, no matter how dismal the situation.

"Mr. Walker! I was hoping we could have met under better circumstances." Commandant Lee began.

"As you know, the death of Mr. Kwon has affected us very negatively. I'm afraid the situation changes the prisoners' status at this facility. We can no longer allow the prisoners to enjoy the freedoms we provided them in the past."

Freedoms? The word was relative to the speaker. To Commandant Lee, freedom meant five hours of sleep a night as opposed to three.

"You should also be aware," he continued, "that your 'friends' in Pyongyang no longer care about your welfare. Your cowardly acts of disobedience to the state sealed your own fate. If it were not for the 'Dear Leader' himself, you would have been executed already. Now, even the 'Dear Leader' has authorized me to do whatever I need to do in order to maintain absolute discipline here."

I doubt Kim Jong IL had really authorized my execution. Commandant Lee just wanted me gone. He was too worried that I might also follow Eric's example, therefore endangering his position as camp leader.

"Therefore," Commandant Lee continued, "the state has decided to transfer you to a more remote camp where your indoctrination will enter a new phase. This camp specializes in prisoners who have selfishly disregarded *Juche* and the teachings of Kimilsungism. You will leave tomorrow."

With those words, Commandant Lee briskly left the room. That night, Peter and I parted by whispering the night away with stories about our hometowns and regaled each other with childhood stories. Now that I think about it, Peter was a great guy. He was simply a survivor. He was tougher than Eric and me. That was why he had made it this far. I have always wondered what happened to him. One thing is for sure; he probably never left North Korea alive. Hardly anyone from the camps was ever actually released. Those fortunate few who were released were reassigned to remote areas that were virtually prisons anyway.

The next day I was forced into a truck, blindfolded, and made to lie on the floor. I felt two other people lying on each side of me. The guards then got into the truck, stepping on us, probably intentionally. The ride was bumpy and long. I couldn't hold myself and urinated in my pants three quarters through the trip. At times, I could hear the truck getting stuck in the mud and the guards and driver trying to get the truck out. I thought about trying to get up and make a run for it, but I never did.

As I finally managed to fall asleep, I woke to the sounds of screams from the guards to get up.

"*Bali wa! Kea seki ya!* (Let's go! You dogs!).

We were pushed out of the truck and led away by different guards. They yelled at us to run. We were still blindfolded when we were running. Suddenly, I felt the earth below me disappear and I fell into a pit. The guy behind me fell right on top of me. We lay there for a few moments, not knowing what to do next. After a few minutes I felt hands on my face. Someone was undoing my blindfold. I could barely see but it was a scrawny Caucasian man by the looks of him.

I looked all around me. It was dark but I could make out people all around me. We were in some sort of pit that was dug into the ground. Above us were steel bars. They were glistening in the moonlight. The Caucasian man began untying the rope around my hands with a makeshift tool he had. As I got a better glance at him, I was surprised at how thin he was. His features were so remarkable. His eyes and cheeks were sunken in to the point that his cheeks had creases in them. The only protruding facial parts were his nose and chin. He had piercing blue eyes that would frighten even the dead. Yet, he was smiling.

"Where am I?" I asked in English.

The man did not answer me. Strangely enough, I wasn't afraid. I had already accepted my fate. I thought Commandant Lee was going to order my execution. I didn't think I was going to survive that day, let alone make it this far. The man finally loosened the rope enough for me to wiggle out of it.

"Thank you" I said.

"Thank you, pajoust" the man responded with a smile.

"Are you Russian? Russkia?"

I asked, being that he said you're welcome in Russian.

"Romany! Bucharest!" the man corrected me.

At that moment another Caucasian approached us suspiciously. He was twitching and seemed very nervous. He asked the Romanian a question in what seemed like Romanian. The man answered him with what looked like reassuring words. The second man then turned to me and asked in English where I was from. I told him I was an American. He seemed surprised.

"American? What are you doing here?"

I told him the gist of my situation and what had led to my imprisonment. After a short pause, the man led me to the other side of the pit where I saw two other Caucasians, also Romanian. They offered me a seat on the floor next to them. The second Romanian spoke in English to me then explained their situation. All of them were once members of several diplomatic missions in Asia.

They had taken asylum in North Korea after the fall of the Romanian dictator Ceaușescu. However, the North Korean government later betrayed them. They speculated that protests from the new Romanian government probably did not help North Korea's position in the world. Rather than confess that they were harboring the Romanians, they decided to deny it and make the asylum seekers disappear. The asylum seekers tried to outwardly protest their conditions and were therefore sent to the "Camp of No Return."

The official name of the camp was number 22, but the Romanians referred to it as the "camp of no return." I was briefed that night about what our duty was. Basically, we were to work in the rock quarry a mile from the camp from dusk to dawn. They showed me the battle scars from the hard labor they endured night and day. One of them lost his toe to frostbite; another had a permanently disfigured arm from a rock that fell on top of him. He kept working that day because he knew that physically handicapped workers were exterminated.

This was, literally, survival camp. No one here would leave alive. The object of the camp was to work the prisoners to death. It was the last insult the North Korean regime could impose on the unwanted population. Killing us would be a waste of free labor. Why not make us suffer as long as possible. Outright executions were considered too good for us. The guards and warden reminded us that if we worked hard and showed that we had been loyal to the state, we would be freed and reunited with our loved ones. There were constant broadcasts on the loudspeakers of Kim IL Sung's and Kim Jong IL's own assurance of the promise to reeducate us and free us. We were supposed to feel thankful that our lives were spared due to the benevolence of the "Great Leader." Yet none of us had ever seen anyone leave the camp alive.

The only exception to the above rule was the few times that the guards would come by and select several of the prisoners for "special duty." That was the only time I saw prisoners allowed to leave camp. We all had a very good idea of what this "special duty" meant. One of the prisoners at the last camp was once a Special Forces commando who told Peter, Raseem, and I that the elite commandoes practiced on "live" targets. The prisoner told us they had an endless supply of able men from the many prisons throughout the country. They would release the prisoners in the mountainous areas throughout North Korea and make the commandoes track them down with only their own bodies as weapons. It was survival of the fittest. That way, the soldiers would be emboldened to be efficient killing machines. We always thought he was crazy and didn't take his word for it. We just couldn't believe this regime could be that cruel.

Now that story seemed to make more and more sense. One day after one of those "special duty" assignments we heard cracking sounds of shots in the mountains around us. These harrowing sounds echoed throughout the camp hours after several prisoners were taken on this "privileged" duty. It didn't take a nuclear scientist to tie in these two events. It reminded me of the story I had read in high school, "The Most Dangerous Game." The story was about a general by the name of Zaroff who was bored with the conventional hunting of animals and wanted a challenge. He purposefully wrecked ships around the island on which he lived so that he could capture the crew and then hunt them throughout the island. Humans are the real barbarians, not the animal kingdom. Only us humans could take pleasure in killing.

In fact, the camp would serve to be hell for every prisoner. Most prisoners were here because of political or ideological "disagreements" with the state. What that meant was open to interpretation. There were Christians and Buddhists here. Kim IL Sung had always feared religion because he himself was the son of a priest and knew how influential religion could be. Kim had created his own religion and delegated himself as God. Other prisoners were in this camp because of an accusation laid upon them by a jealous coworker or because of their family's "questionable allegiance" to Kim IL Sung and Kim Jong IL. It was a frustrating and demoralizing notion to know that anyone at anytime in North Korea could be accused of and sentenced to a concentration camp like this one.

Yet, despite our impending doom, most prisoners wanted to live and endured the harsh conditions. People can't understand this until they live in such an environment. I guess that was what kept people going in during the Holocaust. I used to be a skeptic of how the Jews and others imprisoned by the Nazis allowed themselves to be led to the gas chambers. Why did they not fight back, knowing they were going to a terrible place? Now, I understood. I could relate to the state of mind they were probably in. I also wanted to believe that no human being could put another human being through such misery. I just could not believe it.

The next day we were woken up by screams from the guards above us. A ladder was hoisted down and we climbed it one at a time. Now that it was daylight, I could see that there were more than twenty men in our hole. As we climbed out I was taken aback by all the other holes and other prisoners making their way out of the holes. It looked like a horizontal honeycomb of caverns in an open, muddy field. On both sides of the field were steep hills and barbed wire fences at the bottom of each hill.

I saw a few guards, one with a dog, patrolling the fences (the dog was a *Chindogae*, a native species of Korea that come from the Southern island of Chindo. These dogs are usually aggressive and therefore used as guard dogs.). The only entrance and watchtower I could see was at the southern opening of the field we were in. On the other side, the field came to an end and I could see some sort of barracks with army trucks parked outside.

We headed in the direction of the barracks towards the point where the two hills seemed to meet. There was a dirt road that led up the canyon and eventually into a quarry. That was where we would spend our entire day. The work consisted of the guards placing a stick of dynamite into the rock walls, and then detonating it. After the explosion, we would rush over, pick up the stones, and put them into wheelbarrows. Other prisoners then took the stones all the way down the hill and dumped them in piles. That was all we did all day long. We were not given any break time, food, or water. Luckily for me, it was springtime and the weather was neither too hot nor too cold.

That night I was physically exhausted to the point that I could not feel my limbs. I had blisters all over my feet and hands. I was not used to working so hard. At the previous camp I just had mental, not physical work. A guard came by our hole and dropped a pot of half cooked corn and beans on the steal bars. All of us rushed and grabbed with our hands as much as we could. I forgot how tired I felt and lunged at the food with all the strength I had left. The four Romanians were close knit. They took care of themselves and fought off the other Koreans in our hole. Because they stuck together, they had priorities when it came to food. Luckily for me, they liked me and included me in their group. This became the most important reason why I made it almost an entire year in the "Camp of No Return."

I later learned the names of the four Romanians: Marek, George, Vladimir, and Matei. They taught me some Romanian and I corrected their English. Even under these horrible conditions, I maintained my interest in other cultures. I still remember saying: "Chifache?" to them in the mornings, and hearing a chorus of "bine!" Despite the fact that we knew we had another day of backbreaking work, we greeted each other with a forced smile. I persisted for almost a year under these conditions. A triumph considering the limitations any human can endure. I can't help but wonder whether or not I would have survived without my Romanian friends by my side.

Another bit of solace I managed to find was from the short walk to the quarry everyday. The path to the quarry led us through a ravine, which was lined with pine trees on each side. It was one of the only places where they had not cut down the trees. All over North Korea people were cutting down trees because of the dire energy shortages. These pine trees were on the steep hills, which overlooked our camp and especially the guard barracks. They probably kept the trees there for fear of mudslides during the rainy season. Pine trees were the best deterrent to that. The trees also kept the guards cool in the summer. Seeing those pine trees endure the harsh seasons of North Korea and the grade at which they lived lifted my spirits and reminded me that life can go on even in the most inhospitable places.

Inhospitable was not a strong enough word to describe that camp. Neither was inhumane or cruel. The camp had brought the worst out in human beings. In the camp, people ate rats, bugs, grass, even wood. They ate anything that would provide a source of protein. People died every day at the camp from malnutrition, disease, or exhaustion. The guards did not have to torment us. We were already beaten by the natural elements of hunger and weakness. Luckily for me, I had resourceful Romanians on my side that did not know what the word "beaten" meant.

Two of the Romanians, Matei and Vladimir, bribed a guard with one of their only remaining possessions, a gold crown tooth (Matei pulled it out of his own mouth by using a piece of string), to be on the "graveyard duty." This job was coveted because it was the only time the guards did not supervise the prisoners closely. Everyday, the prisoners had to remove the dead to a remote corner of the camp. The bodies were simply dumped in a ditch and later used as fertilizer. That's right, the guards actually used humans as fertilizer. The place stank so badly that no guard dared follow the prisoners there. Instead, they would wait a few meters away while the prisoners dumped the bodies.

Because the ditch was on a slope, the guards could not see into the ditch or behind it. The prisoners took advantage of the unsupervised time to catch as many rats and mice as they could and also collect any items that were left on the dead bodies such as socks or gold teeth. The place where they buried the bodies was infested with rodents who were eating the carcasses. The tragic irony was that the prisoners ate the rodents that ate the dead bodies. The Romanians would barter with the guards for anything they got from the dead prisoners, like more gold teeth or leather from the shoes. In return, the guards would give them matches and blankets. We would sometimes roast the rat meat and pick it to the bone. This was how we survived.

Winter came and went, so did Spring. I had made it through the most crucial period. North Korean winters are deadly and can be long. Luckily for me, it was a mild year. It rained heavily that year, however, and we sometimes were used to clear and rebuild washed away roads in the province. It was during one of these trips that I realized where we were. We were in the North Hamgyong Province. The guards tried to shield us from any information to keep us in the dark. The prison even had a sign saying we were in South Pyongang province. However, during one of our digging expeditions on a damaged road we recovered a sign that was washed away by the rain. The sign read: "Najin 23km, Sonbong 35." North Korea had very few functioning roads. Both these cities were coastal cities in North Hamgyong Province. From the position of the sun, the season, and the time of day, I calculated that we must be just southwest of those cities.

North Hamgyong was the only province that bordered both China and Russia. It was considered a natural barrier because of its heavily guarded borders and extreme terrain. Jagged steep mountains surrounded the Province with only a thin access to the sea. North Hamgyong Province had been turned into a virtual prison camp due to the recurring acts of rebellion in recent years. It was also a welcoming inspiration for me. Escaping from prison was one thing, but trying to pass as a normal Korean would be impossible once I had escaped. The fact that our prison was so close to the border with China raised my spirits. Maybe I could still make it out of North Korea in one piece.

One piece but a very thin one. I was rapidly loosing weight and strength. I remember how one night I was shocked to learn that I could wrap my fingers around my biceps. I used to have fairly large biceps. Not any more. I was so weak that I could not feel anger, sorrow, and of course, happiness. I was so malnourished I couldn't even shed tears. I was in a constant haze. I kept pushing myself to work hard so that the guards would not pick on me or worse, get rid of me. Those who could not work any longer were executed.

That summer was extremely hot and would signal the most dramatic change in North Korean history. One hot summer day while working at the quarry we were given the news that Kim IL Sung had passed away. The guards were weeping when they delivered the news and barked at us to show our respect. We all bowed deeply in sign of respect. Many prisoners also cried and fell to the ground in despair. We "*Oeguks*" (foreigners) could not put on a show and just kept bowing to show our respects. I am sure that I wasn't the only prisoner there who was secretly delighted with the news. It was the first piece of good news I had received in years.

That night, I couldn't help but speculate what would be the outcome. Would the North Korean regime admit their failures and make room for change? Would there be an internal struggle for power? Would the outside world intervene? What would happen to us prisoners? Kim Jong IL was the heir apparent. His father had groomed him and he had sucked up to his father. The question was whether or not his other half brothers had any power left. Another question was whether the old cronies of Kim IL Sung would let Kim Jong IL take over.

As I mentioned before, Kim Jong IL was no weakling. He was a cunning, methodological killer who had planned for this event. He had made himself useful by sucking up to his father, putting himself in authoritative and military positions, and spinning a web of propaganda promoting his image to North Koreans. He had discredited his half brothers and eliminated their base of support (My first director at Kim IL Sung University, Dr. Han, was one of those supporter). It was very likely that Kim Jong IL would take his father's place and nothing would change.

What did change was the uncertainty that shrouded our camp. The guards, who were already unpredictable, now looked as worried as we were. The irrational system known as *Juche*, coupled with agricultural mismanagement had led North Korea down a spiraling path of destruction. Even before I was arrested, I had noticed the shortages even in Pyongyang of basic goods and foods. It was a sign of worse things to come. Now, the situation was out of hand. Our guards almost stopped feeding us completely and could barely find enough food for themselves. I would see many guards leave their posts during their duty to go look for food and wood in the outlying areas.

Right after Kim IL Sung's death, the guards looked uneasy. To me, it was a message that they did not know who was in control. This was the time we had waited for. I had planned my escape since the day I had set foot at the "Camp of No Return." The Romanians and I would always discuss the possibilities of escape. Marek thought the best way was to hide in the pits with the corpses and escape at night. Vladimir suggested digging around the steel bars at night and escaping as soon as the hole was big enough. That was too risky, the other hole-mates with us would have squealed on us for a reward. I had a better idea. I had noticed that recently there was less and less supervision at the rock quarry. The guards were probably using the time to gather wood or hunt birds. We could make a break for it when the guards were not looking.

Still, how could five of us get the same break and escape unnoticed? I was not planning on that scenario. I was going to selfishly slip away without even telling the Romanians. I thought it was the only way I could escape. The guards would notice if all the "*Oeguks*" made a run for it. Besides, there was a good possibility that we would not all be assigned to the quarry. Mattei and Vladimir played favorite with the guards in order to get more rewarding duties.

A week had gone by since the news of the death of Kim IL Sung and no official word about who was to take over. One day, the guards were late in letting us out of our holes and did not provide any food for us. The guards seemed preoccupied with the current situation and less interested in watching over our work details. I knew I had to act soon. Matei and George did not agree with my reasoning. They thought that just like with the Romanian revolution in 1989, the death of Kim IL Sung would herald in a new era of democratic changes. They were going to wait out the storm in hopes of being freed by the new regime.

I, on the other hand, had seen how manipulative the North Korean regime was and how brainwashed the North Korean population had become. The traditional Confucius system facilitated a culture with despotic leaders and therefore would not influence North Koreans to demand freedoms or regime change. Sure, there was a period of uncertainty right now, but I was sure that Kim Jong IL would soon take over his father's position and that nothing would change. I knew that this period of uncertainty was my only window of opportunity to save my life by escaping the death camp.

That night I glanced for the last time at the lone pine tree that was visible from my hole. It was an unusually warm night and a refreshing wind swept through as if cleaning the death camp with its pure wind. For once, I didn't smell the stench of death and disease. I didn't smell the urine or defecation that usually filled the stale air. That light breeze gave me hope. I felt, for the first time in a while, a sense of optimism. Optimism is relevant to one's surroundings. I thought back about all the times I viewed life through my critical lenses. I remembered how I once perceived my parents, my neighborhood, my school, my city, and my country as authoritarian. That night, my olfactory senses were all it took to put me in such a good mood. I stood there with my head against the cold steel bars breathing in that fresh air. For the first time in ages, a smile dawned my weathered face.

Chapter 23

ESCAPE

1994

The following day brought more good news. Many of the guards at our camp had left in the middle of the night. I had heard a truck leave at night and could only assume the guards were on it. Why? At the moment I didn't care. That day, the guards were late again in opening our cages. Now that most of the guards were gone, the prisoners greatly outnumbered the remaining guards. That day in the quarry there were only three guards supervising us. That meant that they could not watch all of us all of the time. Luckily for me, I was not the only one thinking of escaping that day.

As we made our way down the path to dump the rocks, two prisoners darted into the open field towards the hill. The guards began shooting at them and all hell broke loose. Suddenly, we were all running in different directions. Our hypothesis had proven right, though. The guards discouraged any escape plan we had by informing us of the landmines that were planted around the camp. The Romanians and I had thought it was just a deterrent so that we would not try to escape. As we all ran through the fields, we realized the only threat to our lives were the bullets whizzing by us. As I ran, I heard shots in my direction and then I heard a man groan and fall behind me. I didn't even glance back to look. I just kept running.

After what seemed like an eternity, I finally reached the hillside and took cover behind some boulders. I caught my breath, and then continued to run up the hill. The hill was steep, but small. I made it to the top and began to run down in a perpendicular way, away from the camp. I was now in a forested area. I kept hearing footsteps of someone running in my direction, cracking branches with no regard for the noise he was stirring up. I looked back and saw another prisoner huffing and puffing right behind me. He ran right up to me, tapped my shoulder, pointed straight, and continued running. I followed him with hesitation. I thought my chances might be better alone. Still, I followed him.

We ran alongside a small creek for a few more miles before we stopped and drank some water. Being good at directions, I had noticed that the man was leading me in an Eastward direction instead of Northward, towards the Chinese border. From the direction of the sun I could pretty much tell north from south anywhere in Korea. I asked the man in Korean where we were heading.

"*Amnokgang*" The man replied.

Amnok River, also known in Chinese as the Tumen River, ran along the mountainous border of North Korea and China. This was what I wanted to hear. Joining up with this fellow wasn't so bad after all. As we sat there drinking water, the man began searching the immediate area around the creek. He picked up a log and pulled out what looked liked mushrooms. He started eating them and handed me a handful as well.

"*Mashiseyo!*"

Dong Hak looked at me with a smile.

It was "*Mashiseyo.*" It was the most delicious thing I had had for years. I remember seeing mushrooms all along the woods by my house back in San Francisco. As a kid, I was tempted to eat them, knowing full well that some could be poisonous. As I nibbled on the mushrooms, the man came back with what looked like tree leaves.

Bali moguyo!" (Eat these quickly).

The man explained that the leaves were a good source of nutrients. After eating quickly, the man motioned me to follow him. We walked briskly for a few more miles until it was pitch black. It was cloudy that night and the moon was not visible. We followed the sound of the creek, occasionally stumbling over some rocks or into a pit. It was eerily quiet. Not a single sound with the exception of our footsteps. One advantage we had was that it was the middle of summer and it was actually more bearable at night than during the day.

We continued for a few more hours before we reached a point where the creek approached a dirt road and an open field. We cautiously observed our new surroundings before the man signaled me to follow him. We continued to follow the creek, which was the lowest point in the open field. Occasionally, the man would look over the embankment to see where we were. We finally reached an area of thick shrubbery and high grass. We both decided it would be a good spot to rest and hide. Dawn was approaching and we were both exhausted. We must have traveled twenty or thirty miles that day.

We pushed down the grass in the middle and made sure not to damage the grass around us so that we would remain undetected. While I lay there exhausted, the man began to collect the sticks around us. He used the long grass to tie the sticks together in the shape of a cone. He then left and walked down to the creek. He came back a few minutes later with some plants he had collected. He offered some to me and told me to chew on them. They contained some nutrients that would give me energy, he insisted. I was beginning to think I was very fortunate to have found this guy. He was a survival expert.

He later explained to me that everyone in the village he came from knew these techniques. His name was Bae Gun and he had come from the Northeast. His area had suffered tremendously and many people in his area had to resort to extreme means in order to survive. Bae Gun had told me that rumors about cannibalism were not rumors at all. They were absolutely true. He knew of many places where human flesh was sold. It was sold as pork meat because it tasted like and looked like pork meat. It was also considered the only meat to be found in North Korea. Yet many knew it wasn't pork meat at all. He had even heard of people murdering weaker people, especially street children, and selling their meat.

To make ends meat Bae Gun and his brother sold sheet metal they had stolen from an abandoned factory outside their village. They were caught by the national police and thrown in a work camp. He was later transferred to our camp because he came from a "rebellious" region in North Korea. He was being collectively punished for the attitudes the top brass had towards that region. His brother had died at the camp a month after they arrived. He had also planned his escape before with the goal of making it to the Chinese border. He knew how to swim and the best place to cross the border.

The best place to cross was in the steep mountainous area of North Hamgyong Province. It was so remote that the guard posts were few and far between. We would follow the creek for another few miles until it caught up with another creek coming from the North. We would then follow that creek another few miles up the mountains. On the other side of those mountains was the border with China. We would wait until nightfall and swim across the river. Once in China, Bae Gun had heard there were South Korean missionaries that would hide us, feed us, and transfer us to Shenyang. Shenyang was the largest city in the

Yanbian Korean autonomous region of China. It was also the best place a North Korean and a Westerner could blend in.

That day we laid low in our hideaway. I was physically exhausted, not just from our trek, but from months of excruciating forced labor. I fell in and out of a deep sleep. I kept waking up thinking the prison guards were poking us with sticks to keep themselves entertained. Each noise startled me and put me on edge. One time we heard voices. People were yelling at one another. We later realized it was just a couple of farmers in the fields above us. Still, I couldn't sleep after that. I was afraid they would mistakenly discover us and alert the authorities. The thoughts of killing these farmers ran through my mind. Was I capable of murder? After what I had gone through I was probably capable of much more. I wanted to survive. I didn't come this far to die.

As we lay there, Bae Gun reached through the grass and pulled one of the crops from the stem.

"*Yak Tambae!*" He whispered.

"*Chinja?*" (Really?) I asked.

Yak Tambae referred to the combinations of the words Medicinial and Tobacco. It was the name given to opium. I had heard rumors long ago about the North Korean government resorting to growing opium just to keep the cash flow for the regime and its military. Bae Gun showed me the flower and squeezed it until a white gooey cream oozed out of it. He told me he had see it before. Some farmers in his *Myon* or county were forced to switch their crops to opium by the government. Soldiers occasionally patrolled the fields and strangers were kept out so that no information could be leaked. Another reason for us to lay very low and not make a sound.

As soon as the sun set that day, Bae Gun and I headed down towards the creek. As I was drinking from the creek, Bae Gun walked into the deeper end and pulled out the makeshift cone he had made the night before. Inside were three small fish. I couldn't believe it. His contraption worked. The fish evidently had swum through the wider side of the cone and could not figure a way out. That night we had a feast. Bae Gun had also dug up what had looked like crawfish from the sandbanks. For the first time in months my stomach was actually full.

Right after our feast we headed out. The night was very clear and the half moon reflected off the waters of the creek as we made our way Eastward. After a couple of hours we reached the crossing tributaries of another creek. After inspecting it for a while, Bae Gun became convinced it was the creek we were looking for. I was so happy that we had reached it so soon. What I hadn't realized was how difficult our task was ahead of us.

As we started up the second creek northward, we heard noises. There was a small village just over the embankment and a road that paralleled the creek. We crept our way towards the noises, keeping our heads down. As we approached the village, we could hear people talking. There were many voices, some talking at the same time, some seemed to be angry. We stopped for a minute and tried to listen. It sounded like a community meeting between all the villagers.

One man was complaining about the gasoline shortages. He was afraid that if they could not use the tractor, the crops would be wasted come harvest time. Another man cut him off saying that there wouldn't even be a harvest. Another man chimed in that he wanted to know what the district officer of their *Eup*, or county, had to say about the "current conditions." The radio supposedly had nothing new to report. Another man seemed to be pleading for the sake of his sick child. He wanted to know when the government would permit him to travel outside the *Eup* to seek medical help.

"Comrades, comrades, please! We must bear in mind that our Great Leader had just passed away. Let's show our respect to him." A deep voiced venerated over everyone else.

"We must remember that our "Dear Leader" Grand Marshall Kim Jong IL is still mourning his father and the father of our homelands. We must be patient. We must show our support. In due time, he will reward us for our allegiance to *Juche* and to the Fatherland."

"How do we know who is in charge? I heard that his own troops have moved against him."

One man commented.

"How dare you speak such lies? Do you want the entire village to suffer from your false accusations? Show some respect! We must not get involved in any opposition movements. I am old enough to remember how many times people believed that the government would change. It never happened and it never will. We must accept our fate and worry about providing a good harvest for our Dear Leader, Kim Jong IL."

"The Dear Leader has blessed us with a good life, but what do we do about the shortages? We haven't received any supplies for three weeks now." An elderly sounding woman chimed in.

"I have been in contact with the provincial government. They have assured me all supplies will arrive…"

"My child needs medical attention, what about a doctor?"

Another woman interrupted.

"Such insolence! You don't even let me finish. I told you we will be getting supplies and attention very soon. Your complaints are not constructive to the cause. My generation had it much worse during the war against the imperialists, but we endured. We endured and the victories and benevolence of our 'Dear Leader' were fruitful. Show your patriotism!"

Bae Gun and I listened with great interest to the discussion. At times the conversations were muffled by the wind, but the gist of the conversation was enough to tell us that there was a period of uncertainty sweeping North Korea. Who was in control? Was the army really moving against Kim Jong IL? How would this affect our situation? One thing was for sure; we shouldn't stick around for the outcome. We should take advantage of the confusion and make our escape. Bae Gun then tapped me on the shoulder and motioned me to keep going.

As we continued up the creek bed, I suddenly slipped on some pebbles, igniting a chain reaction of stones falling into the creek.

"*Ya! Gugi nuguya?*" (who's there?) A voice asked.

Bea Gun and I stopped in our tracks and waited. We must have been at the outskirts of the village by now. We heard footsteps heading towards the creek where we were. The footsteps came closer and closer. I was lying behind some grass, while Bae Gun took cover beside the embankment. Suddenly, I saw a man walk over to the edge of the embankment and stop right above where Bae Gun was hiding. I sat there petrified for what seemed like an eternity as the man stood there. He was looking right at the location where I was hiding. The grass I lay behind was only about two feet tall and not so thick. Could he see me? Should I make a run for it? Before I could even make a decision, Bae Gun suddenly leaped up from his hiding spot and grabbed the man's legs with both his hands.

Everything happened so fast. The man let out a shriek as Bae Gun tackled and jumped on top of him. At first, I hesitated as they rolled around, struggling. Suddenly, the man got his breath and yelled for help. At this point I got up, ran over, and jumped on him, grabbing his head. I cupped my hand around his mouth as Bae Gun held his waist. The man seemed to be elderly and not so strong. He did, however, give us a fight. He tried to bite my hand and scratch my face with his hands. Meanwhile, Bae Gun was using his knee to strike sharp blows to his side while holding his legs together with his arms.

As the man continued to struggle and scratch me, I slid one of my arms around his neck and began to choke him. I used every ounce of strength I had in me. Before I realized it, the man had passed out and went limp. As soon as he fell, Bae Gun rushed over to the creek, seemingly looking for something. He picked up a big rock and carried it over. He stood over the unconscious man, raised the rock, and slammed it down on the head of the man. The man's skull dented under the pressure of the blow and a stream of blood rushed down from his head. Bae Gun picked up the rock again and smashed it down against the man head. He did this several times until there was no semblance of the man's head anymore.

Bae Gun signaled to me to help him pick up the body. We carried it over to the tall grass right below where I had hidden. Bae Gun and I began to dig a hole with our hands in the middle of the grassy area. The soil was damp, therefore easy to dig up, because it was so close to the creek. Before long, we had a shallow grave long enough for the body. We dumped the body, filled in the grave, and tried to cover the area by propping up the grass around it. We then crept up the embankment where the man had come from to see if his cries for help had alerted anyone. All was quiet. Feeling safe, we hurriedly made our way along the creek in the direction of the mountains.

We continued for several more miles before we reached the slopes of the first set of mountains. After following the creek for another mile or so, Bae Gun pointed to a small tributary we would now follow. It was a very steep climb, sometimes over big boulders and slippery cliffs. I could hear the sounds of small waterfalls along the way. I felt like stopping several times but kept going. Bae Gun did not stop so I thought it best not to hinder our pace. We reached the top of the first mountain just as the sun was peeking over the second set of mountains. I was surprised that Bae Gun kept going even though it was becoming daytime. I didn't ask him why. I just kept going.

We followed the rim of the mountain for a few minutes until Bae Gun decided to stop. He had found an opening in the forest where he could assess the area. He motioned to me and pointed at the v-shaped area between two sets of mountains. There I saw the river we were looking for. The Tumen River was the last natural barrier between North Korea and China. I was ecstatic to see it. I wanted to run down there, dive in it, and swim as fast as I could.

As I continued to gaze at the river, Bae Gun began the shelter and food search. He found us a nice spot behind some tall grass and a mound of dirt that rolled down a small rock-face. Surrounding it were several pine trees. We laid the pine needles down for bedding. Bae Gun collected some of the pinecones and showed me how to pull out the pine nuts.

That night we had a feast of wild berries, pine nuts, and roots of a plant Bae Gun assured me would build up my energy level. I needed it. As we lay down to sleep, I thought about what we had done to that man. I helped kill a man that day, yet I did not feel remorseful. It was a survival instinct. I wanted to live and that man was in my way. At this point in my life I didn't care about human life, I would have killed Bae Gun if he had gotten in my way. I wanted to get out of North Korea.

We slept that day until late in the afternoon, at which time Bae Gun prepared some food to take with us to eat along the way. We set out around dusk. We made good time because it was mostly downhill. When we reached an opening in the forest, we made our way cautiously. Bae Gun warned me about possible border patrols and guard posts. He was actually surprised that we had not run into any yet. I asked him about minefields, but he assured me they were only along the border with South Korea.

Suddenly, as we were descending a steep embankment, Bae Gun motioned me to get down on the ground. I looked at him to see what had happened. He was looking intently at a certain spot below us. As I looked carefully, I noticed a shack on top of a small cliff. Outside the shack was a small half-domed-wall with a mounted machine gun on it. It was a border patrol station. Bae Gun had told me earlier that there were stations ever few miles. The guards would make their hourly rounds between each station. Either we waited until the next round went by or risked it and went now.

I just had a hunch that the guards would not bother to do their rounds in the middle of the night. I was also anxious to cross the river that night. What if we waited and the guards never did their rounds? That meant we might have to wait until dawn. I worried that during the following day, the guards might discover us. Bae Gun agreed with me. He warned me to watch my step. The guards could have set up booby traps around the border near the river. North Korea was becoming concerned with the growing number of defectors over the past few years. It was possible that the army had set up traps and surveillance of the border areas. It was also clear that the orders were "shoot to kill." North Korea was not taking chances.

We crept by the guard post some distance, always keeping an eye out to see if there was any movement inside. The post was so still that it almost seemed abandoned. This short stretch seemed like hours of snail's pace movement. My heart was beating so fast I actually thought I was having a heart attack. We inched our way past the post and towards the river. I could now hear the roaring river as we approached it. The sound of the rushing water was like music to my ears.

Bae Gun warned me a few nights before that the strong currents might overwhelm us. However, we shouldn't panic and just continue to swim in the direction of the other shore. Bae Gun did not know how deep it was, but he was sure it was over our heads in some spots. The river did not look that dangerous, but Bae Gun warned it was deceiving. Even good swimmers were lost in these currents.

We stopped just short of the river and assessed the situation. There were no fences or warnings in sight. I guess no one imagined people would get this far. We looked over to the Chinese side to discover that there were no army posts there as well, at least none that we could see. We started to walk into the water. I felt the cold waters of the Tumen River fill my worn out shoes. It felt good, refreshing. I walked deep into the river for several meters before the water was up to my shoulders. I then began to swim and found the river to be easy to maneuver in. After a few minutes of breaststroke I could see that I was two-thirds there. I kept silent in the water so as not to arouse anyone who might be around the banks of the river.

Suddenly, I noticed a spotlight on the banks of the Chinese side. I panicked! Were they looking for us? Did they spot us? The light was moving back and forth across the banks of the river. After a few minutes the light faded away. I continued to swim towards the Chinese side. By now, I must have drifted half a mile from where I first entered the river.

I reached the shore of the other side and made my way up to a patch of grass. As I crawled up the bank of the river through the grass, I felt a sharp object stab me in the wrist. It was too dark that night to see much, but I felt it was some kind of bone. I slid my thumb and index finger down the length of this crooked bone until I reached something I will never forget to this day. It was the remains of a human skeleton with patches of flesh and clothing still attached in some areas. I recoiled in horror only to discover two more bodies behind me. I let out a tiny shriek that seemed uncontrollable.

I stopped dead cold and waited to see if anyone had heard my shriek or the noise I had made climbing over these dead bodies. Nothing! I crawled over the two other bodies and into the patch of grass at the top of the bank. I had a good vantage point from this bank yet the grass was tall enough that I could not be seen.

I looked around to see whether or not Bae Gun had made it, but I could not find any trace of him. The sounds of the river muted any other noises. I then crisscrossed through the heaviest part of the grass until I reached some bushes. I looked for any signs of Chinese border posts or patrols. My fears had by now subsided because I knew that even if I were caught, I could lie my way out of any return to North Korea. Unlike Bae Gun, I was a Westerner who definitely did not look like he belonged in North Korea. I would make up a lie and tell the Chinese authorities that I was kidnapped by North Korean agents and taken against my will. They would most surely hand me over to the Americans or keep me in China. At least that was what I thought.

Of course, my ultimate goal was not to get caught at all. I really didn't think too much of what I would do once I had crossed into China because I never thought it was possible. To me, leaving North Korea was a matter of life and death by now. I knew I would have died if I had stayed there. I still wanted to live. A deep sense of relief set into my entire body as I sat there in the tall grass. However, I knew that I still had to make my way inland while it was still dark. The more distance I could make into China, the less likely it would be that Chinese border patrol or police would question me.

I made my way through the grass into a ditch by an open field. I followed the ditch for a few miles, occasionally running across dirt roads and paths. The ditch led me right to a village and ended right behind the village at an aqueduct. The aqueduct ran up the hill behind the village. As I made my way past the aqueduct, I tripped over some rocks and fell. Suddenly, a chorus of barking from the village dogs commenced. I ducted behind the concrete structure and waited. I heard one man come out and yell. After that, the dogs stopped barking and the man went back inside.

It took me about thirty minutes to reach the top of the hill. There was a small clearing with a graveyard in the middle. In the distance, I could see a valley with a few lights around. I thought it must be a good sign considering it was now three or four in the morning. There was probably an urban place there where I could blend in and find shelter.

Bae Gun told me that there were some Christian missions run by South Koreans and Westerners that would help us. I had to decide whether or not I should risk it that night. The sun would rise soon and I didn't want to be caught in my dirty torn rags wandering the streets in daylight. I was also completely exhausted and didn't know if I could make it any further. My wet shoes had almost completely disintegrated and my blisters were killing me.

I decided that the best idea was to stay on top of the hill until the next night. That way, I would be well rested and have the entire next night to wander around incognito and find a mission or somewhere I could take shelter. I found a good spot behind some old graves surrounded by thick bushes. I patted down my bedding with grass and laid down. It was fortunately another clear night and I found myself staring at the stars, contemplating all that I had been through. It was there that it finally sank in that I was free. Free from death, free from tyranny, free from hunger and pain. Nothing could compare to what I had gone through. As I fell asleep, I heard my old companions, the pine trees, swaying in the late-night winds.

The following day I waited patiently until nightfall. The only sign of life on that hill that day was a herd of goats wandering about, eating the tall grass that grew in the graveyard. That night I made my way down the hill and through some fields in the direction of the lights I had seen the night before. I reached a town after an hour or so. The town was still active, with an occasional bicyclist riding by. I tried to look inconspicuous and kept my head down. I reached what looked like the town center because it was in an open square. I quickly turned down an alley when I noticed a police station in the middle of the square.

I kept to the alleys and crisscrossed the town looking for a church. At the end of one of the streets I saw a large building with the sign of the cross on the windows. It was a church or a mission. I canvassed the area before I approached the side door. I checked to see if the door was open. It was. I slowly and quietly made my way in. The door led into a hallway. At the end of the hallway was a large room with chairs laid out in rows and a pulpit at the front. I walked across the room to another door and opened it slowly.

Suddenly, I heard someone talking in Chinese. It seemed to be in a question form. I couldn't understand him so I just stood there quietly. He repeated his question again. He then asked in Korean "*Nuguseyo?*" with a distinct South Korean accent. I repeated that I was a Canadian tourist who got separated from his group tour. I knew better than to tell the truth. By now I was all too familiar how far the North Korean spy agency reached. I could not trust anyone, not even a priest.

The man approached me slowly and asked how I had learned to speak Korean so well. His voice had a suspicious tone. I explained to him that I had learned it in college and had traveled to South Korea several times. By now we were facing each other and by the light of the moon shining through the window we could see each other clearly. He was a tall, middle-aged Korean man with soft eyes and a deep voice. I could tell from the first moment I saw him that he was a warm-hearted person.

"What happened to you?" He asked with surprise as he looked at my ragged appearance. I told him that I had to walk for miles until I had found this town. I then changed the subject by asking him if he had anything to drink or eat. After a few seconds of hesitation, he motioned me to follow him. He took me to a back room, which was the kitchen, and motioned for me to sit down on a mat that was in the corner of the room. He gave me some water and a bowl of cold rice with some pickled side dishes. As I began to devour the food, the man motioned to me to slow down.

"*Chonchonhee!*" (Eat slowly!)

He said as he warned me not to eat too quickly for fear of hurting my digestive system. At that moment I remembered what had happened to the Holocaust survivors who were freed by the allied and Russian troops from the concentration camps during World War II. Some of them had died or became very ill from overeating because their digestive systems were too small to take that amount of food all at once. I remembered those pictures of the bony survivors at that moment and looked over at my own arms. I was now nothing but skin and bones. I could see every bone in my hand. The whole time I was in prison I never once stopped to look at myself. I now looked like one of those Holocaust survivors.

The nice man introduced himself as Reverend Park. He had started this church with the money he had collected from Korean Americans and Korean Canadians. He had made a trip there to explain the situation of the North Koreans and ended up with enough money to start a mission here and another one on the Southwestern border with North Korea. He divided his time between the two missions. The Chinese government allowed him to operate the mission so long as he did not proselytize to Korean Chinese or harbor North Korean defectors. He was only allowed to carry out humanitarian aid and keep a small congregation of existing Christians. Of course, he defied the Chinese government by doing what he was not allowed to: Aid, harbor, and acclimate North Korean defectors into Chinese life.

Reverend Park explained to me that I was in the Yanbian Korean Autonomous region, which was predominantly ethnic Korean. There were a couple of million Korean Chinese in the region and thousands of North Koreans hiding among them. The Chinese and North Korean governments were not very pleased with this and were trying to crack down on North Korean refugees. North Koreans in Yanbian were still not out of danger. North Korean spies camouflaged themselves as refugees and would sometimes kidnap or kill defectors. The Chinese police were also stepping up their inspections of local citizens in order to weed out defectors.

North Korean defectors stood out like sore thumbs because they neither spoke Chinese, nor dressed like Chinese. They looked like lost puppies among the more Capitalist savvy Korean Chinese. That was why it was important for his mission to hide these North Koreans and help them adjust to Chinese life. He knew many sympathetic Korean Chinese who were willing to risk their livelihood by employing and harboring North Koreans in their businesses and homes. There were a few, however, who were selfish and would report North Korean defectors to the local police for a monetary reward. That was why he had to be very careful whom he approached.

Reverend Park sat there for a few seconds and studied me closely. He then sat up straight and slapped my bony knee.

"I know how we can get you home." He began to speak.

"I have a friend who make weekly trips to the port city of Dalian. It is a large port city with a sizeable foreign population. I am sure you could find a way to get home from there. In the meantime, you can stay here and build up your strength."

He showed me to a small room where several other people were sleeping on the floor. I fell asleep as soon as my head hit the pillow. I stayed at the mission for over a week before Reverend Park told me that he had arranged for me to go to Dalian. That week I had learned that my roommates were also defectors/refugees. I got to know a couple of them, the rest of my roommates did not trust me even with Reverend Park's assurance that I was not a "Foreign devil spy who came to kill them and eat their intestines." The indoctrination North Koreans receive is hard to break even for those who escape North Korea. A couple of them would not sleep in the same room with me because they thought I would try to kill them while they slept.

The night before I was to leave, Reverend Park and I had a heart to heart talk with his promise to keep my identity secret. He prayed for my safe voyage and health. As someone who grew up in an agnostic household and believed that Religion was the opiate of the masses, I felt a spiritual connection that night. Regardless of what faith Reverend Park represented, his mission was a just one. After twenty years of living in an atheist country, I was now taking refuge in a holy place.

The next morning a truck pulled up to the back of the church and I climbed into the back. The trip took two days. The whole time I lay behind some boxes with a blanket, a bottle of water, and some rice Reverend Park had packed for me. The following day I could hear the noises of cars, buses, and motorcycles all around the truck. We had arrived in Dalian. The truck made a complete stop minutes later. The driver got out and opened the tarp at the back of the truck. He whispered to me to get out and follow him. It was nighttime and we seemed to be in an alley by the harbor (I could smell the sea).

The driver took me to a small door with a neon light above it. It was some sort of inn or motel. A woman greeted us and showed me to a room. The driver then paid the woman, smiled at me and left. I never got to know his name or anything about him. He was just another honest individual who wanted to help those in need. The room was windowless with a futon, blanket, pillow, and a washbasin in the corner. Although I was dead tired that night, I stayed up most of the night reminiscing about my childhood and what led my life on the Korean peninsula. I tried to put different scenarios in my head of what other course I could have taken in life. It finally dawned on me that what happened, happened. I should now look to the future.

Chapter 24

FINAL NOTES

1995

I spent a couple of weeks in Dalian, contemplating my next moves. I spent most of that time in my room, only going out to the market outside the motel to get food. I also went a couple of times to the American cultural center. Reverend Park had given me enough money to get by for the time being. Still, I was terribly afraid that the North Korean secret police were looking for me. It wasn't hard to figure out that their "top foreign movie star" was missing. There were many North Korean agents in China among the Korean refugee population. They were there to eliminate or bring them back to North Korea. The Chinese government turned a blind eye to this because they did not want the refugee population to grow. I am sure they were now after me because they did not want me to talk about my experiences there. Every day that I stayed in Dalian made me more and more paranoid. It was time to go.

Nevertheless, it was during this time that I realized that I must write down my experiences. I knew there were very few accurate, first-hand accounts existed about life in North Korea. One thing that I have learned is that life is a precious commodity that people take for granted. The only fond memories I have in life are my childhood and the short moments in my life in North Korea listening to the birds in the morning, sitting under the blossoms of the peach trees, the few times I spent hiking in South and North Korea, and the wonderful smells of the eucalyptus trees in the presidio district of San Francisco. The rest of my memories are dark, sinister, and keep me up at nights now. Every foreign sound now startles me out of bed.

As I mentioned in the beginning, do not pity me nor judge me. Learn from my experiences. Learn that regardless of a person's good intention knowledge and awareness is the key to altruism and benevolence. Unlike in North Korea, altruism and benevolence should not be used in propaganda but rather occur naturally by common folk everyday. I searched the world for some mysterious utopia, where good is dominant and evil eradicated. In fact, that good existed right at home because I was just too preoccupied with loathing and criticizing my own surroundings. I blindly followed any system that contradicted that of the United States without realizing the consequences. I was a product of a spoiled generation that championed distrust of the government and the previous generations.

As I write these words, millions suffer from malnutrition and oppression. Travel is restricted for most North Koreans. Children are indoctrinated from an early age to sacrifice everything for their leaders. Hundreds of thousands (maybe millions) are in work camps for crimes they did not commit. Their families are also imprisoned and forced to leave their ancestral homes. Electricity, heat, even running water is an anomaly. Only exclusive neighborhoods in Pyongyang have these amenities and even they have recurrent power shortages. The country is under constant surveillance by its reclusive leader, while the propaganda scares the average North Korean about the outside world. Corruption has penetrated every aspect of life, while the economy is in shambles.

How, then, does the country continue to operate? I think this question is answered to some extent in my diary, yet there is no clear answer. The only one I can think of, lamentably, is that North Korea is unique. Its history, culture, and sad chain of events has led it to this miserable state. I hope that someday North Korea will be liberated or liberate itself from this nightmare that it exists in today. As for me, the future is unclear.

In Confucian philosophy, humans are the root cause of any fortune or misfortune that exists in the world. Like in many religions, random acts of kindness are the root of good fortune, while random acts of cruelty have a negative effect. It is because of the random acts of cruelty that I had suffered so much, just as the random acts of kindness by people such as Reverend Park, Eric, and Bae Gun, have kept me going. Every individual we meet might have a fervent influence on the rest of our lives. I want to dedicate these memoirs to all the kind souls out there.

EPILOGUE

After he entrusted the diary to me, David disappeared. I tried to track him down, I even took some time off from work and traveled around China, trying to get any information I could about him. No such luck. David disappeared as quickly as he appeared.

When I got back home, I attempted to locate someone from his family. David never revealed more than his name (which, as he mentioned in his diary, was a pseudonym) and where he had grown up. The State Department wasn't much help either. At the time, the State Department denied that anyone of such a high caliber had defected to North Korea. The government would only admit to four or five American enlisted men who defected in the 1960's. One of them was Matt, the black basketball player mentioned in David's diary. Another fit the description of Sam. I guess it was hard to ignore and deny their existence. When I questioned a state department spokesman about the famous actor who played so many roles in North Korean propaganda films, he responded by saying that it was one of the four enlisted men.

Maybe after reading this book, someone will come forward and reveal David's true identity. It could more than likely be that his family does not know what has really become of David or simply do not want to be associated with him. I researched the geographical location with the universities David said he had attended and came up with several candidates. However, my search ultimately came to a dead end.

Whatever the case may be, David's story is too important to shelve away in some attic or basement. The world must know more about the degrading state of affairs in North Korea. David's diary is a firsthand account of the hermetic kingdom known as North Korea. It is valuable in the sense that it gives us a perspective of a foreigner's life inside one of the most mysterious places in the world today. My only hope is that this account will someday only be in a history section, instead of current events.

As I put the diary into some semblance of order, I came across a sentence David had written on the margins of one of the pieces of last page that read: "God might be omnipotent in the entire universe, but the Kims rule North Korea." An appropriate summation of this story and of the Hermit Kingdom, known to the world as NORTH KOREA.

0-595-34143-8